THE SLEEPING CAT

Isabel Ostrander

1883-1924

THE SLEEPING CAT

Isabel Ostrander

COACHWHIP PUBLICATIONS
Greenville, Ohio

The Sleeping Cat, by Isabel Ostrander
© 2024 Coachwhip Publications edition

First published 1926
Isabel Ostrander, 1883-1924
CoachwhipBooks.com

ISBN 1-61646-576-X
ISBN-13 978-1-61646-576-6

1

The Mercers' Guest

Mrs. Stanley Mercer paced the station platform at Chichester with a pleasurable feeling of excitement such as she had not known in several placid years. To renew a schoolgirl friendship after a decade would have been interesting in any event, but she and Gloria Warrender had been particular chums and roommates in the exclusive New York boarding school of the Misses Faraday for three years, until at graduation they had gone their different ways; Gloria to Europe with the aunt who had been her reluctant guardian since the death of her parents, and she herself to return to the up-State city of her birth and marry Stan.

What would Gloria be like now, Mrs. Mercer wondered. She recalled her as a long, thin, awkward creature, freckled yet vivid, with bright, red-gold hair and as rangy as a young colt. Ten years—she must be twenty-eight or nine. Had she gone in for art or music, or perhaps politics, like "Jim" Foster? From Mrs. Mercer's own vantage point as the mother of two lively youngsters, an unmarried woman nearing thirty usually "took up" something to occupy her time and attention. The mutual acquaintance, through whom the two women had got in touch with each other again, had told Mrs. Mercer nothing of her former schoolmate except that she had "a most unusual, attractive personality," which might mean anything. Was it going to be awkward, this first meeting? Would she be difficult to entertain?

Mrs. Mercer's speculations were cut short by the whistle and rumble of the approaching train, and in another moment it pulled in and came to a panting halt before the station. Several fellow townsfolk descended, the usual quota of commercial travelers, a guest or two for the country club laden with golf bags, and then a tall, slender woman with a delicate, piquant face and flame-colored hair beneath a small Parisian turban.

Could this be the awkward, freckled Gloria of the old days? For a moment Mrs. Mercer hesitated, and then the other woman caught sight of her and glided forward with a swaying, unhurried grace.

"Gloria?" Mrs. Mercer's voice held the inflection of a question, but she held out both hands and the other smiled swiftly, radiantly.

"Olive!" They kissed and then the hostess exclaimed:

"How good it is to see you again, dear! Do you know, at first I wasn't sure it was really you? After all, ten years is a long time, isn't it? But come, the car's over this way."

She led her guest to a comfortable touring car, by no means a late model, but roomy and glistening with new paint. The chauffeur, a round-faced, cheery-looking country youth, assisted the porter to stow a collection of opulent bags and hat boxes on the floor, and they rolled off, each woman silently taking stock of the other.

Olive Mercer was puzzled. There was a poise and distinction about the older Gloria that had been lacking in the younger, a charm that was almost beauty in the small, colorless face, an indolent grace that was wholly unassumed, and yet something appeared to be lacking. It was as though she were unawakened, Olive thought; as though life had not yet touched her in spite of her years of travel and experience of the world. She who had been so eagerly, vibrantly alive seemed to have remained a bystander.

Gloria Warrender's appraisal was swifter and more sure. She remembered her hostess as a dumpy, dark-eyed brunette, with heavy brows and thick, black hair always decorously arranged; a girl who plodded patiently while others skimmed, and perfectly content with the mediocre result, stolid, unimaginative but reliable. The dumpy figure had become plump and settled, the brows heavier and grown almost together, the stolid face placid, mature, complacent. In matrimony, motherhood, and the small affairs of a small town Olive seemed to have found her groove.

"Ten years," Gloria repeated in her slow, sweet voice. "Have I changed so much or had you almost forgotten me that you didn't know me?"

"No, I hadn't forgotten, but I didn't realize that time would bring changes. You've sort of bloomed out, Gloria."

"I'd have known you anywhere," the other remarked and then changed the subject. "It was so sweet of you to ask me here. When Mrs. Derwent told me she had met you I was delighted, and I'm looking forward to meeting your husband and the babies. You've been home here ever since you graduated, haven't you?"

"Yes." Olive smiled. "I would like to have traveled and seen all the wonderful places you have, but I met Stan and we were married within the year. Then Nancy came, and Stan's father died and he had to step into his place, and the war increased the business tenfold. It's shoes, you know. We'd planned all along to go abroad when the plant was consolidated with the others, but Bill was born four years ago and since then we've settled down. There's the nuisance of traveling with young children, you know, the worry that they'll catch something, and it's pleasant here, although I'm afraid you'll find it terribly quiet."

"I shall love it!" Gloria glanced out at the pleasant, old-fashioned houses set well back behind low hedges, and the towering oaks that bordered the wide, smooth road. "I've been a nomad, Olive, going the rounds of the springs and resorts here and abroad, season after season, with Aunt Ruth. After her death I lived in hotels, for it seemed rather silly to try to make a home all by myself. It's a selfish sort of existence, I suppose, but convenient, and I'm lazy."

"You never were," Olive remarked reminiscently. "You never had to make any effort, things came to you in a flash, but I jogged along comfortably taking everything for granted and always in the middle of the class. Here we are." They had turned in between square, solid gray-stone gateposts and wound up a graveled drive to a square, solid gray house with wide verandas, red roof, and a red brick foundation against which the starry blue of massed hydrangeas stood out in almost startling beauty.

"Oh!" Gloria threw up her hands in a pretty, foreign gesture. "What an exquisite effect! Those wonderful blue flowers bordering the brick paths, too, with no other note of color except the green of the lawns and shrubbery! It's charming!"

There was a trace of surprise in her long hazel eyes as she turned to her hostess, but Olive smiled placidly at the praise.

"That's why our place is called 'Hydrangea Walk,'" she remarked. "It sounds terribly English for an up-State Yankee home, and I think they're almost too vivid and loud-looking, but it was Stanley's idea and he left everything else to me."

Gloria thought it very likely, as they drew up before the veranda steps and she glimpsed the ugly, substantial lines of the dull reed furniture set precisely about. Through the wide entrance doors the vista of the central hall, with the staircase squarely in the middle, displayed the conventional furnishings of the Grand Rapids period, heavy, durable, unimaginative. How very like Olive!

A thin, tow-headed youth of about twenty straightened from where he had been pruning the hydrangeas and came forward to assist the chauffeur with the bags. His temples were slightly sunken, a hectic blotch of color burned in either gaunt cheek, and there was a transparent look about his outstanding ears that told its own tale to the visitor before his dry, hacking cough, quickly subdued, smote her ear. At St. Moritz, in Southern Italy, the heights of the Pyrenees, the Isle of Arran she had seen his like and she glanced pityingly at him as her hostess said pleasantly:

"Thanks, Hans; just put them inside the door. The maids will carry them up."

There was time for no more, for a little girl with fluffy, golden-brown hair and a slim, straight, exquisitely dainty form had appeared at the head of the stairs and came slowly down. There was nothing shy or gauche in her bearing, but an aloof, unconscious grace, and her great blue eyes were fixed upon her mother's guest in appraisal rather than curiosity.

"Come and say how-do-you-do to Miss Warrender, Nancy," Olive called, adding: "She's a queer little thing, Gloria; don't mind if she seems stand-offish; it's her way."

The child approached, gazed contemplatively at Gloria's outstretched, gloved hand and placed her own small one in it, then looked up again as though waiting to hear the visitor's voice.

"Nancy is such a pretty name," Gloria smiled down at her. "I wish it were mine."

"Daddy says it means sit-by-the-fire-and-spin." The child withdrew her hand and backed slowly away as she replied in her clear, childish treble. "I like yours best. It sounds like the sun coming up!"

Then she turned and darted down the hall so swiftly and silently that she seemed to skim through the air and vanish in the shadows. Gloria gazed after her in fascinated interest. Could this actually be a child of Olive's?

"You never can tell what she means." The latter looked after her daughter and sighed. "I can't imagine where she gets it from and I've tried my best to make her like other children. But come and I'll show you to your room. This is Ingred, the housemaid."

A stout, middle-aged woman with mild, cowlike blue eyes and graying yellow hair had advanced from the rear of the hall to shoulder the bags, and she nodded and smiled almost vacuously at the introduction. There was a certain resemblance to the frail youth outside, Gloria thought, and when she and her hostess stood in the sunny, blue-draped guestroom after the maid had departed she spoke of it.

"Oh, Hans is her son," Olive explained casually. "She's as strong and stupid as an ox, but faithful. I never have any bother with servants. Would you like to lie down till tea?"

"Oh, no!" Gloria spoke in an amused tone. Olive would probably "lie down" after a trolley ride! "I'd love to see your boy. May I?"

"He's up in the nursery." Olive led the way. "It's funny; Bill looks like me but he's exactly like his father, talking and laughing and friendly with everybody in the most democratic way, too democratic at times. The garbage man, for instance, is one of his special cronies! Nancy is the image of her father—in a feminine way, of course—but she's not a bit like either of us."

Bill's fat, roly-poly person was astride a battered horse on wheels, which he propelled across the floor with vigorous kicks, but he stopped and hailed his mother and her guest with an affable "H'lo!"

"Bill, come and kiss mamma's friend," Olive said with a fond note in her tones that had been lacking when she spoke to her daughter. "Where's Jane?"

Bill trotted forward obediently and held up his rosy lips to be kissed. He was as dark as his mother with hair and brows already black and thick, and eyes and skin as brown as a gypsy, but the baby features were as exquisite in their way as those of the little girl.

"Dane's dettin' supper," he replied to his mother and then, clinging to Gloria's hand, he asked confidentially, "Is you dot any little boys? I yikes to play wiff little boys."

"No, Bill." Gloria laughed a soft, musical, slightly throaty gurgle of laughter. "Would you like to come and be my little boy?"

Bill reflected.

"I'll tum and wisit," he offered tentatively. "Tan I do out in de wain and wide a weal pony and—not have any nassy ceweal, not never?"

He added the last as a sharp-featured nurse entered the doorway with a bowl of smoking cereal and a jug of cream on a tray, and his mother smiled.

"His pet aversion! And he loves the rain and wants a pony, but of course he's too young yet. Shall we go down? Stan will be home soon and I do hope you'll like him. He's just a big, stupid, lumbering boy, but a comfortable sort of person to have around the house."

She spoke with the calm, indulgent air of perfect possession, and while Gloria changed her gown and redressed her hair she realized, with a delightful and almost forgotten sense of novelty, that such families as this really did exist outside the covers of the semiannual Great American Novel. She had known many house-parties in the last ten years, but none like the coming fortnight promised to be; adorably dull and domesticated, a succession of serene, uneventful days.

She could almost visualize the master of the house, the contented husband of Olive; he would be red-faced, boisterously hospitable, a sort of Yankee squire with a lively interest in his meals and the Big League score. Yet there were the blue hydrangeas and the children! Somewhere in his make-up there must be a streak of the artistic, of the temperamental. Temperament in an up-State shoe manufacturer? Gloria smiled to herself as she went downstairs and out to the broad veranda.

"Stan hasn't come yet, but we won't wait," Olive announced from beside the tea-wagon. "You're a dream in that green dress, Gloria; it makes your hair positively flame-colored! How many lumps, and do you take lemon or cream?"

"No sugar, but cream please, Olive." Gloria seated herself in a long low chair.

"I like cream, too," her hostess admitted, helping herself liberally. "I suppose I shouldn't, I've been putting on weight so, but Stan wouldn't mind if I were the size of a house. I'm sorry he's late, but I'm a golf widow, you know."

She laughed comfortably and her companion asked:

"Don't you play?"

"Not often. It seems sort of silly to me and I'm not fond of exercise. I only have the tennis courts kept up for Stan, and he rides every morning, too."

"And what do you do with yourself?" Gloria crumpled a bit of cinnamon toast and sipped her tea.

"Oh, I have home and the children, and those clubs that Stan insisted on my organizing among the women employees of his factory. I haven't kept up my music, but I play a little bridge; I warned you you'd find it terribly quiet."

"Clubs?" There was an unconscious note of surprise in Gloria's tone. "I didn't know you cared for that sort of thing."

"I don't," Olive replied, taking a second frosted cake. "I don't know a thing about organization, but Jim Foster did the real work for me. She's my best friend; it's funny, because she's everything I'm not, energetic and forceful and a born leader. She goes in for politics and civic duties, and the only really feminine thing about her is her adoration of Bill. He worships her, too."

"He's a darling!" Gloria murmured absently. She felt no interest in the forceful "Jim" Foster, and she turned to glance out over the sloping lawn and driveway just as a tall figure turned in at the gate with an easy, swinging stride. He was bare-headed and the setting sun turned his brown hair to gold, while the golf suit he wore revealed the buoyant youthfulness of his slim, athletic form. This much Gloria noted before her hostess exclaimed:

"Here's Stan now! Doesn't he look like a tramp? He used to put in nine hours a day at the plant, but, now that he only spends part of the forenoon there in executive work, he plays as hard as though he were still in harness. Stan, here's Miss Warrender."

He was coming up the steps of the veranda now and Gloria saw that his eyes were the deep, clear blue of those of the child Nancy, but there was a wearied wistfulness in them which lightened as they fell upon her. For the merest fraction of a second he paused and then came forward with hand outstretched.

"Miss Warrender, I'm more than glad that my wife found you again and that you've come to us." His tones were low and resonant and he spoke with a simple sincerity devoid of surface cordiality. "I heard so much of you years ago that when Mrs. Derwent mentioned you it seemed as though both Olive and I had rediscovered a mutual friend."

"Don't make me feel ancient, Mr. Mercer!" Gloria expostulated laughingly as she withdrew her hand. It was tingling, and there was a little catch in her breath. "Olive always used to put her friends on a pedestal, and I suppose she made you think I was some sort of prodigy!"

"Olive is loyal." He touched his wife's wrist lightly as he dropped down on the end of the settee and his eyes turned

again to Gloria with something like wonder in them. Her
glance met his as though drawn in spite of herself, and
then Olive's matter-of-fact tones broke the spell.

"Tea, Stan?"

"Yes, but iced, please. A large pitcher of it, for Henry
will be along in a few minutes, and tell Betty to get out
some of the old stock for Rider."

Gloria had known Latins and Anglo-Saxons, Teutons
and Danes, but never had she seen such a handsome, god-
like creature as this big, clean-limbed American with his
clear bronzed skin, and features so strong and straight that
they might have been chiseled from marble! The sheer clas-
sic beauty of him was amazing and there was a magnetism
about him that, blasé as she was, made her feel strangely
vibrant like the strings of a harp long untouched. It must
be the utter simplicity of the man, she told herself, the
naive, almost impersonal way he looked at her, as though
she were a being from another world.

She was aware that while her hostess rang and gave the
necessary orders to the trim little maid his eyes strayed
to her again and again, but she kept her own averted.
She felt tongue-tied, almost confused—she, whose wit had
enlivened many an illustrious dinner-table! Deliberately
she turned to him.

"I've been getting acquainted with the children, Mr.
Mercer. Bill has offered to visit me if he may go out in
the rain and ride a real pony, but Nancy and I merely
exchanged opinions about names and then she appeared to
remember an immediate engagement."

"Oh, Stan, you know how she makes some unheard-of
observation and then runs away!" Olive murmured. "I
can't think what possesses her!"

"About names?" Stanley Mercer looked up with sudden
interest. "What was it this time?"

"She said Gloria's was like the sun coming up. Isn't that absurd?" Olive laughed deprecatingly and added, "There's Henry Mott now, and Mr. Rider."

"Neighbors?" Gloria asked as a small runabout turned in at the gate.

"Henry is; he's the head of all our 'Y' branches in this part of the State, and Mr. Rider is a friend visiting him from New York," Olive explained. "I imagine he's a retired broker or something."

Gloria saw a fat man seated behind the wheel with a round, jovial face and sandy hair glinting from beneath his cap, and beside him a heavy-set figure with a graying mustache, square jaw, and huge, bulbous nose that a de Bergerac might have been graced with. She drew in her breath quickly and a little thoughtful frown appeared between her arched brows.

At the same moment the big-nosed man in the car asked without turning his head toward his companion:

"Who's that woman?"

"The red-haired one? That must be the guest the Mercers were expecting; a Miss Warrender."

"Humph!" remarked Daniel Rider.

2

The Lady with a Story

The car drew up before the steps, and its occupants alighted and were presented. Gloria gave the stout Henry Mott a friendly, impersonal smile as she bowed, but she shot Rider a keen, swift glance from beneath lowered lids. She seemed to wait tensely for a moment, then as they dropped into chairs and the conversation became general she relaxed and lay back in her chair.

After a discussion of the afternoon's golf they drifted to Mott's Y.M.C.A. work in Chichester and their host's welfare clubs at the plant. From there it was an easy transition to relief measures abroad, and Olive observed:

"Miss Warrender has lived abroad almost continuously for the past few years; she must have seen quite a little of the reconstruction work. It's funny, we haven't once mentioned the war since she came, but then it is such an old story now! Were you over while it was going on, Gloria?"

Gloria smiled slightly but a fine white line had settled about her lips.

"Oh, yes," she nodded casually. "We were in Paris when it started and I had a dreadful time getting Aunt Ruth to a place she considered quite safe. People at home here seem to think of the continent as one huge scar but really only a comparatively small area was touched by the war."

She spoke coolly, almost lightly, and in her tone was the suggestion that the area she mentioned was of little interest to her, and an indignant half-contemptuous look came into Mott's mild blue eyes, but Rider's lips, beneath the close-cropped mustache, tightened and then relaxed significantly, as Stanley Mercer looked at his guest with a sudden wondering sympathy.

Olive laughed with easy indulgence.

"It must have been rather an experience for your aunt! But, seriously, you have been through the reconstruction sections of France lately, haven't you? We're all interested, Mr. Mott especially, for he had charge of important 'Y' work there during the time our own boys were in action."

Gloria glanced quickly at the little fat man.

"Sorry I can tell you very little," she murmured. "No more than any ordinary observer, I am afraid. I have no penchant, no executive ability; I cannot comprehend the scope of relief measures on such an enormous scale. There is a sameness about the new little villages, to me; a dreary, raw uniformity that lacks interest because it has no background but utter desolation."

This time there could be no misunderstanding of the fact that the subject was distasteful to her, and Henry Mott observed dryly:

"Both the war and afterward must have been highly distressing to other American ladies living in Europe who, like you, lacked interest, Miss Warrender, but no doubt as you say, only a small area of the continent was laid waste; many delightful pleasure resorts must have been available at all times. Are you here for a long stay in your own country?"

Gloria shrugged and smiled brightly upon him once more as though his insinuation had passed quite over her glowing red head.

"I do not know, Mr. Mott. I never decide upon anything until the last moment; that's the advantage of being a solitary nomad, as I've been telling Mrs. Mercer, while I quite frankly envied her. Everything is so peaceful here, your friendships long established, your industries stabilized, your social life going on in the even tenor of its way. To a stranger it would seem that the war, so far away and long ago, had never even existed."

"It wouldn't if you'd seen our roll of honor down on the square, and the ones out at the different plants, Stan Mercer's, for instance!" Mott maintained doggedly. "He was tied to executive work at the training camps but it wasn't his fault, and another one of our neighbors, a splendid fellow, came back a gassed, nerve-wrecked shadow who'll never be the same again!"

"Poor Jack!" Olive sighed. Then her heavy face lightened and she added: "I've been telling Miss Warrender about our country club and the more or less energetic ways you people amuse yourselves. I'm sure she rides and plays tennis and golf splendidly!"

"You ride?" Stan Mercer made the statement rather than queried, and Gloria nodded.

"Yes. I love a good horse and a straightaway."

"Then Stan will ride with you," Olive suggested. "I haven't in some time, it's such a nuisance to change, and then I do like to see to the household in the morning. We don't hunt, although there've been one or two attempts to get up a meet, and we haven't had a polo team since—oh, in several years. Here comes Jack! I'm ever so glad, for he seldom goes anywhere."

At her exclamation the three men glanced out over the lawn where a tall, thin, dark man younger than the others was striding toward them with nervous, jerky steps. Gloria leaned forward and her hands slowly tightened on the arms

of her chair till a ring which she wore on the third finger
of her right hand scraped on the dull, lacquered reed.

Slight as the sound was it appeared to reach the ear of
the huge-nosed, silent man who had taken no part in the
conversation, for without movement of his head his small
gray eyes turned sidewise to observe her.

Gloria's gaze was fastened now on her hostess and she
asked with polite indifference:

"Is this the 'Jack' Mr. Mott spoke of just now? The
friend who was gassed in the war?"

"Yes. Major Hill. He's almost a hermit, lives alone in
the old family house. It's a pity, for he's only forty and
the most eligible man in the neighborhood, but he simply won't look at a girl, Gloria. I'm sometimes afraid that
it's something more than just shell-shock, that perhaps he
isn't quite—well, quite balanced, any more."

She lowered her voice, for the newcomer was approaching the steps, and, as she broke off and turned to greet
him, Gloria slipped the ring from her right hand and
dropped it with a swift but languidly graceful movement
into the front of her gown, down its low Dutch neck. It
was a curious, milky stone shot with varicolored flames,
but so slight had been her gesture that no one observed it
except those keen gray eyes watching her, and no one else
saw her delicate face flush and pale and a shadow of pain
darken for an instant her clear, long, golden-hazel eyes.

"I didn't know—you had guests," Major Hill was saying
stiffly to his hostess in a dull, lifeless voice.

"Only an old school friend of mine," Olive explained
soothingly. "Gloria, dear, may I present our neighbor,
Major Hill?—Miss Warrender."

The major's tall, gaunt frame had quivered at the name
and now he straightened and walked to her chair like an
automaton, his dark, deeply circled eyes staring as though

they saw a ghost. He did not hold out his hand but bowed with military precision before her.

"Miss—Warrender." That was all he said but his voice was vibrant now, alive with feeling which could neither be defined nor disguised.

It was evident that Gloria was aware of the latter fact, at least, for she held out her bare right hand with a gesture of simple friendliness.

"We've met before, on the other side, Major, though it's improbable that you would recall my name. I'm so glad you—won through!" She spoke cordially but with a shade of reserve, and Henry Mott exclaimed:

"Bless me, are you and the major old friends, Miss Warrender? I thought you were never near the danger zones? Jack was never away from them!"

Olive saved her friend the necessity of a reply by saying:

"Isn't that nice? Now you'll positively have to come out of your shell for the next fortnight or so and be sociable with us, Major! Will you have tea, or a long, cool, illegal highball?"

"Tea, please, but long and cool." A faint smile lighted up the dark, stern features, so gaunt that the sallow skin with its network of fine lines seemed drawn tight over a bare skull, and only the eyes appeared alive. "Have I really been unsociable? Not to prove that, but because I do really want you so much, you must all come and dine with me one evening this week, and brave the rigors of bachelor's hall."

He spoke with an unaccustomed effort at lightness, but the unmistakable ring of sincerity was in his tone, although it had dropped almost to a monotone again, and only the tremor of his hands as he took the glass betokened the agitation he was attempting to conceal.

Olive accepted cheerfully for her household, Henry Mott and Daniel Rider nodded their thanks and the conversation drifted off to trivial topics, but Gloria still flushed and paled by turns, avoiding further direct talk with the major whose glance strayed constantly to her, and Rider watched them both with his unobtrusive, speculative gaze.

When the first two guests arose to depart the major got to his feet also with an air of veiled but obvious relief.

"Going too, Jack?" Mott asked. "We'll drop you off at Hilltop; I've got an extra seat, you know."

The major shook his head.

"Thanks, old man. I started out for a good hike and I need the walk home. Delighted to have met you again, Miss Warrender." He turned to Gloria again and bowed. "I'm a wretched golfer but I hope you'll play a round or two with me during your stay."

Gloria murmured a response, farewells were said and the runabout chugged off down the drive while the tall, solitary figure strode down a sidepath and was lost in the gathering shadows.

"Funny, Jack showing up like that," Mott commented as he turned into the road beyond the gateposts. "Wonder where he met her? He had no leave that I remember, and was in the very thick of things till that infernal gas put him out of the game."

"I'm wondering the same thing," Rider remarked. "Where I met her—or rather saw her, I mean. She's striking enough, in all conscience, and I don't often forget a face, but there's something elusive about hers. She had the advantage of me, though—she knows!"

"Knows what?" Mott wriggled as actively as his cramped space behind the wheel would permit. "That she's seen you before, too? Why didn't she say so, then? I didn't see anything mysterious about her; usual useless society woman, charming enough, but, blah! when it comes to a crisis! You heard how she spoke? Probably just another rich American woman preening herself around Europe when the big bust-up came and then running for cover! When I think of that kind, and then some of the splendid women we had in our organization! . . ."

He ended with an indignant snort and then turned to the man who sat chuckling beside him.

"Yeh, Miss Warrender's work was good!" the latter admitted. "She put it over on you pretty, but as soon as I saw she didn't want me to recognize her I began to take notice. Henry, some people don't want to talk about the war because it hits 'em too deep even yet, either because of some one they've lost or some experience of their own. That young woman was taking refuge in pretending to be just what you thought her!"

"Rot!" ejaculated Mott. "You Secret Service guys were always looking for trouble! Jack may be nutty in some ways but he hardly talked to her after she reminded him that they'd met on the other side, wasn't interested, you see? Didn't even recall her name, as she said, and he was glad enough to break away when we did!"

"A man can be struck dumb with surprise, Henry, and he don't have to be nutty, either." Rider gazed straight ahead of him as he spoke and as usual didn't turn toward his companion. "He could leave at the first opportunity, too, if he wanted time to recover himself and think things over. I'll grant you one point, though; the name 'Warrender' didn't mean anything to him. He wasn't familiar with it."

"Oh, come, Daniel!" Henry's tone was shocked. "You don't mean that he knew her by any other! She's not the sort. Why, you've heard Mrs. Mercer say they were old school friends, and I've known the Mercers since they were kids! There's a lot that poor old Jack doesn't remember from that nightmare of a time and maybe names are one of them."

"And maybe a ring is another," Rider retorted obscurely. "The lady took no chances on that score, though. Mind this, Henry; I'm not insinuating that this guest of your friends' isn't a lady and a mighty fascinating one, but I do say there's a story there and I'd like to be able to read the last page of it!"

At that precise moment Gloria, in a gown of shimmering silver cloth and lace with a single strand of pearls about her long white throat, was turning toward the door of her bedroom when the stout, bovine-faced Ingred who had assisted her to dress, stopped her.

"Aye tank you drop dis, Miss Warrender," she said. In her creased, reddened palm she was holding out a narrow platinum circlet mounted with a cabochon of living fire, and Gloria gasped:

"Oh, I did! How fortunate that you found it! It isn't only that it's worth a ransom, but I value it for association more than anything I have!"

She slipped it on her finger once more and then, taking her purse from the drawer of the dressing table, she impulsively offered a bill of large denomination.

"Oh, no, I tank you, ma'am!" Ingred drew back but her gentle, slightly vacuous eyes were shining. "It bane not'ing dat I pick it oop here, and Mrs. Mercer, maybe she not like . . ."

"Of course she will!" Gloria interrupted. "As soon as I missed it I should have offered more than this as a reward. Take it, please! It is I who should thank you, and I do!"

As she went down the staircase she glanced at the ring, which seemed to shoot out sparks in the soft, dim light. How nearly she had lost it, and just on the day when a ghost came back from the dead! A ghost among living men!

Something in the last thought sent a faint color into the clear pallor of her cheeks and it deepened when she entered the drawing-room, to find it occupied solely by a tall, lithe figure whose expanse of shirt bosom brought out his erect, easy bearing and whose brown hair showed golden lights under the lamps' faint glow.

"I'm disgustingly prompt!" Gloria murmured laughingly as he came forward to meet her.

"You mean you thought we should be, and you didn't want to be tardy!" Stanley Mercer laughed, too, and she noticed that the wistful, dispirited look in his deep blue eyes had given place to an eager, glowing warmth. "Olive always sees to the kiddies' going to bed herself, but she'll be here presently before our guests arrive. Do you know, Miss Warrender, you've quite bowled us all over? You won't mind my saying that no one quite like you has appeared among us before?"

Gloria had listened to compliments far more subtle and gracefully put, but now, before the honest, boyish admiration of this man who seemed gauche only in her immediate presence, she felt her heart flutter again as when he had gazed on her on the veranda. She had been a sophisticated belle of several seasons and countries, he a man of achievement and domination in his community; what in the world was the matter with them both? Somehow, she could not reply in her light, bantering way.

"I hope your friends will like me," she replied simply. "I want so tremendously to have them do so! You see, I haven't been in such a thoroughly homelike American environment as long as I can remember, and since I came to-day I've begun to realize just how much I've missed."

The nearness of her, the delicate perfume of her silvery gown and satin skin, the tones of her slow, sweet voice seemed to be casting a spell over Stan Mercer. A flush had crept up beneath his smooth tan, his hand shook on the back of the chair he had placed for her and his voice was all at once low and husky as though a lump had risen in his throat.

"And how much—we've missed!" he returned. "You should have come before, years ago! You . . ."

"Stan," Olive bustled in, her ample form encased in an armor of glittering beads, "the Holcombs' car is coming up the drive. Gloria, that's a marvelous gown! The Holcombs have been to Paris twice and they'll know!"

3

Jim Foster Intervenes

On the following Friday afternoon Olive sat in an old-fashioned woven hammock swung between two tall trees mending a romper of Bill's with a pile of other sturdy but worn little garments beside her. A third tree faced her a few feet away, equidistant between the other two, with a new rope fastened about it, the end of which trailed at her skirt-hem, and the little hollow was densely ringed about with bushes whose intertwined branches formed a hedge, leaving a single opening that looked out on a section of the driveway.

This was ordinarily the children's playground, but today Bill's lusty shouts and Nancy's occasional clear treble came from the rear of the house, where Major Hill was playing with them, and Olive smiled happily to herself. Her two little people seemed to understand this solitary, almost saturnine man better than any of the grown-ups who had been his lifelong friends, and in their company alone he appeared to find surcease of his tortured nerves.

Her reverie was broken by the tinny rattle of a flivver driven recklessly in at the gate, and she glanced up to see a mud-spattered little car dash up the drive, halt with a jerk as its single occupant caught sight of her and descended, and then the engine ceased to sputter with the alacrity of exhaustion.

The woman who approached was about her own age, but short and stocky, with bobbed, straight brown hair and a plain, square, freckled countenance. She walked with a stride that threatened the seams of her rough tweed skirt, and her rather short arms swung with the freedom of a boy's. She waved as she drew near, and Olive called:

"Afternoon, Jim! You've deserted me! Have you found a new candidate for something or other?"

"Yes." Jim Foster, without further greeting, dragged a dilapidated camp stool from beneath the hammock and seated herself squarely facing her friend. "A candidate for the Home for Imbeciles! That's why I'm here."

A slight, puzzled frown gathered between Olive's heavy brows, but she smiled.

"Who is it now?" she asked. "You're my most intimate friend, Jim, but half the time I can't understand you!"

"You will this time, and probably when I walk out of this peaceful dell we won't be friends any longer!" the other retorted darkly as she drew a worn leather cigarette case from the pocket of her sweater and searched further in it for a match. "Why have we been such friends, anyway?"

"I've often wondered," Olive replied placidly. "I'm not a bit interested in women interfering in what has been man's business from the beginning of time, and you haven't any use for a husband and babies, and—and sewing. You tell me."

She picked up Bill's romper again as she spoke and her friend's gray eyes softened as she watched her, then hardened again with purpose.

"All right, then." Jim squared her broad shoulders. "You haven't a mean, suspicious thought in whatever brains you've got, Olive, and there's always been one thing in common between us; we're not scandalmongers. We don't gossip nor carry tales, and we discuss our neighbors' drawing-rooms, not the condition of their kitchen sinks. Yet that's what our friendship has brought me to. I'm here to dish the dirt, and I don't like it any more than you're going to! Where's your guest, Miss Warrender?"

The question came so abruptly that Olive glanced up in mild surprise.

"Over at the country club, playing golf with Stan, of course."

"Where was she this morning?"

"Riding with Stan. He wanted her to try out that new mare. . . ."

"And where was she yesterday afternoon?" Jim interrupted.

"Motoring with Stan. They broke down and had to dine at the Red Coach Inn, but they 'phoned and it was all right."

"And yesterday morning, and the morning and afternoon before that, and ever since she came on Monday, four whole days now?" Jim's square jaw was set.

"Why—why, I don't know what you mean!" Olive stared. "I introduced Gloria at luncheon at the club Tuesday, and that night and the next we dined out, and—surely you don't mean I'm not doing my best to entertain her? She isn't like an ordinary guest; we roomed together at school and she's like one of the family. She knows I would rather look after the children and the house than ride and golf and all that sort of thing, and Stan's been very nice to her."

"He has, you know!" Jim lapsed into slang for emphasis. "Every question I've asked you as to her whereabouts, you've given me the same answer: 'With Stan.' I knew it, of course, and what I've seen the whole neighborhood has seen, too, and it's buzzing like a hive of bees."

"Jim!" Olive arose, dropping the romper, and a slumberous light glowed in her dark eyes. "Do you mean there's silly, spiteful gossip about Gloria and—and my Stan? You've listened to it? I can't believe it!"

"You bet I've listened to it!" Jim lighted a fresh cigarette and then ground the stub of the first viciously into
the turf with her flat heel. "I've listened till I thought it
was time to bring the whole thing to you and make you
see it. I know that every woman who tells her best friend
something that's going to cause her pain always says it's
'her duty' or her friend 'ought to know it,' but I don't
care. Whatever happens will be all your own fault, Olive;
you've got to understand that!"

"My fault?" Olive seated herself in the hammock again.
"My dear girl, nothing is going to happen, except that this
ridiculous gossip will die out of itself. How do you mean
that anything could be my fault?"

"I don't say that anything has or will happen to destroy your peace of mind; I don't mean to insinuate that
Miss Warrender is consciously trying to vamp Stan, or that
he gives her a thought beyond pleasure in companionship
again with a congenial woman! . . ."

Jim paused deliberately and Olive's face flushed darkly.

"Companionship—*again!*" she repeated. "When have I
ceased to be a companion to my husband?"

"So long ago that I can't remember," Jim returned coolly.
"Do you call it companionship to attend to a man's meals
and his laundry, keep his children and his house sweet and
clean and wholesome? It's a lot, of course, that many other
wives aren't so conscientious about, but, after all, who's a
man's pal but the woman who takes a sympathetic interest
in his business, and plays around with him when he needs
diversion? A man's home and children aren't his whole
life; you never encouraged him to talk about the facto-
ries, you didn't know anything about them and wouldn't
bother to learn. You care less for the welfare clubs that he
takes so seriously now that the other burden is lifted from
his shoulders, and as for his sports—how long is it since
you've ridden with him and played golf and tennis?"

"Tennis?" Olive looked down expressively at her stout, flabby form.

"Exactly!" stormed Jim. "Did you have to let yourself get fat? You're twenty-nine and he's forty-three; did you think him beyond the age of romance? He's the handsomest man in three counties and he's been about the loneliest, whether he realized it or not; a kind of a dangerous possession to leave lying around loose if you value it!"

"Absurd!" Olive smiled, but the glint in her eyes had rekindled. "Why, it's almost an insult to Stan! Lonely? Don't we have the neighbors to dinner or go out to play bridge or that silly Chinese game four or five evenings a week?"

Her voice was not quite certain and Jim snorted.

"Hen parties! Whatever regular man goes to 'em unless his wife drags him? Do you think Miss Warrender is pretty?"

The question came so abruptly that Olive replied almost inadvertently:

"No-o, I think she's lovely, charming. There's something about her that's vivid, like a flame. I adored her slavishly when we were girls, and when she first came here to me I thought she was satiated, bored with all her travel and social triumphs; the old, wonderful vivacity seemed gone forever but it must have been because she was just tired; now she's brilliant, sparkling! She's more wonderful than I ever thought her, in my schoolgirl enthusiasm!"

Her championship of her friend had become almost defiant because of a sudden, sick dismay that had shaken her, and Jim smiled a little as though she understood perfectly.

"She has a remarkable personality, but what is her aim in life?"

"Her aim?" Olive echoed blankly. "I don't believe she has any! All of us aren't like you, you know! She isn't interested in any big public questions, she's enormously rich and just drifts about amusing herself."

"It's odd, with all her charm, that she hasn't married, isn't it?" Jim suggested with an assumption of indifference. "I'm not discussing her as your friend, Olive, but impersonally, as though she were a public character. When I met her at the club on Tuesday afternoon I thought her the most discontented, aloof person in the world, but her manner was perfect, of course."

"I don't believe Gloria ever cared for any man," Olive replied, adding: "But don't let us discuss her any more, Jim; it hardly seems loyal or fair."

"A lot of unfair things happen in life," the other retorted, disposing of her second cigarette. "Her clothes are marvelous, though I wouldn't be seen in those slinky things at a dog fight! You're not exactly poverty-stricken yourself, but you wear mail-order things because it's too much of an exertion to go to New York for gowns that would become you, or you wouldn't leave the children and couldn't take 'em for fear of germs on the train! Stan's as lonesome as a lost pup whether you believe it or not and he'd attract any woman; ditto with Miss Warrender. I don't say she'd hurt you if she could, I don't say he'd leave you for her, but would you like to think of him as loving any other woman and only sticking around because it was his duty?"

"Jim, you—you're impossible!" Olive exclaimed with unusual sharpness in her contralto tones, but beneath them there was a note of agony. "I know of other wives, of course, as good as I have been, whose husbands fell in love with some one else, but they weren't like Stan! He's mine, I tell you, wholly and utterly mine, he belongs to me! He wouldn't think of another woman, he couldn't! He don't care how I look, he loves me!"

"He cared how you looked when you were first married and were a real pal, didn't he? Well, I've finished." Jim rose and kicked aside the end of the rope that was coiled about the tree trunk. "You're placid and self-satisfied—and sitting on top of a volcano! Do you think I enjoyed this last half-hour, Olive? I thought I'd rather hurt you a little than have somebody else hurt you a great deal, but I see it's no use! If you'll take an old maid's advice, though, you'll buy some nifty sports clothes if they are forty-fours, and a new evening gown, and resurrect your riding habit and let it out; you'll let the cook ruin the pans, and the dust collect, and the children wallow in nice, healthy dirt, but you'll do everything your visitor does and go everywhere with her and Stan, especially that club dance to-morrow night, and you'll get some reducing treatment! . . ."

She paused, breathless, and with a shout and a sweet, high, welcoming call the two children, discovering the occupants of the little retreat, fell upon Jim, Nancy seeming to float into her short sturdy arms and Bill clasping her ecstatically about the knees. After them, slowly and with apparent reluctance, came the attenuated figure of Major Hill, puffing moodily at his pipe. The nervous, strained lines seemed smoothed out of his thin, high-bred face, however, and he greeted his hostess and her friend genially.

"I'm just off, Jack—" Jim began, but Olive cried:

"Oh, don't go yet, Jim! We'll have a sort of picnic tea out here presently." She spoke with sincerity and an underlying significance which the other understood. Her friend had forgiven her stark frankness and for some reason wanted her to wait at least until the return of Stan and Gloria Warrender. Why? Was it to convince her that her suspicions were groundless? Jim smiled grimly and seated herself again on the campstool.

"I've got a meeting of the Woman's Non-Partisan League at eight and two lukewarm members to see before dinner," she announced. "I'll wait, though, if you think the golfers will return. You are too completely domestic this afternoon to be stimulating, and Jack's bent on poisoning himself with that rotten tobacco."

"You mind?" Major Hill grinned mechanically and sat down on the grass with his back against the tree about which the rope was looped. "Nancy and Bill and I have been having a rare old game but it was a bit more strenuous than golf."

"Henry Mott was telling me you were an old friend of Miss Warrender's." Jim faced him squarely, ignoring the warning glance from Olive. "You met in France, didn't you?"

The major took his odoriferous pipe from his lips and his eyes narrowed.

"I could hardly be so presumptuous as to say we were friends." His brows knit as though he were trying to remember. "It was in France, yes, one of those hurried meetings. I am ashamed to say that I was ungallant enough to be unable to recall her name at first. Miss—Warrender is very charming, Mrs. Mercer; why have you kept her hidden away all this time?"

It was well done, that indolent drawl of polite boredom, but the hand holding the pipe trembled and the man's sallow face had paled. Jim glanced from him to her friend, but Olive Mercer appeared not to have heard. She was gazing out through the aperture in the hedge toward a couple who had entered the gate and were proceeding toward the house unmindful of the semi-enclosed group.

Gloria's long slim neck was bent backward, her piquant face, delicately tanned now, upturned laughingly to her companion's and he was walking very close to her, his face boyishly alight as he looked down straight into her eyes. . . .

"Gloria! Stan! Come over here!" Olive's tones, a trifle deep for a woman, rang out with a sort of command. Then she turned to where Nancy, a little apart, poked daintily at the moss in the rough bark of a tree-trunk. "Run, dear, and have Ingred send us out tea and ginger ale and lots of sandwiches and cake. You and Bill may have some milk, too, if you like."

The little girl started off silently as Bill vociferated his approval from where he lay flat on his back with his short dimpled legs waving in the air and his dark head resting on the major's knees, and Jim glanced at the other woman. Could she have seen the attitude of the two as they entered the gate and read its possible significance? Her serene, untroubled, motherly tone did not convey it, nor the manner in which she greeted Gloria and asked Stan to have Hans bring some garden chairs and a table.

Gloria wore a pale gray felt hat, audaciously tilted, and a gray silk sweater coat over her white satin sports skirt, which made her hair fairly blaze, and her topaz-hazel eyes glowed, yet, when she responded to the major's low-voiced greeting, something of the sparkle died out as though it were consciously dimmed.

"Good round?" Jim asked bluntly.

"No, Miss Foster." Gloria shook her head slowly as she smiled. "I enjoyed it immensely and the greens were perfect but I'm away off my score, and I can't think why. Mr. Mercer is still kind enough to want me to play in the tournament to-morrow with him, but I'm afraid even his game couldn't carry mine through and I should hate to spoil his record!"

This time when Jim glanced at Olive their eyes met, but the latter's were only thoughtful and conveyed no meaning. Hans was approaching, staggering under the weight of the two light chairs he was lifting carefully free from the velvety turf, and Stan following with a round wicker table, when the major spoke.

"We'll all be there in the gallery, Miss Warrender," he remarked.

"Unfortunately I have some canvassing to do," announced Jim dryly. "Are you going?"

She turned deliberately to Olive once more and the latter smiled with a curious feline lift of her full lip on which a faint, shadowy line of down was already visible.

"Of course. I think we'll come home and dress and then return to the club to dine before the dance."

"And the babies?" Jim pursued maliciously.

"The babies," Olive replied decisively, "can be put to bed perfectly well without me for once. I've been in a rut, but Gloria's waked me up!"

Gloria looked at Olive and smiled.

4

In the Garden

A week had passed since Jim Foster had spoken her mind there beside the hammock; a week which had caused rather more commotion than the light gossip of Stan's possible flirtation with their fair guest, for Olive had taken her friend's advice with a vengeance. The more kindly of their little community believed that the coming of her old schoolmate had indeed roused her from the matronly rut into which she had fallen; the others scented competition and smiled in polite derision.

Olive's lately assumed role was too abrupt a change not to awaken comment, and she presented a figure which would have been comic were it not for her grim determination. Her sports clothes were a trifle too sporty, her evening gowns might better have graced the girlish lines of the Olive of ten years ago and the riding habit was a dire failure in itself.

Gloria was pleased and touched at the effort her friend was making for her sake but she felt uncomfortable, nevertheless, and something magic which she could not define was gone from the early morning canters in the sweet fragrant air, the swift runs in the motor over the smooth, rolling hills, the friendly rivalry on the golf greens and tennis courts. It was dear of Olive but oh! if she hadn't troubled!

Stan viewed the metamorphosis at first with wonder, then kindly amusement. Was she trying to be like the radiant vision which was Gloria? Then the swift realization came to him that it was his wife whom he was comparing with another woman and the implied disloyalty made him hot with disgust, but it had been so long since Olive had cared to do the things he liked or bothered even to ask about them, that to have her start now when it had ceased to be looked for was disconcerting.

The poor dear girl was making a mortifying show of herself and if only she really enjoyed it he wouldn't care what the neighbors' criticisms were, but it was so evident that she didn't; shaking and bumping on her horse in a bulging habit, perspiring and digging up the turf on the golf course, trying to lead when she danced and gasping when she bumped into any smoothly gliding couple! He liked her so much better sweet and cool and tranquil in the hammock or the nursery or at the head of his table, even though he hadn't always thought of her that way!

When she came down to breakfast on Friday morning in a striped tennis suit which aggravated her stoutness and accentuated the heavy, close-grown thatches of her brows, he was moved to diplomatic protest.

"My dear, is it going to be tennis now?" Gloria had not yet appeared, and as the children always breakfasted in the nursery the two were, for the moment, alone. "Really, you shouldn't; it's going to be a frightfully hot day."

"It will be good for me, Stan." Olive seated herself serenely behind the coffee pot. "I find I haven't had enough exercise lately. I'm going to the country club with Gloria this afternoon, too. Want to come along?"

She said it naturally enough but Stan stared.

"She—we—we were going to play Mott and Rider!" he began feebly.

"You don't mind a gallery, do you? I didn't say I was going to *play*, did I?" Olive smiled and then added: "Too bad she's going to the city on Monday, isn't it? We'll miss her terribly! Just think, only three days more!"

"Can't we persuade her to stay on, Olive?" Stan flushed. "Just another week? There's a lot going on and it's doing her so much good."

"I'll ask her." Olive turned in her chair just as Gloria entered, with the early sun through the long French windows turning her hair as golden-red as its own first beams and her soft blue tennis flannels into cloud-tinted azure.

"So sorry I'm late!" she exclaimed apologetically to Olive, but her glance, still dewy from sleep, strayed to the tall figure rising to pull out her chair. "There'll be heaps of time, though, before ten. Isn't that when we're due at the Forresters for the first of the elimination sets?"

"We hadn't started yet, Gloria," Olive replied as she nodded smilingly at her guest. "Were you really going to play tennis? Stan was just saying that one shouldn't; it's going to be such a frightfully hot day. Weren't you, Stan?"

He flushed still deeper.

"I advised *you* not to, Olive. You mentioned not having done much exercising lately and I was afraid you'd be overcome."

The thrust went home but Olive observed quietly as she rang for the maid and busied herself with the fruit:

"You'll be astonished how much it will take to overcome me. Gloria, I'm afraid you've been bored to death here—I mean with the dull sort of existence we lead when you are so accustomed to a brilliant one, but we'd love to have you stay with us for as long as you can. I feel that I've seen so little of you, really, and we haven't had a single one of those good, long confidential talks we used to have at school!"

Gloria smiled but it died quickly as she shook her head.

"We will before I leave, but I must go on Monday, Olive. I'd love to stay, you don't know what it's meant to be here and to—to see you again, but I've some tiresome business matters to attend to for a week or two, and then I'm off once more. I told you I was a nomad!"

She had spoken lightly but there was a little note of desolation in her tone of which she was herself perhaps unconscious.

"Where are you going?" Stan asked.

"To Scotland, till the snow flies, then somewhere on the Mediterranean, I think." Gloria added: "It's dear of you both to want me but perhaps sometime I shall descend upon you again to hear that Nancy has become a poetess and Bill an engineer!"

"An engineer?" Olive looked up from her eggs and bacon with a puzzled frown.

"Yes!" Gloria's low delicious laughter came gurgling from her throat. "Nancy's career is already marked in the stars, but Bill has confided his ambition to me; he wants to build bridges and viaducts and great roads—he's pointed out the pictures to me."

"How silly of him!" Olive laughed. "To travel around the world and leave his mother! Bill's going to be a lawyer, like my father, and practice right here in Chichester. Nancy must go to a good, practical school and have all these queer fancies taken out of her head, and then we'll see!"

"You'll pardon me?" Stan interrupted, holding up an official-looking envelope. "This is from one of our vice-presidents and may be important."

For a minute or two the women busied themselves with their own correspondence, a little pile of which lay beside each plate.

"Oh, Stan!" Olive looked up. "The Pearsalls are coming in a fortnight to week-end with us on their way to Canada!

Now you'll have a chance to teach Fred that new mashie stroke of yours."

"Sorry, but I won't, my dear." Stan folded his note and replaced it carefully in its envelope. "I've got to run down to New York on Thursday and I'll be away at least ten days to a fortnight; just a business matter that wouldn't interest you but it's imperative."

"Will you excuse me?" Gloria rose. "I've received a letter that requires an immediate answer, but I won't be late for the tennis."

When her light footsteps had vanished up the stairs Olive laid her letters aside.

"Stan, I'll go to New York with you."

"Eh?" He glanced across at her in surprise. "But you can't! The Pearsalls . . ."

"Their hostess is no more—and no less—necessary than their host." A certain hard deliberation had come into her tones. "I shall wire them that we are to be away and they must stop on their return trip. We'll go to New York together."

"It can't be done this trip, Olive. I'll be too busy, and think of the heat in the city for the children!" Stan did not look at her as he spoke but fingered the second envelope he had taken up.

"Oh, we'll leave them home!" Her tone was still pleasant, but her face had whitened till the faint line of down on her upper lip stood out plainly. "Don't you want me, Stan?"

"Of course, my dear girl, but you haven't wanted to go before, not in years." Stan fidgeted in his chair. "I told you I'd be busy! . . ."

"So will I," Olive assured him. "I need a lot of expensive clothes and beauty treatments and ever so many other things."

"Look here, Olive, what's got into you?" Stan demanded. "Order your things by mail just as you always do, and as for beauty, nonsense—you know it doesn't matter to me how you look, you're you!"

His deep blue eyes were troubled and the flush which had subsided was rising again.

"It should matter to you, Stan! Do you realize that I'm only twenty-nine—just a year older than Gloria, for instance? It gives one a nice satisfied feeling to have a man's meals as he likes them, and his laundry checked, and his home clean, and children healthy, but it isn't exactly thrilling, would you think?" She was hurriedly recalling bits of Jim's diatribe of a week before, to turn them to her own ends. "A woman's home and children are a great deal to her but they're not everything in life, any more than they are to a man. I think I shall go to New York with you, Stan."

"Do you mean that I've been neglecting you, Olive?" His tone was very quiet. "I shan't attempt to defend myself or recite my possible virtues, but I think I've been always at your service to go wherever you wanted to go and do whatever you wished. This time, however, it's out of the question; I must go on this trip alone!"

There was a little pause and then Olive rose, gathering up her letters.

"I didn't know it was as urgent as that." She spoke from the doorway. "I'm playing tennis at the Holcombs', but of course I'll be home at lunchtime and then we three will go to the club together."

She played only one set, however, went down to utter defeat before the older but more agile Mrs. Holcomb, and returned to Hydrangea Walk, long before lunch, exhausted and hot and longing for an afternoon in her hammock, but more grimly determined than ever.

When the others appeared they found her already in golfing attire, cool and tranquil and ready to laugh with them at Mrs. Holcomb's victory and listen to the story of their own. There was no indication that she recalled the argument of the morning, and Stan was apparently relieved. This new phase was only a passing one, he concluded, and she hadn't really cared about going to the city at all.

At the country club, a little later, they were joined not only by Henry Mott and his guest, Mr. Rider, but by the major, although the latter explained he had only come to play a few holes with the Prof., just to get his hand in again.

"Oh, dear!" Gloria exclaimed to Olive on the porch. "I forgot I had this ring on! Bad form, and it interferes with my play. Will you keep it for me since you won't join us?"

She thrust the circlet into Olive's hand and turned away to join Stan, who waited with Mott and Rider for her coming, and the woman she had left glanced down at the ring she held. It was the enormous, fiery cabochon opal she remembered seeing frequently on her guest's hand, but she had never studied it closely before. It was all milky blues with swirls and darts of scintillating greens and angry reds through it, and deep in its heart a burst of orange appeared in a strange form, like a misshapen fleur de lis. Olive would have liked to examine it further, but a group of ladies, seated under a wide-striped lawn umbrella, called to her, so she slipped the jewel into her beaded purse and joined them.

After the foursome was over Henry Mott and his guest had a discreet libation in the locker room and started back to The Rafters, as the former called his roomy, rehabilitated farmhouse because there had been little else left of the original house when it came into his hands. Both men felt aglow and at peace with the world as they set out down the lane back of the caddie house to avoid the clamorous invitations of the various tea-parties on the porch and lawns. Mott was pulling contentedly at his pipe and Rider's

graying mustache was tilted at one side by his inevitable
cigar, and they walked almost to where the lane crossed a
patch of woodland beyond which lay the rough between
the seventh and eighth holes before either spoke. Then
Henry Mott broke the silence.

"Plays a mighty good game for a woman," he observed
grudgingly. "Made up your mind about her, Dan? Remember where you met her? It must have been when she went
slumming some time, if she did really recognize you and
hasn't mentioned it."

Rider shook his head, ignoring the pleasantry.

"Nope. It's the darnedest thing! Her face, that's all I
remember; everything else is hazy, like smoke."

"Sounds like a crystal-gazing faker," commented Mott.
"It's kind of funny, though, that Jack won't talk about
her."

"She doesn't talk about him—or *to* him very much,
does she?" asked Rider. "They've met before, she was the
first to spring that, but there's some kind of a tacit understanding between them that further reminiscence is out of
order. When's that chap coming you spoke of, the one who
was a liaison officer over there?"

"Captain Staverton? Craig is his front name and you'll
find him an interesting fellow. He's coming next week just
for the night and he'll wire when . . . Great guns! Look at
that!"

Mott had suddenly seized his companion's arm with his
fat fingers and drawn him back, adding the exclamation
in a surprised whisper, and Rider looked in the direction
the other pointed out. They were midway in the patch of
woodland just before the lane twisted away from the rough
beside the green, and a few yards from them a woman sat
on a rustic bench, her hands, palms outward, held in front
of her as though in rejection or possible defense, while,
standing fairly over her, his hands clenched at his sides—

and his face distorted with some violent emotion so that it was scarcely recognizable, was a man. They were both recognizable, however, for the man's tall, frail figure was a familiar one and bright red hair showed beneath the pale, mauve hat of the woman—Major Hill and Gloria Warrender!

"Jumping Christopher!" Mott breathed excitedly, his ruddy face empurpled. "Is he going to strike her? He isn't altogether responsible, you know! Think we ought to interfere?"

"Not by a jugful!" Rider returned. "Whatever it is, they're having it out between them! Walk on and talk naturally. If they see and hear us, we don't know they're there; get me?"

If the couple knew of their proximity they gave no sign, and Mott did not dare to look back, but he couldn't draw a free breath till his own gates were reached.

"By Godfrey!" he gasped. "I didn't like the look of that, did you, Dan?"

"Quite an interesting little scene," Rider said appreciatively. "I'm glad we're dining with the Mercers to-night. I'm going to watch the lady's reaction."

But from Gloria's appearance that evening there was little to be gained in explanation of the earlier violent tête-à-tête. To Rider, glancing down his huge nose at her across the table, she seemed merely a well-poised, light-hearted woman, witty, clever and supremely attractive even to his coldly unimpressionable eye.

Her gown seemed to be composed of some cloudy opalescent gauze which ran from palest yellow into the rich red of her hair, blending with the glint in her long eyes and the flash of the strange ring which she wore.

Without effort or apparent desire she held the attention of all in the circle, and it was with reluctance that Rider permitted himself to be dragged away by Mott immediately after dinner to a "Y" meeting down in the town.

"Remarkable woman!" he observed as they chugged off in the little runabout. "After that scene this afternoon, no matter what caused it, a weak sister would have pleaded a headache and remained in her room, an ordinary one would have appeared limp and nerve-racked, but she seemed merely stimulated by it! Lord, I wish I could recall where I saw her before!"

There was a full moon that evening, turning the gardens of Hydrangea Walk into a fairyland, and to Stan, strolling there with Gloria, she appeared like a creature from another world in her softly luminous gown, an indefinable perfume seeming to rise from her arms and shoulders, as smooth and pearly white as marble, and from her hair, vivid even under the silvery light.

"It's strange," he spoke as though to himself, "how perfectly I understand you—and yet I don't understand you at all! That first day, at tea on the veranda, when you made Henry Mott so indignant at your apparent callousness about the war—only *I* saw that it was still so near and terrible that the very mention of it seared your heart—I've known every mood of yours but not what caused them, and yet there's something mysterious about you, Gloria! Something that no man can ever grasp, if I cannot!"

They had reached the dimmest recesses of the arbor, but the moon peered down through the leafy arch and, in the opening beyond them, the gleam of the sundial threw their figures in silhouette. The man beside her had never spoken to her so intimately, emotionally, before and never had he made her tremble and thrill with vibrations that seemed to be of her body and spirit in one.

With an unsteady, low murmur of laughter she asked:

"Why such conceit, my friend? Can no man do what you cannot?"

"None, because I love you as no man ever did or shall, and you love me!" He turned and caught her close to him, holding her trembling form still for a long moment, then, pushing back her soft hair, he kissed her brow and eyes and lips and throat as a starving man would touch the food and wine of life, but with a tender reverence in his passion.

Faint, torn with her own emotion, Gloria leaned against him and he raised his eyes for a moment to the brilliant night sky between the whispering leaves.

"God!" he breathed. "God!"

All at once Gloria's reeling senses steadied and she put both her hands against his breast to thrust him from her, but with a little sob her head drooped upon them.

"You see, dear!" he whispered. "It just came to us—caught us up in a whirlwind! You can't help it, nor can I, and no one's to blame! Gloria! Gloria! You're in my arms and I'll never let you go!"

"You must!" The words seemed to tear her heart apart, but she lifted her head and looked straight into his eyes. "We can't help—love, maybe, but we can help . . ."

Stan closed her lips with his.

"Not this love of ours! We've been waiting all our lives, but from the moment we met—well, there wasn't anything else! You knew it, you felt it just as I did! Oh, I knew you were trying to fight it; that's why you wouldn't stay any longer, and when I asked you this morning where you were going you answered vaguely because you knew I meant to follow you, to the ends of the earth. You spoke of coming back—back, when a new generation had risen! I knew what you meant, but it wasn't to be like that! This thing which has come is a force greater than we! How I've dreamed of you, here close to me!"

"And it must be always a dream!" Gloria slowly drew herself from him. "Have you thought . . ."

This time she paused of her own accord and he bowed his head, replying humbly:

"I know! I've wondered desperately what we could do, but there's nothing! There's no crazy infatuation about this, it's swept us off our feet and it will carry us on forever! Do you think I could let you go?" He lifted his head and his breath came quickly. "Let you go your way through the world with other men making love to you, other men feeling the flame of you, knowing you are alone and free? I'd rather see you dead!"

"No, Stan!" Gloria said softly. "I'll never be free, and I don't want to be! Wherever I go I shall feel that you are with me. We'll be forgiven for this moment, I know, but it is the last, the end!"

He took one step forward and crushed her to him.

"It is the beginning! It's the very beginning of life for both of us!"

Suddenly his voice died in his throat and his arms fell limply from about her as he stepped back. In the full glow of the moonlight just beyond the arbor's end stood Olive!

5

The Hammock's Burden

For an instant they stood motionless, transfixed, and then Olive's voice came to them, its contralto tones raised in query.

"Stan! Gloria! Are you in there? I can't see."

Stan gasped with relief and opened his lips, but before he could utter a word Gloria called, her drawling notes a little shaken: "Yes, Olive, 'way down here near the sundial. We're coming."

"I've been looking everywhere for you!" Olive laughed. "I suppose Stan was trying to show you that queer shadow the moon casts on the sundial sometimes when it's just right, but it's damp under that arbor."

"I couldn't see it." Gloria spoke more calmly as they emerged and went toward her, but Stan was still silent. "How's Bill?"

"Only a little feverish; some berries, or something, I suppose. He's always cramming whatever he can find into his mouth and the nurse is an alarmist," replied Olive tranquilly. "I came to tell you that the Forresters have 'phoned to invite us all to the dance at the Waterfall Inn over by the lake to-morrow night."

"Good!" Stan had found his voice. "It'll be a change at least from the country club, and they give such original affairs."

They talked on casually and Gloria, forced by sheer need to rise to the occasion, found herself wondering if Olive had seen. But, no; she was not actress enough to play a part; there were no depths to her good, honest nature, only quiet contented shallows which the swiftest of winds could only ruffle on the surface.

The evening seemed interminable, but Gloria, seated where the shadow cast by one of the drawing-room lamps shielded her face, talked on of trivial things, her spirit in torment, until Olive asked suddenly:

"That's an opal, isn't it, Gloria? That ring you're wearing which you gave me to take care of for you at the club this afternoon? It's very strange and beautiful."

"It's rare." Gloria glanced down with a little shudder at the jewel. "In fact, I understand there isn't another like it in the world! I don't know that I consider it beautiful; it's rather terrible to me, sometimes."

"Well, opals are considered unlucky, but you'd hardly call yourself that!" Olive smiled, adding: "Where in your wanderings did you pick it up?"

"It was given to me by a ghost." Gloria's tone was very low.

"My dear!"

"It's my one superstition. It repels me and yet I feel bound to it. I couldn't sell it and I wouldn't give it away with that thought of ill-luck following it. The friend who gave it to me was dying—in fact, they thought he had already passed away. I happened to be near and they sent for me, when all at once he sat up and spoke."

"What an experience!" Olive murmured. Stan was sitting with his eyes shaded by his hand, motionless, listening.

"That's why I said he was a ghost," Gloria explained. "He had no people, and he wanted me to wear it always, so I took it to please him, although it actually terrified me!"

"I should think so, under the circumstances," commented the other woman. "I noticed an odd orange light in the center, not a streak, but almost a compact mass, like a conventionalized lily."

"Yes." But Gloria made no move to take the ring from her finger and offer it for further examination. "That is what makes it so valuable; the jeweler who looked to the settings for me in Paris offered me enough for it to keep a person in humble circumstances for life. . . . Goodness, can it be as late as that?"

The old tall clock had clanged eleven strokes, and Olive rose.

"You've had a more strenuous day than I," she said indulgently. "We really must all rest up a little to-morrow in order to be fresh for the dance at the Inn."

Alone in her own room, Gloria fell to pacing the floor, her soft negligee flowing about her and her hair a fiery cloud to her knees. Till Monday! She must bear the strain of this mingled joy and suffering till Monday, and then it would be over, a memory to cloud and yet lighten all the experiences of the past and those to come. Was she equal to it? Would the weakness which had come to her in that magic moment in the arbor return to beat down her defenses? She, didn't know, she couldn't trust herself! The only safeguard would be to avoid a moment alone with Stan until she went out of his life. . . .

The little runabout which had taken Henry Mott and his friend to the "Y" meeting in Chichester broke down ignominiously when they started homeward and had to be rolled into a garage across the street, but it was only a two-mile walk and the midnight air balmy and fragrant.

Their way took them past a hedge at the side of Hydrangea Walk and they paused, for the moonlight, still flooding the perfect garden, made it a scene of arresting beauty and peace.

All the lights were out in the house save one on the second story, and inadvertently they glanced up at it, then Mott turned quickly with his hand on his companion's arm. A tall, graceful woman had passed before the window, with flowing draperies and rippling masses of ruddy hair, and just as the light from within the room fell full upon her she had flung her slender arms out and upward with a gesture of infinite despair.

"Wait!" Rider said suddenly in a cautious tone. "I'm not spying on the lady, Henry, but some one else is. Look!"

Beyond the hedge, and almost directly beneath Gloria's window, stood a clump of well spaced, tall bushes, their leaves turned to silver in the clear, white radiance, and as Mott's eyes followed Rider's pointing finger it seemed to him that something moved in the shadows beneath them.

"What is it?" Mott whispered excitedly. "What's anybody doing around the place at this hour? Hadn't we better . . ."

"Hush! He's watching that window, don't you see? There, he's coming out into the light!"

A tall, gaunt figure emerged from the shadows and stood with his back to them staring up at Gloria's window, and involuntarily their gaze followed his. She passed again, unaware of the three watchers, and this time her head was bent, her face covered with her hands and her hair falling like a veil about her.

When she had disappeared the man by the bushes turned suddenly, the glow falling full upon his face which appeared to be twisted in a maniacal fury, and, with a wild wave of his arms, dashed toward the front of the house. A moment later they heard the crunch of his flying feet on the gravel of the drive leading to the gate.

"By Godfrey, this is going too far!" Mott drew a deep breath. "That was Jack, and I'd swear he was out of his mind! We've got to do something about it, Dan! He might harm her!"

"Not to-night, anyway, for he's gone," Rider responded practically. "There goes Miss Warrender's light out, too, and it's time we were getting on ourselves. The curtain has fallen, but I'm glad I've seen her with the mask off, at last!"

If mask she wore, it was safely on again the next morning, however, and declining to ride she spent an hour or two with the children, and then wrote letters till lunch. During the meal, although she felt Stan's reproachfully wistful eyes upon her, she forestalled any invitation by announcing that she meant to read herself to sleep in the hammock, and wouldn't Olive come out too, if she was going to remain at home and mend that black feather fan, as she had said?

The afternoon was very hot and still, with the brooding promise of a coming storm in the air, and little Nancy, unable to fall asleep, when no diversion offered, like her more phlegmatic brother, wandered restlessly about the garden, her sensitive spirit depressed by the sultry atmosphere, until she felt a tremulous foreboding, she could not have told why.

Mother was sewing in her room, Daddy had gone out somewhere directly after lunch, and he'd looked sort of angry and hurt about something, too. Perhaps dear, wonderful Miss Warrender hadn't fallen asleep yet and would tell her some more about the glorious places she'd seen, but Nancy would slip very softly between the circling shrubbery and see. . . .

What she saw made her blue eyes widen, become distended, and she crushed her hands down over her lips to stifle the shriek which arose to them as she staggered back, swaying against the trunk of a tree. Something lay at her feet, a tiny, fragile object, which had no place in that scene, and stooping, the child picked it up and fled to the house.

Five minutes later the telephone at The Rafters rang with an insistency which made Mott mutter exasperatedly as he rose from the card-table where he and Rider were spending the warm hours over a chess-board.

"Hello!" he yelled, then lowered his voice swiftly. "Oh, Mrs. Mercer? Yes? . . . No, he hasn't been here. Did you try the country club? . . . Why, what's wrong? . . . Of course, at once! May I bring Dan Rider? . . . All right, you can count on us, Mrs. Mercer!"

There was a sudden ring as of the authority of the overseas days in his tones and his rotund figure was erect as he returned hastily to his friend.

"What's up?" Rider demanded. "I heard your end of the talk of course, and I gathered she couldn't locate Mercer. What did she want you for?"

"I don't know, but come on!" Henry snatched up a cap and started for the door. "Thank the powers they brought the car back from the garage this morning!"

Only when they were skittering wildly over the short distance which separated them from Hydrangea Walk would he pursue the subject, and then he explained jerkily:

"She asked first if I knew where Stan was—she'd already tried the country club—and I could tell from her voice that she was all broken up about something and as near hysteria as a woman of her type could ever be. When I asked what was wrong she said it was something terrible, something she couldn't talk about over the 'phone, and as she couldn't locate Stan would I mind coming over? You heard my reply. I wonder if anything could have happened to Nancy or Bill?"

"Must have, if it's a matter of physical injury, and she was able to talk to you herself." Rider paused and gave a quick, habitually sidelong glance at the other. "That is, if Miss Warrender is golfing or somewhere with Mercer. She didn't mention her, did she?"

"No. No one but her husband." Mott swung perilously in at the gate. "She'd know where he was if Miss Warrender was with him! Jumping Christopher, you don't mean . . ."

"What's that boy doing there?" Rider interrupted sharply. "What's inside that circle of bushes?"

"That's Hans, the assistant gardener—t.b., poor kid." Mott glanced quickly at the place indicated by his companion. "Wonder what he's walking up and down like that for? There's just a hammock and a couple of camp-chairs in that little hollow and the children play there. Look! Here's Mrs. Mercer!"

They had drawn up before the steps of the veranda, and as they sprang out of the car Olive came forward to meet them. Her sallow skin was ghastly in its pallor and her eyes within their reddened rims stared unseeingly as those of a sleep-walker.

"Oh, Mr. Mott—and Mr. Rider!" Her deep tones were hoarse and shaking. "I don't know what to do—I'm almost insane! Nancy—Nancy came shrieking into the house a few minutes before I called you, fairly beside herself with terror! We couldn't get anything out of her except 'the hammock! Go look in the hammock!' I left her with Ingred and ran out to that little circle of shrubbery—you know, Mr. Mott—and there—there my friend is lying!"

"Miss Warrender, you mean?" Mott demanded. "What's the matter with her?"

"I—I thought she was asleep, but her head was hanging over the side of the hammock in an odd way, and when I called her name and rushed up to her, I saw a—a rope twisted about her neck! I don't know how I did it, but I turned her so that I could see her face and it was black! Oh, go—go and see her yourselves!"

"Murder! My God!" Mott's eyes met his companion's for an instant, and then he turned and sped over the lawn toward the copse as fast as his short legs would carry him, while Rider gently forced Olive into a chair and sat down beside her.

"Now, Mrs. Mercer, let's have it over again," he said encouragingly. "If this is true, it's what Mott called it, right enough, and we . . . I mean the local police will have to have every detail."

"Murder!" Olive repeated in a horrified whisper. "I can't believe it! It's like a nightmare! Gloria—Gloria and I were like sisters years ago at school—it can't be that she's dead, killed! I—I think I'm going mad!"

"Indeed you're not!" Rider assured her. "Won't you tell me everything down to the very least detail from the moment your little girl came screaming into the house?"

"But I have!" Olive protested.

"Where, for instance, were you?" he asked.

"Why, up in my own bedroom, sewing." Olive eyed him wonderingly. "I supposed the children and the maids were about somewhere, and at lunch Gloria—Gloria said she was going down to read in the hammock. I hadn't thought about my husband—he'd gone off somewhere immediately after we arose from the table. I heard Nancy rush in the side door, shrieking with every breath she drew, and Ingred's heavy feet hurrying to her, and, of course, I dropped my work and flew down the stairs. Nancy was crouched on the floor in the hall, covering her face with her hands, and cowering away if we tried to touch her as though she were in mortal terror. She's a queer child, morbid and sensitive, but I'd never seen her in such a state before.

"The parlormaid appeared, and cook came up to see what was the matter and the nurse ran down, and then Bill woke up from his nap in the nursery and fell downstairs trying to reach us! Altogether it was the wildest confusion, but I finally got Nancy to speak and she cried out about the hammock. That's—that's all, Mr. Rider. Who—who

could have done such a fearful thing? Gloria hadn't an
enemy in the world, I'm sure!"

"You saw your friend lying there with the rope twisted
about her neck, and when you lifted her you saw that her
face was black," Rider prompted. "What did you do then?
Are you sure she was dead?"

"Sure!" Olive shuddered violently. "Her eyes were staring and her tongue . . . oh, don't ask me any more, I can't
bear it! I suppose I dropped her back into the hammock,
and I don't know how I got to that opening in the bushes
nor whether I screamed or not, but Ingred, the housekeeper, came running from the house, and then her son Hans
appeared—the head gardener has gone away for a week—
and my only thought was to find my husband and tell him.
Ingred helped me into the house and I composed myself
enough to call up the country club, but he wasn't there.
Then I thought of Mr. Mott and I knew he'd help me! I—
I'm sorry to drag you into this, Mr. Rider . . ."

"I'm glad to be of any service I can, Mrs. Mercer, and
I've always taken an interest in such tragic affairs as this,"
Rider was beginning, when Mott appeared at the break in
the hedge and hurried to them.

His round, usually ruddy countenance had taken on a
greenish tinge and his sandy hair was standing straight up,
but when he spoke his voice was brisk and authoritative.

"Mrs. Mercer, has any one touched the body or, indeed,
been in that hollow at all except your little girl, and then
you?" he asked.

"Of course not!" She shuddered again. "I told Hans to
stand guard until Stan or some one came."

"Some one must come, and at once," Mott asserted.
"The Chichester headquarters must be 'phoned to without
a moment's delay, and till they come Dan Rider and I'll
mount guard out there. Will you call them or shall I?"

"Oh, you, please, if you'll be so good!" Olive faltered. "I feel almost prostrated! Poor Gloria, what a thing to come to her here!"

"You are quite sure Miss Warrender had no enemies?" pursued Rider as the other man went to the telephone. "It's a delicate question, I know, but more people in all walks of life have deadly enemies than you would believe."

"I can't imagine—I can't conceive—of Gloria having an enemy on earth," Olive replied slowly. "Of course, we literally dropped out of each other's lives when we left school, ten years ago, and I heard nothing of her since, until a mutual friend came here to visit the Holcombs, a Mrs. Derwent. It—it seems odd when we were so intimate years ago, but the time was too long to gap, I suppose; we haven't had a real, confidential talk since she came, and I know nothing of who her friends may have been except that, of course, they were the best people. Mr. Rider, who on earth could have any motive to harm her?"

He shrugged.

"That's what the police will have to discover. You don't know if there was any romance in her life? Who will profit financially by her death? If any one was in fear of her, or trying to blackmail her? These are the most common reasons for murder, you know, but when a woman is young, attractive, rich and with no ties, the possibilities are almost limitless."

"I haven't an idea who will profit by her death for she's—she was—absolutely alone in the world, and I can't think of any one wanting to injure, much less kill, such a happy, harmless, adorable girl! Oh, if Stan would only come home!"

"The Chief of Police will be here himself as soon as his car can bring him, together with two or three subordinates, Mrs. Mercer." Mott rejoined them in the big entrance hall. "Is there any one you would like me to call up in order to locate Stan?"

"I'm here! Why all the fuss about finding me?" Stan's tall figure, hatless as usual and with his coat flung over his arm, appeared in the entrance door. He had bounded so lightly up the veranda steps in his rubber-soled shoes that none of them had heard him. "Hello, you fellows! Olive, you look terribly upset, and didn't I hear some one say something about the police?"

Mott and Rider glanced from him to each other, and in the pause Olive sprang to her feet.

"Stan!" she cried, "Gloria is dead!"

6

The Ghost's Gift

Stan staggered back, catching at the side of the door to save himself, but as he stood silhouetted against the sunny background of the veranda his features were blotted out in shadow.

"You—I must have misunderstood!" he spoke in a choking whisper. "Did you say Gloria—*was dead?*"

Rider took a step forward, but Olive sank back in her chair.

"Yes! Isn't it terrible, Stan?" she moaned. "Who could have killed her!"

"Killed her!" Stan gazed wildly at the two other men. "It couldn't be possible that you mean—murder!"

Mott nodded gravely.

"It's true, old man. I've seen her, it's—it's horrible!"

"God! It can't be true! Who—where is she?"

"In the hammock down in the copse—" Mott was beginning, but, waiting to hear no more, Stan turned and rushed away, and Olive buried her face in her hands.

"I knew he'd take it that way!" she sobbed in muffled tones. "He'd grown to—to look on her as an old f-friend, too, and he liked her immensely. Every one did! Only a maniac could have committed such a frightful crime! Oh, may I go to my room till the police arrive? There'll be endless questioning and I—I must have a few minutes alone!"

"Certainly, Mrs. Mercer." Mott assisted her to the staircase. "Rest by all means and I'll ask the chief not to disturb you until it's absolutely necessary."

"I knew I could count on you as a real friend, Mr. Mott!" Olive's hand rested on his coatsleeve for a minute. "I suppose I ought to have gone with Stan; he'll feel dreadfully, especially as she was our guest, under our protection. He'll think that we are responsible in a way, and I suppose we are, but what forewarning could any of us have had?"

"That's morbid, dear lady!" Mott's pallor was tinged with pink in his earnestness. "We don't any of us know what—er—what may lie back of this, and it would be ridiculous to blame yourselves! Of course, Stan will be stunned, we all are, but we'll find out who did it, never fear!"

"I—I hope so!" With her head bowed Olive turned and went on up the stairs, and Mott looked about him to speak to Rider—but Rider had disappeared.

He was, in fact, outside the opposite semicircle of shrubbery, concealed alike from the house and the little hollow in which the hammock was slung, but staring through at the scene before him with his huge nose thrust between the interlaced twigs.

Stan had halted and stood staring down at the thing which lay in the hammock as one in a trance, but his head was so averted that the watcher could not read his expression. Suddenly he wheeled at the sound of a motor and started for the house.

The car, however, did not turn in at the gate, and Rider crept around the screening shrubbery to the opening and passed in, in his turn. Gloria Warrender's slender limbs were contorted in the struggle which had evidently come upon her unawares. Her face was bloated and discolored almost beyond recognition, her hands fell limply on either side as though they had been tearing at the thin, strong rope which had cut deeply into her white throat and had relaxed only in the moment of dissolution, and her head still hung grotesquely over the edge of the hammock, her unbound hair rippling in great masses to the short-trodden grass beneath.

It was too soft and springing for any definite footsteps to have been outlined, but there was a recently flattened space close to the body where some heavy person had stood within the hour, with both feet pressing firmly into the turf. Rider glanced up at the two ropes which, anchored about the trunks of two trees, supported the hammock at head and foot. They were weather-grayed, not as new as the rope wound so tightly about that pulseless throat, but the one at the foot was still sound and that at the head of the hammock was frayed, showing the raw glint of hemp through the worn outer strands. It was at the head, then, that the greatest strain had come when the brief, silent struggle had taken place!

Had Miss Warrender been asleep when the murderer came? Surely the crime had been unpremeditated; no one in their senses would have planned to kill her there so near the house in broad daylight, with children and servants constantly about! Then, where had the rope come from? It was quite an ordinary bit, scarcely the thickness of one of the victim's fingers, but new and strong, and no slip noose had been made in it; it seemed rather to have been passed around and around the unfortunate woman's neck and then the ends pulled tight with almost superhuman strength until her struggles ceased.

There was something odd about the ends of that rope, too; one had been knotted into a sort of ball, but the other appeared to have been actually torn apart from a longer section, its ends frayed and bearing no mark of having been severed with a knife. That would have taken

strength far beyond that of a normal human being, and
Rider turned perplexedly to find himself confronting a
similar rope looped around the trunk of a tree a few feet
away, with a short, dangling end, frayed and torn as the
other had been. This, then, was where the weapon had been
found and Miss Warrender had not even had time to rise
from the hammock before death had been upon her. That
she had struggled, her unbound hair and certain abrasions
on her limp hands proved; that she had been taken by surprise was evident, either in the sudden appearance of her
assailant or in the attack itself, but Rider's keen eyes could
discover no other clew.

A book, opened and turned upside down, lay on a
camp-chair, as though Gloria Warrender had placed it
there herself, and although Rider was scrupulously careful
not to touch it, he recognized it as one from the Mercers'
library. The murderer could have left only by that opening
in the circle of hedge which practically faced the house; a
nervy job, the unofficial investigator decided, with long
odds against his escape undiscovered, but apparently he
had accomplished it.

He made haste to pass through it himself as the police
car turned in between the gateposts, and with no desire
to encounter them now, he strode toward the side porch
and the little door through which Nancy must have gone
screaming with her dreadful news. The house seemed op-
pressive with silence, but from the library came Henry
Mott's voice, low and intent, and an occasional monosyl-
labic response from Stan Mercer. Rider turned toward the
rear and entered the deserted billiard-room to lean over a
pool-table, jotting down various notes with a pencil on the
back of an envelope from his pocket, and as he wrote his
heavy face grew sterner, his jaw more squarely prominent
and the nostrils of his great nose were distended now and
then with a labored breath as those of a hard-run horse.

When he had finished he dropped into a leather chair and listened to the arrival of the chief and his subordinates, who were greeted quietly and composedly by Stan and taken out to the scene of the crime. Mott appeared in the billiard-room doorway and grunted with relief when he saw his friend.

"You disappeared when I was talking to Mrs. Mercer!" he accused, mopping his brow with a capacious handkerchief. "Pretty fierce business, isn't it? Did you see the body?"

"Yes, after Mercer. He just stood and looked at it for a minute and then turned away." Rider got out of his chair. "I don't believe we're needed here for a while, and out of sheer curiosity I'm going down to the town to send a wire or two that I don't want to 'phone in. Ring and ask if Mrs. Mercer wants us to do any errand for her; say we'll be back within an hour."

The stout, huge-framed Ingred answered the summons, her wide face placid no longer but white and drawn, and her mild blue eyes filled with a dumb, helpless terror. It seemed some time before she could comprehend their message, and when she returned after delivering it she shook her head.

"Missis say not to tall nobody not'ings, pleass. Ef anybody bane want dey should see har, she got seeckness."

"All right, Ingred; I understand," Mott said, but the woman still barred his way, her huge, reddened hands twisting a corner of her apron.

"Ef you coom 'crost little Mees Nancy, sir, vould you pleass to send har home?" she asked in grave trouble. "She bane gone the whiles har marmer talk to you on de wire, and never she done dis before, but she is scairt from out har senses. Ve don't like ve makes more troubles so ve don't tall Mister and Missis yet."

"Look here, who does she play with, Ingred? The Holcomb kids? Where does her mother let her visit?" Mott asked.

Ingred shook her head and the terror in her eyes deepened to a haunting dread.

"She bane gone no place," she insisted stubbornly. "Mees Nancy, she looked on somet'ing dat a child's eyes should not see, and she vant to run from all de vorld!"

"I guess Ingred's right, if she wouldn't even let her own mother touch her." Mott turned to his companion. "We'll keep an eye out for her, eh?"

But Nancy's disappearance was soon forgotten, for in the mysterious manner in which news of a bizarre or tragic nature travels in a small city, it had become known that somebody was dead up at the Mercers' and that Henry Mott himself had telephoned for the police, and they were besieged at every halt and turning. Rider sent off his telegrams from the office at the railroad station and they started back to Hydrangea Walk, replying to the excited, peremptory gestures of Mott's fellow-townsmen merely by an answering wave. When the village street gave way to the winding country road, a silence fell between them; Rider had vouchsafed no further information concerning the telegrams he had sent, and his companion knew that his confidence would not be withheld when the propitious moment for it came.

"I'm curious about something," Rider remarked as they neared the spot where the tragedy had taken place.

"Don't say so!" Mott responded with heavy sarcasm. "I'm curious about the whole wretched business! It's the worst thing that ever hit this county!"

"I was thinking of that slow-witted giantess of a maid— Ingred, you called her? She spoke of the little girl being scared out of her senses, but she was the one who was terrorized!"

"Nancy! We forgot her!" Mott ejaculated, but the other shrugged.

"What can we do? Start a lost-child cry in the town without the parents' permission, or wander about the neighborhood at random looking for her? We'll make sure first that she isn't anywhere in the house or grounds and then tell Mercer. But did you notice Ingred particularly?"

"No, I didn't; she seemed about as dumb as usual. She's been working in this section of the country for sixteen or eighteen years to my knowledge and you heard what English she speaks!" Mott paused and then added in a different tone. "You said she looked terrorized, Dan, but why wouldn't she, considering the murder and then Nancy running away like that?"

"I'm asking myself just how dumb she is." Rider appeared to be looking straight ahead, but the other was conscious of his glance. "She seemed chiefly concerned with the child's absence, but could she be held responsible for that? She could have had no guilty knowledge concerning the murder, but could she have seen or overheard anything, become suspicious, in fact, as to the identity of the murderer? There was fear in her eyes, I tell you, Henry, and the fear wasn't entirely on Nancy's account. I'd give something merely as a bystander, for a confidential talk with Ingred!"

They had reached the gates of Hydrangea Walk, and the presence of several men from police headquarters loitering about made them realize that the crowd of curiosity seekers had been anticipated.

"It's all right, Mr. Mott." A man just inside the tall posts waved him on up the drive. "Chief's waiting for you, and the coroner, too."

Several other machines including the last named individual's grim little closed car were drawn up beside the chief's at the porch steps, and as they alighted from their own and crossed the porch, the door was opened by one

of the local police who grinned broadly at Mott before
the seriousness of the situation reoccurred to him. Rider
recognized him as one of the Y.M.C.A. members he had
met at the meeting the night before.

"The District Attorney's here and one of his men,
Ridgeway, Mr. Mott." He glanced over his shoulder at the
closed library door from behind which the subdued murmur of voices arose. "Doc Todd's in the parlor with the
Chief and Mrs. Mercer."

"All right, Ben." Mott nodded and turned toward the
drawing-room on the other side of the hall. "I guess they'll
want to see my friend here, too."

Olive Mercer was seated between two men at the center
table and, although pallid from shock and gravely troubled, her face as she turned toward her neighbors seemed
composed once more.

"Here's Mr. Mott now, Doctor!" she exclaimed. "Do
you know Mr. Rider? The coroner, Dr. Todd, and Chief of
Police Clark."

Dr. Todd, an insignificant, undersized individual of
early middle age, bowed with professional aplomb, but the
chief's small, twinkling eyes widened in his lantern-jawed
face as he gazed at Rider, and after a moment he asked in
a slow nasal drawl:

"Mr. Rider, you're visiting Henry Mott up here, ain't
you? How long you been with us?"

"About a month, Chief," the other replied gravely, but
there was a twinkle in his own eyes.

"New Yorker?"

"Yes."

"Know anything about Miss Gloria Warrender?" the
chief pursued, to the obvious surprise of the rest of the
group. "Ever hear of her before she come here to visit?"

"I never heard of Miss Warrender until her prospec-
tive visit was announced by Mr. and Mrs. Mercer," Rider

responded as though he thought there was nothing unusual in the query, adding: "I'm taking a vacation here and happened to come over with Mott when Mrs. Mercer 'phoned for him."

In the slight pause which ensued Dr. Todd turned rather significantly to Henry Mott.

"You were the third to view the body, I believe?"

"To the best of my knowledge, Doctor," Mott replied carefully. "Mrs. Mercer tells me that her little daughter discovered it, then she herself went to the garden where it was lying in a hammock, and when I came she requested me to look at it. I did so and with Mrs. Mercer's permission I telephoned to the police."

"And now Nancy has run off somewhere!" Olive interjected in a vexed tone. "I suppose she is frightened, but why didn't she come to me? It's a mere matter of form, but naturally she must tell what she remembers seeing when she first came upon my—my poor friend!"

"That can go until later—any time before the inquest," Dr. Todd remarked indulgently. "Mr. Rider, did you too, view the body?"

"Yes, later, after Mr. Mercer himself had done so," Rider nodded.

"Did you see any possible clew?" the chief asked suddenly. "Any suggestion come to you, Mr. Rider?"

He slightly emphasized the "mister" as before and this time Rider smiled but shook his head.

"None. Miss Warrender had apparently been strangled by a piece of the swing-rope attached to a tree close by, but of course I touched nothing. In fact, I went to the scene of the crime merely because I inferred that Mrs. Mercer's request for Mr. Mott to do so included us both."

There was a trace of impatience in the coroner's manner as in his turn he addressed the stranger.

"You did not wait here for our arrival, Mr. Rider?"

"No. I had some errands to attend to in the town and Mr. Mott drove me down. We didn't discuss this affair with any one, of course, and came directly back here."

"Very good. Now then, Mott, will you tell us exactly what happened from the time Mrs. Mercer telephoned to you?"

Henry Mott complied and when he had finished Mrs. Mercer spoke suddenly.

"I've told you that I knew practically nothing about my friend or her associates until Mrs. Derwent, who was visiting the Holcombs a few weeks ago, mentioned her as being a guest in the same residential hotel in New York in which she lived herself. I hadn't seen Gloria since we graduated from school, but one of our neighbors has, for when I started to introduce them she reminded him that they had met before, on the other side, although that probably he would not remember her. I'd forgotten to ask her about it, but they didn't appear to be at all well acquainted. However, he might be able to tell you more than I can about her. It's Major Hill!"

"I may use your telephone, Mrs. Mercer?" Without waiting for her conventional permission, the coroner turned to the instrument, while Mott stared hard at Rider, and the latter regarded Olive's harassed, strained face with quiet understanding.

After some delay Hilltop's number responded and they all listened to the coroner's end of the brief conversation.

"Hello, Major? . . . Oh, where is he? . . . When did he go? . . . This afternoon, eh? What time? . . . Who are you? This is Dr. Todd, a friend of the Major's, speaking. . . . Well, Hiram, when do you expect him back? It was arranged that I should call him this afternoon. . . . He did, did he? Where did he go? I'll write him. . . . Oh, all right. When he gets back just tell him I called up, will you?"

He rung off and turned to the tensely listening group.

"Major Hill went away suddenly about two o'clock this afternoon. Some old man named 'Hiram' who keeps house for him answered me; hasn't any notion of where he's gone or when he'll be back. You're rather a good friend of his, I understand, Mott; did he say anything about this trip the last time you saw him?"

"We're pretty good friends," Mott responded with slow significance. "He's a silent sort of fellow, though; doesn't often talk about his plans. Certainly when we met him at the country club yesterday afternoon he didn't say anything about going away."

His eyes wandered cautiously to those of Rider to find them regarding him in a quizzical way, but the coroner's next remark turned their thoughts into a different channel.

"There was no jewelry of any kind on the body when I saw it in the hammock. Of course, Miss Warrender may have worn some concealed about her person, but do you know how many pieces she had with her here, Mrs. Mercer, and where she kept them?"

"The second day she was here I showed her a small drawer with a concealed lock in the back of her dressing-table; we haven't any safe in the house," Olive Mercer began almost absently. "I don't know what jewels she may have had with her, but I remember her wearing a string of pearls, a diamond bracelet and several rings and brooches. She brought them with her in a leather jewel-case, so I don't believe she has any means of carrying them about her. Would you like me to get them for you? I know how the lock works; it's a patent affair. Perhaps you'll come with me?"

She rose and the coroner passed with her out of the drawing-room and up the stairs. Chief Clark turned to his two companions.

"I got it myself that the choking was done with a piece from the swing-rope," he announced. "Miss Warrender couldn't have been anything but a lady, going to the fine school Mrs. Mercer did and getting in with all the folks up here so easy, but it's common sense that it was somebody who followed her to Chichester killed her, and I'm going to look up everybody who left town to-day or tries to leave it! Yes, sir! This c'munity ain't going to have a thing like this fastened onto it—not while I'm Chief of Police!"

"But no one at all is under suspicion yet, Chief," Mott expostulated. "That is, unless you've got some one up your sleeve!"

The official's high-pitched, nasal disclaimer was cut short by the reentrance of Mrs. Mercer and the coroner, the latter carrying a folded case of pale mauve satin which he spread out on the table before his colleague.

"These were what we found," he declared as Mott and Rider approached also at a nod from the chief. "They were all in the little drawer Mrs. Mercer spoke of and she identifies them as having been worn here by the deceased during her stay. She can't recall any missing jewels."

Mott gasped as from pocket after pocket of the case small boxes appeared and were opened; the string of pearls, diamond bracelets, brooches and rings lay in a glittering array before him. Then he glanced up suddenly.

"We dined here last night and I noticed a ring on Miss Warrender's finger, a queer ring, all fire, and color, and light! Don't you recall it, Mrs. Mercer?"

Olive drew her heavy brows together and then suddenly she gasped:

"The opal! The ghost's gift!"

7

Nancy

The sun was setting as Mott and Rider drove away from Hydrangea Walk with a promise to be on hand for the coroner's inquest on Monday. The latter, together with the other officials, had long since departed, Olive had retired prostrated to her room and Stan Mercer, dazed by the sudden tragedy, was roused only by the knowledge of his small daughter's disappearance. The three had searched the entire grounds with the negligible aid of Hans, who was so shocked by the afternoon's event that he could do little more than follow them about vacantly, his pathetic, hollow cough forever in their ears, but no trace was found of the missing Nancy, while Ingred reported that a further search of the house had proved fruitless.

Stan had insisted, however, that the child would come home by nightfall, and as the two friends started homeward themselves Henry Mott observed:

"Well, they've got something to work on anyway, if Doc Todd doesn't find that ring on Miss Warrender. That Paris jeweler told her it was worth a fortune, according to what Mrs. Mercer said, remember? That was sure a funny story about that friend of hers coming to life and giving it to her, wasn't it?"

"Funny but quite possible." Rider's thoughts appeared to be far afield. "This is a pretty well-to-do section up here, isn't it? Lots of rich manufacturers whose wives have plenty of jewels?"

"Yes, but there hasn't been a robbery of any importance in years, if that's what you're thinking of!" laughed Mott.

"Yet you believe some one followed Miss Warrender up here, waited two weeks, almost, and then killed her in broad day for the sake of that one ring?" Rider demanded. "I'm no judge, but I should say that string of pearls was worth more than the opal, to say nothing of the rest of the junk."

"I don't mean anything of the kind!" protested the other, twisting his fat body impatiently behind the wheel. "I said the police would have something to work on, and the county authorities as well. They're at loggerheads—politics, of course—but they'll have to hang together now. I want to stop up here a minute and see old Hi. I feel kind of worried about Jack going away like this."

He had turned the car into a side road which branched off the main highway and Rider glanced at him down his long nose.

"You're worried about him anyway, aren't you, Henry? Remember that little scene just off the golf course yesterday afternoon and the other last night in the Mercers' garden under Miss Warrender's window? Why didn't you tell the chief about them?"

"Because I wasn't going to trail a bag of anise seed in front of him, and have him think it was a real fox!" Mott retorted, reddening. "He'd grab at anything as a starter and old Jack's been through enough; besides I'll never believe he did it, no matter what was between them!"

"The major was gassed during the war and came home a nerve-wrecked shadow, you told Miss Warrender the first time you met her," Rider reminded him. "She didn't volunteer that she knew him till he stood before her, though.

I told you there was a story behind that young woman and I'd like to read the last page of it; well, the last page is open before us, and I'm darned if I can read it."

"You said that she knew you but didn't want you to recall her!" Mott exclaimed suddenly. "If it's true, can't you place her even after this shock?"

"No." Rider dismissed the subject with a gesture. "Tell me how your friend got his, and what happened to him afterward?"

"Jack? The way hundreds of others did; led his men over the top, got a vile dose of gas and a couple of wounds, but it was the gas that put him out of the game for keeps. He was moved from station to station back to one of the base hospitals and finally sent home. His brain is all right, it's just his nerves. What's the idea, Dan?"

"Was the central 'Y' hut anywhere near where he was sent through?" his companion persisted, ignoring the query. "You said, I believe, that he didn't have any extended leave from the time his regiment first went into action till he was wounded and gassed; do you know anything about his condition before he was sent home? Was he ever given up for dead?"

"I shouldn't wonder, though I only got a rumored report of him from friends in the same sector." Mott gave a jerk of the wheel as a sudden thought came to him, and the runabout swerved almost into the ditch. "By Godfrey! You don't think he—that ring . . ."

"I know that he would have recognized it if he saw it— or Miss Warrender thought he would," Rider replied dryly. "I saw her slip it into her gown when he came up on the Mercers' veranda the first day she was there, and yesterday she had it on at her arrival at the country club, but it had disappeared a few minutes later when she joined us on the green—after seeing the major there, too."

"But he couldn't have been the 'ghost' she spoke about, then!" Mott exclaimed. "She wasn't afraid of his recognition—she welcomed it, commanded it! Why should she be afraid to have him see the ring?"

"Why did neither of them mention where or how they met on the other side?" retorted Rider. "Why that quarrel yesterday afternoon, and the major's behavior under her window last night? Why his sudden disappearance an hour, approximately, before her death this afternoon?"

"I'm going to find that out now!" declared Mott determinedly. "This is Hilltop—or was, before he let it go to seed."

The road had gradually ascended with a low graystone wall winding along at the right in a sad state of disrepair, with huge gaps in it clothed with trailing green vines, and now they turned in between rusty iron posts on a grass-grown road. It was bordered by huge old trees among whose leafy branches gaunt dead ones stood out, and the unmown fields and ragged lawns gave the place a deserted air in the fast-coming twilight.

"I should think it would make him jumpy to live here!" Rider remarked. "Why doesn't he keep it up? Is it lack of money or of pride?"

"Neither, I think," his companion replied. "He's got a settled income for life—rather a bad thing, I expect, for a fellow in his condition to have nothing to fight for—and he's proud of the old place. The way I dope it out, he wants to be as solitary as possible and couldn't stand servants about him. He got rid of the caretaker's family when he came home and no one knows where he picked up this old fellow, but he keeps the house as clean as Jack will let him and cooks astonishingly well. Jack comes out of his shell now and then and gives a few of us a mighty good dinner."

"He invited us all to one that day Miss Warrender arrived, but he never named a date—" Rider broke off and added: "Good Lord, is this the house?"

They had halted before the steps of a staunch, old dwelling of the earlier farm type, half stone and half clapboard, and before Mott could respond the door opened and a thin elderly figure in black peered out at them in the waning light.

"Oh, it's you, Mr. Mott!" He spoke in obvious relief. "The major is away."

"I know he is!" Mott sang out cheerfully. "I was with Dr. Todd when he got you on the wire, but I don't think you know him, Hi. Has the major really gone without letting you know where, or when he'll be back?"

"Yes, sir, but he'd no call to tell me," Hi replied defensively. "It's nothing unusual and he knows I'll be waiting . . ."

"Well, it's too bad, because I'm expecting a friend of his up whom he knew in the old days—like this gentleman here." Mott indicated his guest with an elaborately careless gesture and then continued: "We've both been worried about the major the last day or two; he oughtn't to have gone away alone.

"That's what I told him, sir, but he just told me where—where I could go instead!" The old man, thoroughly reassured as to his audience, shook his gray head disconsolately. "You know what he is in one of his black moods, and it's been more like two weeks than two days! A week ago Monday night it started; he wouldn't eat a bite and didn't seem to hear when I spoke to him, except to tell me to go to bed and let him alone. In the morning I found him fast asleep in the same chair I'd left him in, with the tobacco jar almost empty beside him and the pipe on the floor where it had burnt a great hole in the rug.

"He rushed out without any breakfast, but when he came in dog-tired after a long tramp he was all excited. That's been the way of things for all the time since—either strange with excitement as if something was burning him up inside, or numb like a man that'd been struck down and couldn't get up again."

"What struck him to-day to go off like this?" Mott asked as his informant paused. "Was he all right yesterday?"

"Better than for days, when he went off to the country club with the golf sticks he hadn't used more than two or three times this season." Hi's voice shook a trifle with affectionate pride. "He's a fine figure of a man, the major is, and he seemed to be in good spirits, but when he came home he was in a state! His nerves was gone worse than I ever saw them, and he could hardly lift the cup of coffee—which was all he'd take—to his mouth, but he went to his room right after and to bed, for I heard it creak.

"Thinking things would be better in the morning, I went to bed, too, but I couldn't sleep, and about midnight I got up and went to his room. He'd gone!"

"Didn't you see him again?" demanded Mott. "You said he didn't leave till this afternoon."

"He didn't," Hi protested. "He came in at dawn all dusty and tired but real quiet; he didn't even let out on me for waiting up for him, but there was a look on his face I didn't like, more desperate than if he'd raged and ranted around. He flung himself on his bed without breakfast or even taking off his boots, and I thought I'd better let him rest. It was past noon when he woke up and called for me to get him something to eat. That was a good sign, but when I brought it he was all dressed in a sack suit, with a little grip already packed, and said he was going away for a few days. It was when I said he oughtn't to go by himself that he swore at me, but he shook hands before he left."

"Haven't you a notion where he might have gone, Hi?" Mott's voice was more and more grave, although he strove to lighten it. "Perhaps he received an invitation from somebody to visit . . ."

Hi shook his head again.

"No, sir, for he hasn't had any mail in nearly a month. The major kept himself to himself, as you might say, and he would never even go to the post-office or the bank. I put in his checks for him regular and drew out what he wanted."

"Then you'd know how much he had in ready cash and we could tell from that how long he meant to stay away and how far he went," Mott suggested eagerly. "I'm not trying to pry into his affairs, but I want to be sure he's all right and able to take care of himself. Men do queer thing; when their nerves are all gone to pieces, and I knew his folks before him."

"I know you did, sir!" Hi paused and then went on hesitatingly. "We ran no bills and the major always liked to have a little aside in the house, and it was my business to keep account and tell him when we was running low. There was just thirty dollars in the house last Tuesday and he sent me to the bank with his check to draw two hundred. I'd still ten left this afternoon of the thirty and before he went he gave me ninety more, an even hundred: forty for my month's wages due next Monday, fifty to run the house on and ten to pay for having some carpentering done. Except for what he might have spent at the country club or in town he had a hundred and ten dollars."

"Well, he won't go far on that, and he didn't leave you enough to run the house forever, so I guess we needn't worry." Mott turned on the switch key and reached for the self-starter. "When the major comes home tell him to run down to my place, and if you hear anything, Hiram, let me know."

The old man stood in the doorway and looked after them as they disappeared in the gathering dusk, and Rider spoke for the first time since they had approached the house.

"Well, you drew a blank there, except that it doesn't look so good for your friend the major, does it? If we only knew the motive. . . ."

"Huh!" Mott grunted in derision. "What's motive got to do with it? What's it got to do with any case? I hate old women's gossip as much as the next one, but it's the talk of the whole neighborhood that a certain leading citizen has lost his head over this woman, and if any one had cause to kill her for jealousy, wouldn't it be his wife? Of course, we know she didn't, but there's motive for you!"

"Especially as Miss Warrender was to have left on Monday," Rider suggested satirically.

"That didn't need to have been the end of it!" retorted Mott. "The man could have followed, couldn't he, and another family been busted up for keeps? Why, some of the fellows have even discussed it at the country club, the way the wife's been gallivanting around this past week trying to hold him and making a fool of herself instead? It's all bosh, but if the motive wasn't jealousy, or else the possession of that ring . . ."

"Slow down a bit!" Rider interrupted in a low, curt command. "Run along as quietly as you can and don't talk! There's something creeping through the bushes at the right of the road just ahead and it didn't look like a dog to me!"

Mott obeyed in silent wonder, his round eyes trying to pierce the gloom where he could faintly see the clumps of sumac and wild berry bushes swaying as something passed beneath them. Whatever it was the creature appeared to scent pursuit, for as the car approached nearer it flung itself into the depths of a dense mass of shrubbery and the swaying branches above were still.

"Quick, turn on your lights!" cried Rider. "I saw a flutter of white! It's a child!"

"Nancy!" Mott exclaimed as he complied. A faint, moaning cry came from the hidden recess and he stopped the car with a jerk, but before he could squeeze his rotund body from behind the wheel his companion was out and across the road, thrusting the bushes aside.

When he reached him with a pocket flashlight from the car, Rider was dragging a small limp form gently toward open ground where he might take her up in his arms. The fluffy, golden-brown hair was bedraggled and snarled with leaves and twigs, the lips colorless and the great blue eyes half-closed as they bore her to the car, but she uttered only a little sighing breath.

"The child's been—been hurt!" Mott gasped hoarsely as he pointed to streaks of red on her face and arms.

"Only scratches from the berry bushes," Rider assured him. "She's got a pretty high fever, though; shock and exhaustion, I guess. We'd better get her home as quickly as we can."

"Home!" Henry Mott glanced about at the dark, deserted road. "Why, she's come more than six miles! You don't think she—she had any reason to be trying to reach the major's, do you?"

The question seemed dragged from him but the other growled.

"She hasn't any reason at all! That's what's the matter with her. Ingred wasn't so dumb when she said the child would want to run from all the world, frightened out of her wits. She's tried to do it, poor kid, and now don't let's waste any more time. You drive and I'll hold her as easy as I can."

Rider settled the little head on his burly shoulder, holding her as tenderly as a woman might have done, but scarcely had the car started than her lips moved and he said sharply to the man beside him:

"Shut off that engine quick! She's trying to speak, and we've got to hear!"

The engine purred to silence and Nancy's eyes opened wide but there was no wonder in them, for she did not see her two rescuers. She was staring instead at the stark horror of that afternoon and her whispering voice rose to a shriek.

"That thing around her neck! Seemed's if it was 'round mine too! I couldn't call!" A little pause ensued which neither of the two listeners dared to break and then there came in a raucous whisper, filled with horror unspeakable, "I found it! It came off—I knew! I buried it and I'll never tell! Oh, I want to go dead, too!"

8

Two Telegrams

"Nancy meant the ring, I tell you!" Henry Mott thumped down his coffee cup with unnecessary vigor, beginning again at the Sunday breakfast table the argument which had lasted far into the night between the two friends. "What else could she have found and buried? Of course she knew where it came from—Miss Warrender's finger! That she buried it and won't tell about it was sheer childish fright, and so was that cry about wishing she was dead. Mrs. Mercer has always said she was a queer little thing."

"Then you admit there was something queer in her actions?" Dan Rider pushed back his empty plate and lighted his cigar, tilting it at an argumentative angle. "I only hope she didn't talk any more after that Miss Foster met us in her flivver and relieved us of our charge! Exceedingly forceful young woman!"

"Awful!" Mott's round face flushed more than its natural wont at the memory. "From the way she ran on, one would have thought we'd kidnapped Nancy! Let's 'phone and find out how the kid is?"

But "Central" informed them with official mendaciousness that the Mercers' wire was out of order, and Rider remarked:

"After all, I saw her first and I think I'll stroll over and ask about her—that is, if you haven't any plans for us both this morning?"

Mott eyed him knowingly and chuckled.

"I haven't, you old faker! I knew you couldn't keep out of this to save your life, and as a matter of fact I've other fish to fry myself for a while. Meet you home here for lunch."

"Got to see Mr. Mercer. Message from Mr. Henry Mott; I'm his guest, Rider, from New York." This personal introduction was offered a half-hour later at the gate of Hydrangea Walk, and its guardian proving to be the young policeman of the "Y" meeting, no obstacle was presented, although already vehicles of many vintages thronged the roadway and reporters from the nearest large cities were taxing the ingenuity of the local officials.

Stan Mercer greeted his guest in the library with quiet courtesy, but his blue eyes, so like those of the child Nancy, were sunken and dull and the hand he extended shook.

"Rider! I can't thank you and Mott about Nancy—last night!" he said brokenly. "When I think what might have happened if you hadn't found her!"

"It was the sheerest luck in the world!" Rider exclaimed. "How is she now?"

"She doesn't know any of us, but thank God she doesn't seem to remember yesterday, either." The father's tones trembled. "I never knew how dear she was to me till now! She shrinks from all of us, but the doctor says that is always the way, and he won't let any one see her, not even her mother, only the two nurses he has installed."

"Does she say anything, rave, I mean, in delirium?" Rider hastily amended the form of his question. "She isn't violent?"

"Oh, no!" Stan looked his surprise. "Was she delirious when you found her?"

"She just moaned a little and sighed when I picked her up," replied Rider evasively. "What did Miss Foster tell you?"

"That Nancy seemed to be in a coma and never uttered a word or knew anything. The doctor says it's going to be a long siege, but we'll pull her through physically; she'll come out of it either normal or with her mind permanently gone! I'll never forgive myself for taking her disappearance yesterday as of so little account, but in the face of what had happened I was dazed, beside myself!" He passed his hand over his eyes and forehead. "Mrs. Mercer is bearing up wonderfully considering the long friendship that existed between her and—her friend, but she is certain that the solution of this terrible mystery lies somewhere back during the years when they knew nothing of each other."

"And you are not of that opinion?" asked Rider quietly.

"I haven't any, I don't know what to think!" He shook his head and his lips tightened. "It's a nightmare that I can't even realize! I've notified the management of the hotel where Miss Warrender lived in New York to ask for the names of her bankers and her attorney. I doubt if they can throw any light on the matter even if it's as my wife thinks, but we must try everything! The local police, the men from the District Attorney's office—they've concentrated on the fact of the missing ring—believe some one saw her asleep there with it on and killed her for it. They've tried to get an alibi from every one in the house— and nobody appears to have one!"

"What?" Rider stared.

"The cook was in the kitchen until nearly four, preparing some complicated adjuncts for the dinner we were to have given to-night, nurse was with Bill getting him to take his nap, the housemaid cleaning one of the upper floors, and Ingred mending linen in the sewing-room. That accounts for the household servants, and as the gardener is away on a vacation, only Hans was left, and he was priming the vines of the pergola around on the other side of the house. Any one of them could have slipped out there to the hammock and—and committed that fearful thing, but it's preposterous to think that they did."

"Mrs. Mercer tells me that she was in her own room, but where was the little girl during those early hours of the afternoon?" Rider paused to light the cigar which his host offered and then added: "Is it possible that she could actually have witnessed the murder?"

Stan started.

"Good heavens! I never thought of that!" he exclaimed. "But no! Nancy's first words were: 'The hammock! Go look in the hammock!' She had seen what—what was there after the murderer departed, but no more. She had been out wandering around the grounds by herself, though; Hans says that she stopped and stood under his ladder talking to him not ten minutes before she rushed screaming into the house."

"It's lucky you came home as early as you did." Rider's head was slightly lowered as though he were regarding his cigar, but beneath their lids his eyes were fixed on the other man's face. "You were out at the plant, weren't you?"

"No." Stan's lips were twisted into a faint, mirthless smile. "I've no better alibi than any one else, if it could be considered that I murdered our guest, my wife's old schoolmate! I went for a long walk quite by myself out on the Lake Valley way and I didn't meet a soul I knew, or any one else, for that matter, except an old farmer with a load of the first cut hay!"

"What do you think of the police theory, leaving your household, of course, out of the affair?" Rider had settled back in his chair.

"I don't think any one would risk capital punishment, when, without resorting to murder, the ring could have been so easily slipped off Miss Warrender's finger while she slept." Stan brought his hand down with a nervous gesture on his knee. "She must have been attacked in her sleep, or she would have cried out and given the alarm. I can't, I won't believe that she had any enemies from the past; the robbery theory seems equally untenable! I tell you, Rider, this thing is driving me mad!"

There was sheer agony in his tone and his guest nodded understandingly.

"Yet the ring is gone; that's a concrete fact," he reminded him. "By the way, when was the last time you saw it on her, Mercer?"

Stan frowned thoughtfully.

"I don't recall seeing it since Friday night, when you dined with us. Later my wife remarked upon its beauty, and she told us its strange history. I'm positive she didn't wear it at lunch yesterday. Great heavens!" he broke off. "What if she didn't have it on at all when the crime was committed! Perhaps it's still in the house somewhere! I'll send for Mrs. Mercer!"

He rang the bell and after an interval Ingred appeared. Her face was stolid and impassive once more and her eyes stared vacuously as she listened to her instructions and then turned without a word and lumbered up the stairs.

"That would eliminate the police theory," Rider agreed. "If the ring's not found, however, it's always possible that she put it on after lunch. I hope Mrs. Mercer won't think I'm intruding in this tragic affair."

"After finding Nancy for us?" Stan interrupted. "Man, if you can make any possible suggestions we'll be only too thankful! We'll know no peace until the truth is discovered!"

His tone was tremulous again and before the agony in his haggard eyes Rider averted his own. This man was not merely deploring the tragedy which had taken place practically under his roof; he was in stark grief, obvious to the most casual of observers. What could Mrs. Mercer's attitude be?

But Olive, when she came into the room with hand extended to greet the guest, was apparently blind to her husband's real emotion. Her face still bore traces of grief and shock, but she was wholly in command of herself.

"Mr. Rider, I hope Stan has told you of our gratitude, for I can't find words! If it were not for you Nancy might be wandering about yet, crazed and suffering, or even dead from exhaustion and fever! I can never cease to reproach myself for not starting a search for her at once when she was missed. To think that I, who have always been over-careful of my children, should have failed her when she most needed me!" Her eyelids fluttered beneath her heavy brows. "What can you think of me?"

"It was perfectly natural under the circumstances," Rider assured her. "I'm quite sure little Nancy will recover in mind as well as body. But your husband has a suggestion to make to you."

"It was you who suggested it to me, Rider. I see that now; you led me deliberately to viewing that possibility." Stan turned to his wife. "Olive, did you notice that opal ring on Miss Warrender's finger at lunch yesterday?"

Olive's brows drew together till they seemed a strong, unbroken line upon her forehead.

"Not particularly, that I remember," she said slowly, at last. "She must have worn it, though, for it wasn't with her other jewels in the little drawer and she was seldom without it. Besides, we searched . . ."

"Then we must search again," Stan interrupted. "See that none of the servants are upstairs and we'll go over every room ourselves."

"But, Stan!" Olive protested. "You don't think that a single servant of ours would *steal?*"

"We can't think, we've got to know!" he retorted, then turning to their guest: "Would you mind waiting, Rider?

Since you're good enough to help us, as a friend, there are some other points I'd like to go over with you."

Rider acquiesced and Olive departed to give some orders. Presently, through the half-open door, they saw the housemaid descend and go toward the rear with Ingred close at her heels, and then Olive returned for her husband.

Rider finished his cigar in their absence and then strolled out on the terrace that overlooked spreading lawns leading to that innocent appearing circle of shrubbery with tall trees waving leafy branches within it. On a small table just outside the high library window through which he had emerged Ingred stood arranging flowers awkwardly enough in several bowls and vases. Her son was clipping the grass at the edge of the path just below and his patient cough floated up to their ears.

"Excuse me, sir." Ingred smiled shyly and a trifle anxiously. "Could I ask you somet'ing?"

"Surely, Ingred." Rider concealed his surprise beneath a casually pleasant tone.

"You bane from New York, sir?"

"Yes," he replied and waited. What could the woman want of him?

"You know goot doctors dere? Goot doctors for a cough?" She lowered her tones and glanced significantly toward the stooping figure down on the path. "It's my boy, Hans. He ain't so well, not for a year, and las' week I take him to a doctor—de best in Chichester. He tell me dat Hans' chest, it eats avay vit dat cough inside and dat soon he die unless he go to Arizona for one, maybe two, t'ree year. I tank maybe a from New York doctor, he makes me some medicine dat cure Hans home here, so dat he don't have to go avay off like dat?"

Her tone had grown incredibly rich and full and tender, and the glance she had given toward her son glowed with a maternal love that was a veritable passion. Rider was moved but he shook his head.

"I can tell you myself, Ingred; no great doctor could help him here. The one in Chichester is right. The boy has got to get to a dry climate to live, and he'll have to go mighty quick or it'll be too late."

He hated to tell her and when he had finished there was a little pause.

Then Ingred lifted her head and he saw to his amazement that a certain peaceful expression, more like satisfaction than anxiety, had settled upon her heavy features, giving them a sort of dignity.

"Thank you, sir." Her voice was respectful and perfectly composed. "Hans shall go, den. It is goot dat I know de truth."

An hour later, when Stan and Olive descended, they found their guest back in the library, idly turning the leaves of a book from the shelves.

"It wasn't any use," Olive replied to his questioning look. "We even took the maids' beds apart and looked in the pockets, and hems, and linings of their clothes, and in their hats and shoes. I'm so relieved that we weren't successful, but then I never had the remotest idea that we would be. Whoever killed Gloria took that ring, and it needn't have been exactly robbery, either!"

"You see, Rider," Stan explained, "my wife thinks that some one may have wanted that ring for a reason quite apart from its value. Her friend admitted to us both that she thought the opal more terrible than beautiful; that she only accepted it to please a dying man, and that it repelled her, but superstitiously she felt bound to it. She would gladly have disposed of it, but she actually didn't dare. In the face of what has occurred, my wife believes that some one had a motive strong enough even for murder for the possession of the ring. I tell her it's absurd!"

"It isn't," Olive interrupted with the calmness of finality. "I felt from the first meeting with Miss Warrender that something had changed her more than the years; she didn't seem like the same girl I had known at school at all. I'm grieved, of course, and horrified that such a thing should have happened here, but I can't grieve as I would for the old Gloria. I am the last person in the world to slander the dead, but there are possibilities in those years that in justice can't be overlooked. I regret that I asked her here without learning more of the years between."

"Olive!" Stan exclaimed, but there was a shade of uncertainty in his tone. "You should be more loyal, my dear! I shall never believe that there could be anything in the past that could warrant your friend's murder!"

After half an hour's vague conjecturing, Rider took his leave and started for The Rafters again, conscious of unrelated and seemingly unimportant impressions. Stan Mercer's evident emotion and his wife's blindness to it, his remorse and anxiety over the condition of the child, Nancy, whereas Mrs. Mercer's thought seemed to be chiefly of the censure of the neighbors as to possible negligence on her part, yet there had been terrific fever in the hand she had held out to him on greeting and his departure, as though she were indeed suffering an inward torment over the little girl's illness.

Mercer himself had been ostensibly frank and open in his manner, yet there had been something covert in his nervous tension, something very like apprehension, and he had asked a stranger for help when lifelong friends and neighbors were at hand—and he was a popular man!

There was the woman Ingred, too! She was merely a servant of the household, supernumerary in this drama; why did she loom so largely and irrelevantly in his thoughts? Was she as stupid as people supposed, or was a strong character there, strongly repressed?

When he came up on the porch of The Rafters he heard masculine voices within, Mott's and another's, slow and nasal and drawling, which he recognized as that of the chief of police, Clark. They were obviously too excited to hear him and he opened the door without knocking. Then both turned to him.

"Good morning, Mr. Rider!" The chief grinned. "I got a telegram this morning and as there was one there for you I thought I'd bring it along. I kind of guess what's in yours from my own, which is in answer to one I sent myself late yesterday afternoon. We may be slow up-State here, but I rekernized you the minute I laid eyes on you and heard your name, and I'm willing to admit this case looked too big for me, with the district attorney so hot on the job. I wired the New York Police Headquarters to ask for the help of their biggest detective who happens to be here on the spot. My answer tells me I've got him, if I let him work in his own way. What's your telegram say?"

Special Deputy Commissioner Daniel Rider opened the yellow envelope, glanced at its contents which detailed him for duty on the Warrender case at the request of the Chief of Police of Chichester, and smiled at Mott's blank expression.

"My vacation is over," he said.

9

The Jury's Opinion

"Yes, sir!" Clark grinned again. "Rekernized you from your pictures in the papers in c'nection with the Willis murders a year ago; mighty nervy to join that gang and work right in with 'em for weeks and weeks to get the goods on 'em. Knew you wasn't up here vacationing as you said, but they got ahead of you with the killing, didn't they?"

"No." Rider shook his head. "You're on the wrong track, Chief. Mott and I've been friends for years and I never heard of the Warrender woman till she came up here. If I'd been on any lead I would have called on you, of course. Now, let's get down to business and if you've no objection we'll keep Mott in the conference."

"Suits me!" The chief seated himself. "Looks like anything you say'll have to go, as far as your own work goes."

"Have a cigar?" Rider tendered his leather case. "That's one reason why I wanted to have Mott in on this. He's introduced me as a friend to all the neighborhood and I don't want him to think I'm using that as a cloak to pull off anything like betrayal, even in the interests of justice, but if I take this case with you I've got to work under cover. How many people know about these telegrams?"

"Only the day operator at the station." The chief puffed appreciatively at his cigar.

"Got any means of keeping his mouth shut?"

"Reckon I have!" The nasal drawl was punctuated by a chuckle. "He's got a flivver 'bout the size of a go-cart, but lately he built a garage to 'commodate four cars and he's got lots of stop-over tourist friends that come down from Canada. I ain't interfered because that's Fed'ral business and besides I calc'lated he might come in handy some time. No, C'missioner, he won't talk!"

"Very good. Remember, then, that I'm interested in this case merely as a curious bystander. Mercer has already accepted a harmless suggestion or two of mine and asked me to help him, as a friend, to clear up this mystery. What do you know about this case so far? What did you get from the scene of the crime?"

"That the woman was strangled with a piece of the swingrope and her opal ring stolen." The chief replied promptly as though the question were a superfluous one.

"Got any evidence that she had it on her finger or anywhere about her?" Rider demanded briskly. "Just because it wasn't with the rest of her jewels and can't be found in the house doesn't prove that, and she certainly wasn't wearing it at lunch, an hour or so before. Did you notice one fact about the murderer?"

"What the Sam Hill?" The chief's lantern jaw dropped.

"Didn't you take a look at the rope-ends?" Rider's tone was impatient. "Where the piece around the woman's throat was separated from the one on the tree?"

"Only that it *was* separated!" There was a bewildered but defensive note in the chief's voice.

"How? It wasn't cut with a knife or sawn off on some rough, sharp surface; it was torn apart as you or I would break a bit of string. We're average muscular customers, both of us, but I'll wager neither of us could do it; if you don't believe it, take a piece of that rope and try. That murderer was strong, with a strength far beyond the normal; that narrows the field considerably, don't you think so?"

"You betcher!" The chief's small eyes were alight. "Goddamighty, why didn't I think of that! 'Strength beyond normal,' eh? Folks that ain't in their right minds are stronger'n three men sometimes, ain't they?"

He darted a glance at Henry Mott who reddened indignantly.

"Dan!" the latter appealed. "The Chief here's got it all wrong about Jack; just because he was acquainted with Miss Warrender before she came here . . ."

"No." The official shook his head slowly. "Just because her caddie happened to follow them on Friday afternoon to that patch of woods by the golf course and saw what you saw, caught you watching 'em, too. Just because he disappeared 'bout the time the murder was c'mitted and you and this 'curious bystander' was the first to go to his place asking questions of Hiram 'bout him right after you left Hydrangea Walk. Just because the whole town knows he wasn't all there in the upper story since he come back from war, and he's been acting plain crazy the last couple of weeks. Maybe he took that ring and maybe he didn't, but if he don't come home soon he's going to be brought, to tell where he was between two and four yesterday afternoon!"

"The major might have been acquainted with Miss Warrender before she came here, he may even have quarreled bitterly with her on the golf course on Friday afternoon, but if he hasn't any alibi at all it's as good as several other people have," Rider remarked smoothly. "For instance, the entire Mercer household. As to the ring, it may have been stolen for a purpose we know nothing about before Miss Warrender ever went out to that hammock."

The chief mopped his forehead with a blue polka-dotted handkerchief.

"This is getting more mixed than ever!" he exclaimed. "Not a soul has left town without giving a satisfactory

account of themselves since the murder was discovered
except Major Hill, and no trains went out either way between two and four yesterday. She couldn't have done anything in the scant two weeks she was here that'd make anybody want to kill her, and as for a giant of strength—h'm!
I'm putting it up to you, C'missioner. What are you going
to do?"

"Ask you to stop calling me that; I'm just plain 'Rider,'
or you'll forget some time; next, tell your men to lay off
me if I seem to be nosing around too much. Say I'm a kind
of a crank, but you've got a notion you can use me. That'll
account for it to them if we seem to be pretty good friends,
but at that we'd better hold our talks in private as much as
possible because of neighborhood gossip. Better fix your
telegraph operator as soon as you can, for I'm expecting a
wire or two myself from my own headquarters. I sent word
to them yesterday afternoon to get a line on Miss Warrender and her friend, Mrs. Derwent, who first mentioned
her up here to Mrs. Mercer. Want a suggestion?"

"Like a dog wants a bone!" the chief declared fervently.

"Then if you've got a reliable man or two you can spare,
set 'em to watching the jewelry shops, even as far as Albany. It's just possible that ring'll turn up. And I'd give the
major time before I set the bloodhounds on his trail; don't
do any good to get the department held up to ridicule in
case that guess happens to be wide of the mark. That's all
I've got to say now, Chief, but I'll see you at the inquest
to-morrow, if you'll see that a place is made for me among
the spectators."

"Decent of you to put in that word about Jack!" Henry
Mott remarked when their visitor had departed. "After you
left this morning I went up to see old Hi again to find
out if he'd had any news from Jack and he bu'st out at me
like an old turkey-cock. It seems the chief was up there
soon after we were yesterday afternoon and blew the whole

works about the murder, and that Jack was kind of under suspicion. You saw how loyal Hiram was, but I could tell this morning that he was scared, too; scared that maybe Jack did know something about it, though he vowed that Jack never gave a woman a thought except to steer clear of 'em as much as he could, that he hated 'em so he wouldn't even have one working around the house! Well, Dan, so you're on the job again!"

"Yes," Rider answered soberly. "You couldn't have a fire, could you?"

"In this weather!" Mott's eyes rounded.

"I mean the house—anything that would necessitate repairs so I'd be driven to the inn for a week or two. I'll have to stick around for a while to play in those golf tournaments I've engaged for, but I needn't stay under your roof."

"For Pete's sake!" Mott half rose from his chair.

"No, for the sake of common hospitality. I'm not going to abuse it, and we've been friends a good many years." Rider's tone had deepened in gravity. "There's no friendship in my work and I'm working now, Henry. I may have to bring notoriety and trouble on people you've known all your life, and I warn you now that no consideration can stop me. Arrange some excuse for me to go to the inn."

"No, by Godfrey!" Mott brought his hand down on his fat knee. "In the cause of justice, as a law-abiding citizen—oh, I'm not making a speech! I'm going to see this thing through with you as far as you'll let me, if I have to get the chief to appoint me deputy, and that's that! I like the way you got out of telling him what you were going to do! When he asked you pointblank you told him what to do instead, and I'll bet he hasn't realized it yet!"

Rider smiled but did not take the bait so temptingly offered, and they sat down to a belated luncheon, after which Mott suggested slyly: "Golf? We'll find a couple of the usual nuts to make up a foursome."

Rider laughed frankly and shook his head.

"No. I'm going down to Hydrangea Walk to play with Bill."

"Wha-at!"

"Oh, you can come along with me and ask about Nancy, then talk to Mr. and Mrs. Mercer; give 'em your opinion of the case even if you haven't got any, and chime in with hers. Mrs. Mercer doesn't think so much of her old school friend as she did. She's afraid there's something in the past that'll make it look bad for her, for introducing a woman she's known nothing of for years so promiscuously to all her neighbors. Help it along and don't bother about me, whatever I do."

"Why this sudden interest in the Mercers?" Mott cast a wary glance on his friend, who laughed again.

"I like to start things at the scene of the crime, old scout. Come on."

They found Olive in a secluded corner of the porch and presently Stan came out to join them, but Mott played up nobly and as soon as Rider—who had kept carefully in the background—saw that his ally was fairly launched, he sauntered away around the south side of the house in the direction of the pergola, from whence came sounds of defiance and wrath in a lusty if infantile voice.

He found a thin, sharp-featured nurse gripping Bill's round, creased wrist, and trying vainly to drag him to the house while he held back with all the weight of his chubby body.

"Not doing to take nap!" he declared belligerently. "Want to pyay, Dane. Do take nap you ownse'f!"

"Hey there, what's the matter, Bill?" Rider asked jovially.

"Oh, sir," the long-suffering Jane appealed to the visitor, "it's time for his afternoon sleep and besides I've got to relieve the day nurse for an hour. He knows there's everything upset and he's taking advantage of me!"

"Suppose you leave him with me, and I'll soon get him sleepy," Rider suggested. "Mr. and Mrs. Mercer are on the veranda with my friend and they'll tell you it's all right. Nancy needs your attention now more than Bill does if the nurse is going off duty for a while."

With relief and gratitude Jane relinquished her charge, and Rider contemplated Bill, who smiled affably up at him.

"Tell you what we'll do!" he proposed. "Let's play we're miners, shall we? The men who dig in the ground for gold for mamma's rings and coal to keep you warm in winter, you know. Can't tell what we'll find if we dig for it! What do you say?"

Bill wriggled enthusiastically.

"Nanthy and me digged last week down by de house where de auto lives, but all we dot was a deaded pussytat," he observed, adding with relish: "It was werry dead-ed, and Hans took it 'way f'om us 'tause Nanthy dot sick. Where s'all we dig now, mans?"

"Where do you and Nancy usually dig? Not always there behind the garage, do you?"

"Yots of pyaces, where it's soft. Turn on, I'll s'ow you!"

For the better part of an hour, until Bill's eyelids grew heavy in spite of himself, they wandered from one spot to another in perfect congeniality, getting equally warm and grubby, but making no discoveries save for a shining new quarter, which Rider planted judiciously when he fancied that his partner's enthusiasm was waning. He took him at last to the back door and left him nodding in Ingred's arms, then, making himself as presentable as possible, he rejoined the others on the veranda.

Tea had been served and he noticed that Stan Mercer had grown even more reserved, but his wife was more than ordinarily gracious in her manner toward Mott, whose fat face bore signs of strain. Evidently he had succeeded in holding his audience, but the effort had told on him.

Rider accepted a cup of tea, laughingly explained that he had been having the time of his life with Bill, and adroitly extricated his friend.

"You're a sight!" Mott declared acridly as he turned the little car toward home. "Look at your cuffs! Have you been making mudpies?"

"Something like that!" Rider chuckled. "I've exhausted Bill as a source of information and that's one job done!"

The inquest was held at ten the next morning in the library at Hydrangea Walk. It was brief and its conclusion as foregone as the result of the autopsy. Olive Mercer was called first, then Henry Mott and after him every adult member of the Mercer household, but none threw any new light on the mystery, nor did the various neighbors who were called. The chief had not taken the coroner into his confidence concerning the caddie, so the latter was not a witness nor was Major Hill's disappearance referred to, and after the most superficial pretense at deliberation the jury brought in the verdict of murder at the hand of a person or persons unknown.

Rider had been seated just behind Henry Mott and stopped him as the latter started to rise and file out after the jury and spectators.

"The chief's looking this way; he'll want a word with us," he explained, then turned as Stan Mercer came up to them. "It must be a relief to have this over, especially for your wife. Just a formality, of course, but a distressing one under the circumstances."

"Very," Stan replied as he shook hands with them. "Miss Warrender's attorney will be here on the noon train and take charge of the final arrangements, but this frightful affair is not ended nor will it be if the district attorney himself shelves it. I intend to employ the greatest talent in the country if need be, but I won't stop till the murderer is found!"

"I don't believe your chief of police will drop the case even if the district attorney does," Rider observed. "How is Nancy?"

"About the same. She doesn't sleep much, for her eyes are open most of the time, but she appears to notice nothing of what is said to her and hasn't uttered a word. That's all the doctors can tell me and they won't speak of the future," he broke off with a sigh. "You saw how pale my wife looked on the witness stand? This double grief and shock has been almost too much for her, but she s fortunately self-contained."

His own eyes as he spoke were sunken and deeply lined, his face colorless and haggard with an expression of haunting sorrow, and Rider contrasted his appearance with that of Olive Mercer. She had been pale, but gave her evidence with the utmost composure and lack of all emotion, telling of her daughter's discovery of the crime without visible sign of anxiety for the child's critical illness. While he was thinking of her she came toward him and held out her hand.

"My dear Mr. Rider, has Stan told you that even he and I are excluded from Nancy's sickroom? Through all this horrible ordeal I haven't been able to keep my thoughts from her. Don't you think it's very hard?" Emotion enough trembled in her tones now, and again Rider noted the feverish heat of her hand. Self-contained and strong of will this mother must be, he concluded, beneath her placid, commonplace exterior, and he replied with ready sympathy:

"Not if it means that she will get well more quickly, Mrs. Mercer."

"I got more telegrams," the chief drew him aside to announce briefly. "Two for you and one for Mott, besides a couple of my own. Here's yours."

While he gave Henry Mott the yellow envelope Rider opened the first which had been handed to him. It read:

"Derwent widow money o.k. socially lived same hotel eight years knows nothing of subject's affairs or history casual acquaintance only."

The second message was longer but more to the point.

"Subject lived alone hotel with maid. Maid discharged month ago not located yet. When subject first came hotel four years ago was much broken in health, said had been invalid some time but recovery swift then. Absent for long periods but retained apartments. Rumors not verified subject had given services war. Much attention society several admirers no special one no intimate woman friend. Detailed report follows."

Rider deliberated for a moment then advanced to Mrs. Mercer where she stood a little apart with Mott and held out to her the last telegram.

"Mrs. Mercer, on Saturday afternoon I permitted my name to be used by certain authorities in sending a message of inquiry concerning your friend. I think you should see the reply."

As she held out her hand to receive it Mott exclaimed:

"Your hand! Have you burned it?"

"Yes, slightly, when an alcohol stove was overturned in the excitement of caring for Nancy when she was brought home." Mrs. Mercer glanced at the puffed, reddened palm of her hand and then took the telegram. A frown drew her brows together as she perused it and she shook her head thoughtfully as she handed it back.

"War work? I'm sure that rumor isn't true, Mr. Rider," she remarked. "Miss Warrender never mentioned it; in fact, from the little she did say, I was under the impression that she and her aunt remained as far from the battle zone as possible."

So the fever in her hand had been from a mere burn, not anxiety or sorrow! Rider shrugged but Henry Mott took his attention.

"Look here!" He spoke in an excited whisper as he held out his own telegram. "That fellow I've been expecting will be here to-night, Captain Craig Staverton! He knew Jack overseas, remember! Now perhaps we'll get some real dope!"

10

Mr. Gildersleeve Arrives

Low as Mott's whisper had been the chief's quick ears had caught it, as Rider could tell from his expression, but he turned away to talk to Stan Mercer.

"I'll be glad to meet Captain Staverton," Rider replied to his friend. "Don't mind if I ask him some questions, do you?"

At Mott's nod of acquiescence the other turned and crossed the room to where the hammock lay in a heap in the corner, brought in as Exhibit A after the jury viewed it at the undisturbed scene of the crime. With a backward glance to assure himself that no one was paying attention to him, Rider stooped and examined it strand by strand, but only a bit of fluff caught in the fringe near its head rewarded his search, and straightening up, he strolled out on the terrace, drawing a cigar from his pocket.

The air was clear and pleasantly cool and after a little he sauntered down a path which led to the rear of the house.

"Good morning, sir." Ingred looked up with a respectful little nod from the bench beside the steps of the back porch, where she sat preparing vegetables. She wore a checked apron over the black silk dress she had donned for the inquest, and her limpid blue eyes were as docilely ingenuous as when he had first seen her. "Dere is some-t'ing you vish, maybe? Der cook is sick from a scare over de inquest, she bane yoost a fool, and I take her place."

"No, I don't want anything, Ingred," Rider shook his head smilingly. "Now that everything's over you'll all have a chance to get things running again as usual and forget all about Miss Warrender."

"Poor lady!" Ingred's full lips drew down at the corners. "I could never forget dis terrible t'ing! Der little Nancy too! Her cries, I hear dem yet, and ven dat Miss Foster bring her home so near dead, I t'ought I vould get crazy!"

"Naturally everybody must have been anxious and ex-cited then," Rider conceded carelessly. "Mrs. Mercer tells me she burned her hand . . ."

"Dat vas my fault," Ingred interrupted. "Mrs. Mercer go to take de little alcohol stove from me ven I ain't ex-pecting, and it slip. Could I bodder you yoost again 'bout my Hans, sir?"

"Your son?" Rider glanced about but the lad was no-where to be seen. "Have you spoken to Mr. and Mrs. Mer-cer about him? Of course, I'll be glad to give you any advice I can."

"I don't vant dat dey should be boddered now, vit all deir ot'er troubles, and you bane so kind, sir." Ingred spoke with half-hesitant apology. "I read dat dere is a place dat bane mooch nearer as Arizona, a place vit sooch a quare name, vere dey cure people vit sick chests like Hans got. De Ad-derondacks. Der is big voods and hospitals all t'rough; could be you know a doctor in dere?"

"Several of them," Rider replied promptly. "Messiter at Saranac would be the best for you. I'll give you a letter for Hans to take to him if you like and he won't charge as much as the rest would at their sanitariums, but at that it will be expensive for you."

"It bane cheaper as Arizona, and I got de money for dat," Ingred declared. "I be so grateful for dat letter, sir, yoost if you don't mind."

Rider promised and strolled once more to the front of the house just as a doctor's sedan came up the drive. He saw that its occupant was not the coroner and turned to find the chief at his elbow.

"The physician in charge of Nancy," the latter explained. "Dr. Ross, his name is. Like to see him the next coroner. Todd and I ain't had many murder cases, but he holds out on me and we don't pull well together."

"How about you holding out on him?" Rider chuckled. "I didn't see that caddie on the witness stand to-day. Tell you what, Chief; get that doctor alone and ask him just how soon this stupor Nancy's in will turn to delirium. It's bound to, in the ordinary course of an illness like this, and I've seen such cases before. We want to be on hand when she begins to talk, do you understand? Just you and I, with even the nurse excluded if possible. I want to know what she says."

"But there won't be any sense to it if the little thing is out of her head!" Chief Clark remonstrated in honest bewilderment.

"There'll be more sense to it for us than if she was conscious," Rider insisted. "We've got to hear and nobody else must if Dr. Ross has to keep her doped from then on till this mystery is cleared up!"

"Good Lord! You don't think . . . ." the chief began, but Rider deliberately turned away and entered the house just as the sedan stopped before the door. Mott met him in some little excitement and drew him hastily into the drawing-room.

"Say, Dan, I wish you wouldn't keep disappearing!" he exclaimed. "We thought all the neighbors who had been

called at the inquest went home, but while I was looking for you after you left the library Holcomb was having
some trouble with his car halfway down the drive and I
went to help him. Mrs. Holcomb said she couldn't wait,
so she got out to walk home. I shouldn't be surprised if
she wanted to write that friend of hers, Mrs. Derwent, all
about the inquest—and then Holcomb got talking. Ever
notice what an old scavenger he is for news and gossip? Do
you remember what you and I were talking about ourselves
when we drove away from Jack's place on Saturday just
before we found Nancy?"

"What's this, anyway, a cross-examination?" Rider
asked good-naturedly. "I haven't noticed anything about
Holcomb except that he smokes vile cigars and his stance
is all wrong, and as for what we talked about coming back
from our interview with Hiram—seems to me we were gos-
siping ourselves, weren't we? Or rather, you were; something about the talk of the neighborhood?"

"Yes, and it's getting worse!" Mott retorted. "Seems the
women have been gabbing a lot more than we thought,
to their husbands, at that, and according to Holcomb the
locker-room barnacles are beginning to take it seriously."

"What you hinted about a jealous woman?" Rider's
tone was amusedly incredulous. "Who's the Amazon with
double a man's strength?"

"Ha! I thought you remembered!" the other grunted
with satisfaction. "It's the other way 'round, though. We
were talking of motives and how absolutely ridiculous
some perfectly possible ones could be. We spoke—or as
you say I did—of the gossip about a certain man's rumored
infatuation for this Warrender woman. Now, whether his
wife suspected it or not, it's going around that—that he
might have been crazy enough about her to kill her because
he couldn't have her himself and wouldn't give her up to
any one else. Sounds like rot, I know, when the man's been

known to them all his life, but this whole case is fantastic! I can't believe Jack did it either, and I'd consider every other possibility first, Dan!"

"If he didn't, he must know of the murder by this time from the papers," Rider remarked. "Why doesn't he show up? Mercer's going to push this case to the finish; you heard him say so."

"What's he done? What's he going to do?" Mott demanded, now that the name had been mentioned between them. "Wouldn't that be a natural enough bluff? Where was he on Saturday afternoon?"

Rider shook his head.

"He was at home within half an hour after the murder was discovered, and the major hasn't been seen or heard from since," he said. "I can read you like a book, Henry; you think in your heart that the major is guilty and you're catching at straws, refusing to admit it even to yourself. As for me, I'm not expressing any opinion till I have proof."

"All right, but I've heard enough from Holcomb to go after a little of the talk at first hand," Mott asserted. "I'd hate to think it was true at that, but I'm going to hang around the lounge and the tea-fiends on the veranda first and the locker-room afterwards, and I'll get all that's going!"

Rider was scarcely listening, for the sound of a motor driving rapidly away had turned his attention to the window. The doctor's sedan was still there, but the Mercers' own car, with the chauffeur at the wheel and Stan Mercer himself in the tonneau, was whirling out of the gate.

"Fixed it with him, all right! Oh, you here too, Mott?" The chief had stuck his head in the door and now came slowly forward. "Mercer's gone down to the station to meet Miss Warrender's lawyer, a fellow named Gildersleeve. Ever hear of him?"

"If it's Alexander Gildersleeve he's one of the biggest men of his kind in the city," Rider replied. "Settles up estates, you know, arranges about probating wills and managing trust funds. Little old chap with a smooth face and very bright, dark eyes. I'd like to sit in on the conference with him but it's not important."

"Not important!" the chief stared and then grinned. "You don't think anything he'll have to tell us will help, eh? Well, we'll see!"

The trio waited until the car returned, and after one glance at the visitor seated beside Stan, Chief Clark hurried out on the porch, anticipating Mrs. Mercer, who had halted at the foot of the stairs.

"Mr. Alexander Gildersleeve?" His high nasal twang was wafted back to those waiting just within. "I'm the Chief of Police! Know you anywhere, Mr. Gildersleeve, from your pictures in the papers. We up-Staters don't miss much that's going on down to New York! Like a word with you first, sir, before you settle 'bout the funeral arrangements with Mr. and Mrs. Mercer."

The hint was broad enough, but Olive Mercer came forward in her turn.

"How do you do, Mr. Gildersleeve. I am Mrs. Mercer, Gloria Warrender's old school friend, and you can imagine how anxiously my husband and I have awaited your coming! I'm quite sure Chief Clark doesn't intend to exclude us from this conference, since we are all deeply interested together, and we'll discuss arrangements later."

Olive's level gaze turned upon the chief and he shifted uneasily from one foot to the other.

"Guess there ain't any harm in it, Mrs. Mercer, since we're all interested as you say. Fact is, I'd like to have Mr. Mott and Mr. Rider in on it, too." He turned to the attorney. "Mr. Mott's a neighbor here and Mr. Rider's visiting him, and they've both given me quite some pointers."

"Rider, did you say?" Gildersleeve lifted thin eyebrows.

"Yes, sir, Mr. Dan'l Rider; a broker from New York," the chief explained, emphasizing the word "broker" clumsily, and the other gave an almost imperceptible nod.

"I have no objection," he observed. "All that I have to tell even Mrs. Mercer could very well be printed in the newspapers to-morrow. The—er—sudden death of my client is a great shock to me, I assure you, for I have been in close touch with her during the years I have taken charge of her estate, and I only wish it were in my power to aid you in your investigation."

"Let us go into the drawing-room then," Olive suggested and opened the door, starting slightly with surprise at finding it occupied already by Mott and Rider. Then she smiled faintly. "I'm glad you are here to join our conference with my poor friend's attorney, Mr. Gildersleeve."

Introductions followed, the lawyer darting a quizzical glance at Rider as they were presented and seated with easy tact by Olive. Chief Clark waited for no further preliminaries.

"Mr. Gildersleeve, how long have you known Miss Warrender?"

The attorney smiled.

"Since she was ten years old and became a ward of her aunt, the elder Miss Warrender," he replied. "I had control of Miss Ruth Warrender's affairs for many years before that, for she was an almost constant globe-trotter. She placed Miss Gloria in a school selected by me, where she remained until her graduation."

"The Misses Faraday's," murmured Olive.

"Precisely," Gildersleeve bowed slightly to her. "It was there you must have known her."

"Where did she go on her vacations?" The chief resumed his interrogation.

"With her Aunt Ruth occasionally, but that lady detested American summer resorts and was seldom in this country during the season." The attorney turned again to him. "I was practically Miss Gloria's guardian—by proxy, as one might say—and usually her vacations were spent with a governess of my selection as a paying guest in some private family in the country, that I knew personally. Miss Warrender took her niece abroad and plunged her into society and I heard little of them until the war started; nothing, in fact, except business letters from the elder lady and later frequently from Miss Gloria in her stead. It was apparent that Miss Ruth Warrender was failing at last—not in the least incompetent, you understand, but her age and her efforts to keep up a constant round of social activity were telling on her."

"You say you heard little from them until the war started," the chief repeated. "What did you hear then?"

"Nothing whatever for the first few weeks, although I made every effort to reach them by cable and letter. They were caught in Paris, but Miss Gloria succeeded in getting her aunt to Biarritz, and there the elder Miss Warrender remained until the spring, when she went to England with relatives."

"And where was Miss Gloria?" The chief bent forward and at his question Gildersleeve shrugged slightly.

"She was an exceedingly active young woman and had many friends among the highest circles in England and France," he remarked. "I fancy Biarritz bored her when all the rest of the continent seemed to be at such high tension, and she left her aunt in good hands, with two maids and a companion in the hotel where she had been going for years. I received a cable from Miss Gloria there for money from their incomes to maintain them both for six months, and later Miss Gloria wrote me from Paris acknowledging its receipt and asking me to sell certain securities of hers and send her the proceeds to contribute to relief work. As she had recently become of age, I complied."

His tone expressed disapproval, and the chief asked:

"Was it much? Miss Warrender—the deceased here—had money of her own, apart from what her aunt left her?"

"The amount I sent her was fifty thousand dollars, one-third of the entire estate left her by her parents." The attorney compressed his lips. "Needless to say I remonstrated at such a sum, and several cablegrams were exchanged between us, quite—er—emphatic on her part, so I had no choice. Miss Gloria was always impulsive and self-willed but most—most lovable, as you know, Mrs. Mercer."

He had turned to Olive and she nodded.

"Gloria was lovable," she said quietly. "I know."

"Miss Ruth Warrender died shortly after the Armistice, leaving her entire fortune of over half a million to Miss Gloria, and I have continued to take charge of the estate," Gildersleeve resumed. "For the last four years she has kept an apartment permanently at her hotel in New York, taking occasional trips of only a few months' duration, and I have seen her frequently. Never has she seemed in better health and spirits than of late, and I cannot conceive of any one wanting to take her life! It is horrible, incredible!"

Olive moved slightly in her chair.

"Was Gloria in good health when she first went to that hotel, Mr. Gildersleeve?" she asked. "Was she with her aunt when she died, and where did that death take place? What kind of war work was Gloria engaged in? Where did she go after you sent her that large sum in Paris? You've told us really nothing and we want details of her life. But wait! Mr. Rider permitted his name to be used by some of the Chichester officials in making inquiries in New York about Gloria and he knows just what we want to learn from you. Will you reply to his questions, Mr. Gildersleeve? My husband and I will appreciate it."

The attorney silently bowed his acquiescence, but it seemed that a faint shadow of a smile curved his mobile lips as he turned again in his chair and waited for Rider to speak.

"Mr. Gildersleeve, as a mere bystander I have no authority, and no excuse except curiosity and a desire to help my friends here," he began at last. "I think Mrs. Mercer's final question would be my first. What do you actually know of Miss Gloria Warrender's whereabouts and associates from the date on which you sent her the money from her own property, to Paris. That was, I gather, in the autumn or winter of 1914?"

"In November, 1914," Gildersleeve amended and there ensued a pause. Finally he held out his hands with an eloquent gesture. "When this interview first started I said that I had nothing to tell even Mrs. Mercer that could not very well be printed in the newspapers to-morrow. Unfortunately that ceases to be true. I must ask that you respect my confidence and I only give it because you could obtain it, perhaps, from other sources, and I prefer to have you know the real undistorted facts. On receipt of that money in November, 1914, my young client disappeared."

11

Buried Years

"'Disappeared!'" Olive was the first to recover her voice, and its shocked accents rang through the room. "How could it be possible! Was no effort made . . .'"

"Every possible effort was made, Mrs. Mercer, in a quiet way through influential channels; Miss Ruth Warrender insisted upon that," the attorney retorted with dignity. "I received an acknowledgment by cable from Miss Gloria for the receipt of the money, then nothing more till a letter came after long delay from her aunt begging me to use every means that would not entail publicity in trying to locate the young woman. I did so, exhausting every resource at my command and finally going over myself, but I was unsuccessful. You can scarcely comprehend what conditions were like over there, but Miss Gloria seemed to have vanished from the face of the earth! The old lady failed rapidly, although I assured her unceasingly that her niece was safe, and possibly gone as a nurse to some remote theater of war. The air-raids in England prostrated her and I personally escorted her to Spain, where I was obliged to leave her in the care of a physician and nurses, for I was compelled by my duty to my other clients to return to this country, and Miss Ruth Warrender could not be persuaded to do so while a hope remained that Miss Gloria might be found."

"All search for her ceased on your return to America?" Rider took up his inquiry once more.

"No. I had agents everywhere searching. Privately I feared that she had been killed in some accident either in Paris or elsewhere in those feverish days, one of the hundreds lost or unidentified among the noncombatants, but I knew that she must, of course, with her ardent nature, have flung herself into active war-work of some sort. I knew, I say, but it was only my instinct that told me so, then or since. I have never succeeded in learning where she was during those four buried years."

"So Miss Warrender actually disappeared for four years?" Rider pursued.

"The first news of her was when she reappeared a week after the Armistice. That was at the American consulate in Paris, asking for news of her aunt, and that they cable me for funds in order to reach her. I have been informed that Miss Gloria was in a shocking state due to seeming privation, and overtaxed mentally and physically, but she refused to give any account of herself then or ever after as far as we have been able to discover. She was supplied with her aunt's address in Spain and immediate funds to set there, reaching the old lady's side just ten days before she died." He paused, smoothing down the fine white hair on his well-shaped head. "I arranged with the consulate in Madrid to have the body sent home and Miss Gloria accompanied it. That was in the spring of 1919."

"Where did your first meeting with Gloria Warrender take place after her return, Mr. Gildersleeve?" Rider was drawing invisible scrolls on the marble top of the table with an ivory paper knife as he spoke, and apparently he did not glance up.

"On the dock, when her steamer came in." The attorney shifted his position, resting his elbow on the arm of his chair and his chin on his hand. "She looked much older to me and still very ill and frail; there was a dullness, a sort of lack of all interest about her, too, which contrasted sharply with the vivid, not to say fiery, personality I remembered that impressed me most painfully, and as soon as her aunt's will was probated and the matter of the estate settled, I persuaded her to go away to a health resort. She was quite docile on every point except concerning those four years of the war; although I lectured her like a—a grandfather, she simply would not discuss them. My conviction remains that she was one of the unknown heroines of that terrible period!"

He spoke proudly, almost defiantly, but Rider's next question was uttered in the same dryly unmoved tone.

"Was no trace ever obtained of the funds you had sent her? No mention of her in any records of relief contributions of any country, any registrations of nurses or workers of whatever sort?"

"None."

"You say that you had previously sent to her at Biarritz the amount of her expenses for the following six months," Rider went on. "How much was that?"

"About six thousand dollars for the half-year. Her inheritance was advantageously invested." Gildersleeve dropped his arm and sat back in his chair.

"So that for four years, as far as you know, Miss Warrender lived on what remained of fifty-six thousand dollars after she had presumably donated the rest to war relief of one sort or another?"

"As far as I know, Mr. Rider!"

"Did Miss Warrender ever offer any explanation as to why she had not communicated with her aunt or yourself during that period? What were her relations with her aunt? Had she ever wished to contract a marriage which the older woman disapproved of? Do you know of any romance whatever in her life? Have you ever heard rumors concerning one?"

The queries came in a volley now and when they ceased a sharp intake of breath was audible, but from whom it came would have been difficult to tell.

"Miss Gloria said just once that it would have been 'useless' for her to write to her aunt or to me. I inferred she meant that we would try to dissuade her from whatever work she was doing and it would have been futile." The attorney proceeded to reply to the questions in turn. "A very warm affection existed between her and her aunt in spite of the differences in their ages and temperaments. The elder Miss Warrender was world-weary, bored to extinction and inexperienced in dealing with a young girl; narrow in spite of her cosmopolitan life, and bound to tradition and convention. Miss Gloria was independent and impetuous in those days, unconventional and democratic to degree, but generous and warm-hearted, and from the general tone of their brief communications with me I gather that within a very few months after her graduation Miss Gloria had completely won her aunt—er—'wound her around her finger' as one might say. It was a source of great satisfaction to me, for I had been apprehensive of their congeniality."

A smothered exclamation came from the chief, but Gildersleeve continued:

"I have never heard of Miss Gloria desiring to contract any marriage with or without her aunt's approval; I fancy she would have thought that of little moment if she really decided to marry. As to romance or rumors of it, the international society news will give you any quantity during the first year—the last, I should say before the war—but I don't think she herself was ever sentimentally involved. Then came the four years' eclipse and since then, as I say, she has been much changed."

"In what way? You said that she had never been in better health and spirits than lately," Rider reminded him.

"But of a different sort. Her health and strength returned during the following year or two after she came back to America, but not her interest in life. She was quiet and well-poised but no longer impulsive nor unconventional; if you know what I mean, she did the usual thing in the usual way, but merely because every one else did, as though it were a task. Personally, I think she had seen so much of suffering and horror during those four years that she was drained of any possible emotion. Nothing else could explain her apathy."

"I felt it—the change in her—when I met her at the station a fortnight ago to-day," Olive Mercer said slowly. "You know, of course, Mr. Gildersleeve, that I have known absolutely nothing of her for the past ten years, and I attributed her languid, detached air to the natural boredom of a woman of the world in our quiet, simple community, but she changed again quickly enough, didn't she, Stan?"

She appealed directly to her husband who nodded without speaking and she went on:

"Indeed, you would scarcely have known Gloria the—the last few days, Mr. Gildersleeve! She was positively radiant, more self-assured of course than the girl who had been my friend, but irresistible! I do believe every man in our set was fascinated by her, even Mr. Mott here—even my husband!" Olive had spoken in a tone of unusual enthusiasm, but now her eyes drooped and she said sadly: "Poor Gloria! I wonder what dreadful thing from those four years of mystery could have shadowed her here!"

"Surely, Mrs. Mercer, you cannot be under the impression that the past could have any connection with the brutal crime which took place here!" The attorney sat forward in his chair.

"What can we think?" Olive raised her eyes sorrowfully to his. "Surely no one here could have had any reason for taking her life, and you admit yourself that you don't know how she spent four years of it! Did you ever see her wear a strange opal ring, and hear its history as she told it to my husband and me last Friday evening?"

Gildersleeve gave a slight start and countered evasively:

"I have seen an opal ring on her finger, and when I read of the disappearance of one at the time of—of the murder I concluded it must be the same. It never occurred to me to inquire about it, for she was constantly changing her jewels. Will you tell me its history as she told it to you?"

Olive complied, turning occasionally to Stan for corroboration and he responded as before by a silent nod. When she had finished the attorney exclaimed:

"Extraordinary! She never mentioned it to me, but, as I said, I didn't ask! However, that ring, of course, can have nothing to do with her death. She could have lost or mislaid it temporarily, or it might even have been stolen from her before or after the tragedy; it is immaterial. As to the period during which her aunt and I were out of touch with her, please allow me to impress it upon you, Mrs. Mercer, that nothing which occurred then or later could account for this crime!"

"I'm afraid only proof can do that." Olive shook her head, and although she continued without resentment, it was with the stubborn note of the placidly implacable in her tones. "There was a mystery, you know; there has never been one here. We, too, like Gloria's aunt, but in our own fashion, are perhaps narrow and bound by tradition and convention, but our families have been in close association for generations, our lives are open books to one another. You ask me to disregard this singular not to say equivocal episode in Gloria's past and seriously consider the possibility that one of us, one of our friends, or at least a member of our own community, did this frightful thing? I would be the last to believe Gloria other than the splendid, generous, good woman that she was, but, leaving sentiment and affection aside, you as a lawyer and a man of common sense and intelligence must realize that you are asking too much of us."

"Olive, my dear, we must remember that we know nothing, we haven't even a suspicion as to the truth." Stan leaned toward his wife and spoke in a voice of mild reproof. "We are all equally in the dark and we must work together!"

"Well," Chief Clark caught a meaning glance from Rider and rose reluctantly, "I guess we won't keep you any longer from making your arrangements 'bout the funeral and all the rest of it. Do you expect to remain over night, Mr. Gildersleeve?"

"No. I must be back at my office to-morrow." The attorney rose as Mott and Rider got to their feet preparatory to departure. "There is a train later this afternoon, I believe?"

"Yes, at 'bout five. It's usually behind time but don't bank on that. I'll want to have a little talk with you, sir, down at headquarters before you go, and one of my men'll be here with a car for you in good time," the chief drawled genially. "You'll understand it's just to fill in my report?"

"Certainly. I shall be at your disposal." Gildersleeve bowed while the Mercers nodded in a friendly, less formal fashion and the trio departed.

"What's he know?" the chief demanded, jerking his thumb over his shoulder in the direction of the drawing-room door which had just closed behind them. "Acted kind of funny 'bout that ring, didn't he? What reason in the world has he got to hide anything? The girl was no kin to him!"

"But she was a client of his and he can't afford scandal with his fashionable practice," explained Rider. "The

notoriety of the whole affair with him being mentioned
as Miss Warrender's attorney and former guardian, practically, will injure him as it is. If the crime can be traced to
some one up here, some one entirely unconnected with her
former life, well and good, but he'd rather the case were
never solved than to trace the motive back to those four
years. You saw how carefully her disappearance and the
long search for her was kept from the newspapers, and he
did his best to avoid speaking of it till Mrs. Mercer pinned
him down."

"Till he saw you meant to drag it out of him, you
mean!" Mott corrected him. "I was sure something like
that would turn up—the mystery, I mean! It's going to let
our community out, by Godfrey!"

They separated at the porch steps, the chief to rattle
off down to his headquarters and the other two returning
home. Little was said during lunch, but when later they
sat with pipe and cigar, tilted comfortably back in the
shade of the grape arbor, Henry Mott made a seemingly
irrelevant remark.

"She certainly didn't mind using me as a smoke-screen!"

"Who?" Rider asked innocently, but his mustache
twitched.

"Mrs. Mercer. She said every one was fascinated by
Miss Warrender, even I—even her husband. It was Stan
she meant, and she wanted him to know that she was aware
of it! What do you think of that disappearance, anyway?"

"I'm inclined to believe Gildersleeve was right, if he
told all he knows. Do you remember when we drove away
after our first meeting with her you were indignant with
her lack of interest even after all this time, in the war? I
told you it had hit her too deep for her even to talk about
it and I've never had reason to change that opinion. I told
you, too, that her face was familiar although I couldn't

place her. Henry, it was some time during those four years that I saw her!"

Mott shrugged his fat shoulders.

"A lot of help that's going to be if you can't remember where, and we won't stand much chance of tracing her back through that time if the attorney and his agents couldn't do it!" he observed witheringly. "She recognized you, but she didn't want you to recall her, you admitted that. You were right, though, when you said she had a story! Even if we never get it all, the reason for the murder lies somewhere in those closed chapters and they can never accuse any of us up here!"

"I thought you were sure that one of your neighbors . . ." Rider began facetiously, but Mott reddened.

"How could I be sure?" he growled. "I didn't know then what I do now, and that theory was the one best bet. Anyway it was better than having none at all and standing pat for a bluff! Want to come along over to the club?"

He knocked the ashes from his pipe and rose, and Rider shook his head.

"Still going scandalmongering, eh? No, thank you. You can retail it to me when you come back, and I have a little problem of my own I want to try to solve."

Left to himself Rider finished his cigar and then wandered aimlessly through Mott's orchard, skirting the fields to a wooded ridge beyond, a ridge that twisted like the tracks of a huge mole to Major Hill's dismal home.

But that was apparently not Rider's objective, for once within the dense growth of trees, he seated himself on a fallen log, and drawing a second cigar from his pocket, he puffed contemplatively upon it. Every indication, and not a shred of evidence! From the moment that he had been summoned with Mott to the scene of the crime he had been feeling his way and everything confirmed the mad hypothesis that leaped to his brain—everything but an atom of proof!

Never had he investigated a crime at once so simple and so complex! Could it be that, after all, his instinct, his science, the reading of character, which had been his greatest asset, were for once at fault?

If only he could remember where he had seen Gloria Warrender! It had not been a mere passing glance; of that he was sure, although he had remembered less distinctive faces than hers from a single glimpse and for a far longer period. It had been in some crisis, some moment of supreme importance, but when? Her piquant face with its aureole of flame-colored hair, her hazel eyes shining with a golden light! And the rest? Mist, vapor, clouds that obscured his vision!

Then, as he concentrated, gradually, imperceptibly the veil lifted and a single scene swept across his mind as a picture is flashed on a screen, livid but magnificent, horrible yet sublime, and in the midst of it the face of Gloria Warrender!

With a cry Rider leaped to his feet. He had remembered!

12

The Tiger Lily

"Well, if this affair turns out to be a matter of local talent, there's enough circumstantial evidence in the talk at the club to start the ball rolling and it's bound to reach the chief's ears sooner or later!" Mott dropped into a chair on the porch beside Rider and mopped his glistening forehead. "I'll bet every member was there to-day though the course was practically deserted, and the tea grew cold. It was just as I told you; between the veranda, the lounge, and the locker-room, I got what the boys call an earful!"

"So Stan Mercer is the villain, eh?" Rider smiled, and then his face grew serious. "We might as well mention names, we're not sitting on his jury! Your neighbors don't know about this episode in Miss Warrender's past, and so they think that he, a man with a good wife, fine children, comfortable home and settled income, took a chance on going to the chair for an infatuation that would have died of inanition anyway, for the lady was to have gone out of his life in two days more! Go on, tell me the worst; I can stand it!"

"Look here, Dan, you needn't be satirical!" Mott's own expression was almost solemn. "Personally I still believe that some secret from the past was the cause of the crime, but if it wasn't—well, there isn't any doubt but that Stan was mad about her! You saw how he practically carried her off by himself from their very first meeting. Oh, I admit that he did it conventionally enough, riding, golf, tennis and all that, quite openly! So all-fired openly that the whole neighborhood was on from the first few days, and the women quacking like a lot of ducks by the end of the week! Then came the change in Olive Mercer. Every one knows that she hasn't gone out of her way to be much of a companion to Stan for years and she's let herself get fat, and unattractive, and all that, but she's the best mother and housekeeper in all Chichester! After the first few days of the Warrender woman's visit, poor Olive Mercer starts in all of a sudden to try to pal around with them, and why?"

"You seem to have the answer," Rider observed.

"You bet I have!" Mott exclaimed explosively. "I talked confidentially with seven different women in turn this afternoon and each of them says that somebody put her wise to what was going on and advised her to wade in to the rescue. And who do you think that somebody was? The seven votes were unanimous—that spell-binding Foster girl!"

"The one who took charge of little Nancy after we found her?"

"Yes. She's Mrs. Mercer's best friend, and a good listener for all her electioneering; she got all the gossip and was seen driving away from Hydrangea Walk a week ago Friday afternoon. The very next day Mrs. Mercer broke out and made a fool of herself trying to play the game when she'd let herself get out of practice for so long. Everybody laughed but they were sorry for her too, and most of the men are sorry for Stan, not only because she brought ridicule on them both, but because he's been practically a married bachelor for so long. They all say that his wife's interference only fanned the flame, and that he must have been crazy enough to propose to the Warrender woman that they run away together! You can say what you like about his being a settled married man but, by Godfrey, they're the hardest hit when it comes to an infatuation like that; they lose their heads and wreck everything!"

"Then your club gossips don't imply that Miss Warrender agreed to spoil Mrs. Mercer's happiness?" There was a peculiar note in Rider's tone.

"We-ell, women are more cautious, especially women of the world who want to stay *in* that world! They've seen what happened to other romances that started that way, and the world-well-lost stuff doesn't apply to the present vintage when they've everything to lose. No, they think she was just amusing herself in the way that's perfectly recognized in the set she traveled with, only Stan didn't know the rules, and when she saw how desperate he was she enlightened him and it drove him half out of his mind."

"But all that you got from Holcomb this morning," Rider objected.

"I've had corroboration since, in detail. How Stan looked at her, spoke to her, helped her down from her horse! How their hands touched when he gave her a cup of tea or selected a golf stick for her! Jumping Christopher, I feel like the third act of a 'drammer'!"

"And you talk like one!" Rider assented dryly. "When is Captain Staverton due?"

"I forgot all about him!" Mott scrambled to his feet. "Just time to clean up and get down to the train!"

He rushed into the house, to reappear a few minutes later and chug away in his disreputable little car, and the sunset dimmed to twilight and deepened to dusk while Rider still sat there smoking meditatively.

He was engaged in making himself presentable when the car came back and he heard the sound of masculine voices and clink of a shaker from below. From the head of the stairs he reconnoitered for a moment before descending.

The man in the deep chair under the glow of the bridge lamp was long and lean, sprawled in the utter relaxation of a body in perfect condition under perfect control. He looked to be about forty, with a well-shaped head covered with mouse-colored hair, keen gray eyes and a thinly arched, aquiline nose above a firm mouth and chin. Despite his ease there was an alert air about him as though he could snap into instant action, and beneath the geniality of his laughter at some sally of his host there was a cutting edge to his tone.

Rider had scarcely finished his survey when Mott glanced up and saw him.

"Come on down, old scout, and meet Captain Staverton!" he called.

"Glad to know you, sir!" Staverton's voice was crisply cordial and his handclasp hearty. "We've been talking shop, going back to five or six years ago, but Mott tells me that you were over with us, though in a different capacity than this fat old noncombatant! More in my line."

"Captain Staverton was a liaison officer, I think I told you, Dan," Mott explained. "Polite name for spy, since he's started this, and what were you in the Secret Service but a glorified policeman? Come on, let's go!"

He filled a glass for Rider from the shaker, took mineral water for himself, and the flow of reminiscence began. Throughout dinner they talked war, and as anecdote after anecdote was related Rider glanced with growing wonder at their host, for not once was Major Hill mentioned. Mott had said the captain was a friend of his; what had passed between the two before he joined them? Were they waiting for him to mention the name, or because of recent events and his own official duty now, did they mean to ignore that topic?

The meal concluded, they settled again in the living-room, for the rumble and flash of an approaching thunderstorm warned them off the porch, and then, as the captain produced a pipe even more malodorous than Mott's the latter asked with a desperate side glance at Rider:

"You remember old Jack, don't you, Craig? Jack Hill, who was invalided home a major after the gas got him?"

"Great guns, yes!" The captain paused with a lighted match against his pipe bowl. "I haven't seen him since, but what a fine chap he was! Never knew such nerve in the outfit! I don't suppose you happen to have run across him?"

"Every now and then." Mott cast another glance at Rider and this time there was no mistaking his meaning; he was signaling for help. "You see, he lives right in the neighborhood here. He's away just now or I'd have had him over to-night."

"Jove, is that so? Sorry I missed him. You know him, Commissioner?" The captain turned courteously to include Rider in the conversation and unconsciously gave him his opening.

"Met him when I first came a month ago, poor fellow! It's hard to see a mere shell of a man like that and realize what he must have been."

The captain glanced up quickly.

"You don't mean to say he hasn't recovered in five years?" he asked in shocked accents.

"Well, Henry could tell you his condition better than I, perhaps, for I can scarcely say I know him, yet I've seen men like him when they've gone to pieces," Rider returned and leaned back in his chair.

"It was that infernal gas, you see, Craig," Mott explained hastily. "The wounds, of course, got him physically and pulled him down, but the gas shattered his nerves and he came home to a solitary existence in a lonely house without a relative in the world or an interest in life to buck him up. He doesn't dissipate, and once in a while he appears at the country club or some informal affair at a neighbor's, or has a few of us to dinner at that ramshackle old house of his, but you can see it's an effort. Most of the time he lives like a hermit, takes long walks in the woods or moons around his place with just one decrepit old manservant for company, and naturally he's not getting any better."

"Humph!" Captain Staverton grunted sympathetically. "Too d—n bad! The gas, eh? Of course, if he lives as you say, it's the worst possible thing for him and yet it's unusual for the effect to be so lasting when his physical health is restored. Isn't it, Commissioner? You say you've seen men like him before."

"Yes." Rider paused and then added musingly as though to himself: "In my experience there's just one thing in life that can take the heart and soul out of a man, and that's a woman. Not a bad woman either, but perhaps among the finest, straightest, bravest characters on earth."

"I thought you said you didn't know Jack Hill!" The captain rapped out the comment like an accusation, and Rider smiled.

"I never met him till I came here to visit Henry but—I was in the Secret Service, you know," he replied quietly.

Mott uttered a startled exclamation beneath his breath and for a space there was silence in the room, broken only by a nearer crash of thunder.

Then Rider resumed:

"You two are his friends and perhaps you think I'm overstepping the bounds, Captain Staverton, but there's a certain fact you don't know yet that exonerates me. As to Major Hill, I do not presume to say or think that he may even remember one of so many individuals with whom he came in contact in the brief but brilliant period of his active service; I am leaving him out of the subject completely, digressing, if you will permit."

"You were thinking of some one else?" There was a tense note in Staverton's tones, and Mott leaned forward to hear the answer.

"I was wondering if either of you had ever heard of—the Tiger Lily?"

As though in response to his question there came a sharp peal and a blinding flash, and the storm was upon them.

"Gad, yes!" There was a fervent, almost reverent look upon Staverton's lean, clean-cut face. "You know everything, I see! So poor Jack never got over it? What a hopeless, pitiful thing!"

"Good—God!" Henry Mott, who abjured profanity, stared from one to the other of them. "I heard of her, of course, but I never saw her—unless . . . Dan, am I going crazy? Who *was* the Tiger Lily?"

"Nobody ever knew, I think." Rider gave him a level glance. "Just a young slip of a girl with flaming red hair, who appeared to have a roving commission just back of the front lines—a commission of mercy and aid. We were simply told to serve her in every way we could as long as she didn't disobey the rules laid down for all women war-workers, and I never heard of her doing that. She must have had great influence, of course, and she had a habit of appearing miraculously where the need for her was most urgent. They tell me she'd been at it since long before we got in, but that I can't say. I don't know what the French and English called her, but our own boys nicknamed her the 'Tiger Lily' in sheer worship and out of deference to her vivid coloring and temperament, I suppose. Officers or buck privates, it made no difference to her, and I understand she always worked alone with plenty of supplies that she got the Lord knows how or where! Isn't that so, Captain Staverton?"

The captain nodded.

"You'd hear of her taking possession of an abandoned wreck of a farmhouse, giving soup and coffee to the poor devils staggering back for a few days out of hell, and the next you knew, after some attack miles away, you'd find her with a little dressing station of her own right back of the lines, handing out first aid. I never saw her and a lot of us thought she was a myth until we learned something personal—after Major Hill was gassed and wounded—and then later when she did something, I never knew what, that was pretty average heroic, and a certain general came looking for her to pin a decoration on her. She promptly disappeared and wasn't heard of again in our sector."

"I happened to be very much present when she did that particular heroic thing," Rider remarked. "It's the only time I ever saw her during the war."

"So you did remember!" Mott exclaimed bitterly. "It's a pity . . ."

"Wait, Henry!" Rider interrupted sharply, and their host subsided. "She had a bunch of wounded, French and our own, in a little hut that was bombed, and she got every one of them out—alone. I happened to get there with a bunch of linemen, one of whom I was watching, just as the ambulances she'd been waiting for came rolling up, and I'll never forget her face and her hair like flame itself in the smoke and glow of that burning shack!"

"That's what you said!" Mott exclaimed irrepressibly. "You said you could only remember her face, and the rest was all hazy, like smoke!"

"I suppose more of the boys owe their lives to her than you could imagine," Rider went on hastily but smoothly. "Individual activities didn't reach the papers very often in those days when the heroism of a group only got a paragraph now and then. A lot of them must have fallen in love with her, too, and perhaps some of them remember even yet!"

"Perhaps," assented the captain gravely. "That chap, for instance, who begged for her when they thought he was dying in a base hospital and she came. You heard of that case, Commissioner?"

"Yes," Rider nodded, avoiding Mott's eyes. "I understood at the time that it was the real thing on his part, one of these romances you read about, but the Tiger Lily had only pity and mercy in her heart for any one then, they tell me. She was as austere as a nun and as tender as a mother! She only went to him because she believed him to be dying—but he didn't, I hear?"

"He—didn't." The captain knocked out his pipe on the empty hearth and then resumed his seat while the storm still roared, and flashed, and swept in driving sheets against the windows and on the porch roof.

"So Jack was the ghost, after all!" Mott said at last. "We all three know who we're talking about so why beat about the bush? We're all friends,—his friends! He gave her a ring and she gave him a promise!"

"Only because she thought he was dying!" the captain reminded his host. "She did it to ease his last moments, as she thought, and it wasn't a promise of love or marriage; it was only that if he lived and came to her after the war was over and found her wearing that ring, he might ask her. Then he suddenly turned delirious and cried out that if she ever ceased wearing it a curse would be upon her. I learned this from a girl who was visiting her brother in the same ward and she only knew Jack's name; she never heard of the Tiger Lily, but we all knew who it was. She was a mystery, from first to last. Have you chaps ever heard of her since?"

"Look here!" Mott had grown suddenly discreet. "If it happened that her picture should appear in all the big city papers, to say nothing of the small syndicated ones, don't you suppose some of the boys would remember her and blazon her to the world, no matter what her real name was or—or why she happened to be in the public eye just now?"

"Undoubtedly." Staverton looked from one to the other of them. "What's the idea? Do you know, after all, who she is? I mean, of course, if it's going to be made public after all these years?"

"Yes," Rider glanced again at his host, and Mott crimsoned as he went on: "We have even had the honor of knowing her—recently. You say you've never seen her, Captain Staverton, but from what you've heard of her would you consider her the sort of woman who would flirt with a man for mere idle amusement till he was ready to wreck his home for her?"

"Never, by God!" the captain exclaimed just as a louder blast of wind and rain swirled against the door and it flew open. "Has any contemptible cad dared to say that? The Tiger Lily is . . ."

From behind them a hoarse voice cried out suddenly:

"The Tiger Lily is dead!"

13

A Shot at Dawn

As the harsh, half-demented voice burst upon their ears
the three men seated around the library table sprang to
their feet and wheeled to find a strange apparition confronting them from the doorway. In the jagged fork of
lightning that flashed just behind him they saw that he
was tall and gaunt to the point of emaciation, with his
drenched garments clinging to his spare form, and in his
bloodshot eyes there was the wild, wolfish look of one who
had known no food nor rest for days.

"Jack!" cried Henry Mott, starting forward. "Thank
God, you're back! Here's Craig Staverton. . . ."

The words died on his lips, however, for the grotesque,
pitiful figure that was Major Jack Hill had laughed and
flinging up his arms whirled and disappeared in the driving storm.

"Was that—that actually old Jack?" Staverton demanded,
and then, without waiting for a reply, he strode toward the
door, with a ring of command in his tones. "Come! He's
half-crazed! We can't let him get away like this!"

Rider followed with Mott in his wake, and it seemed to
the former that a lanky but spryly animated shadow leaped
from the porch before them and vanished in the inky dark-
ness. When another flash of lightning came, however, it
revealed nothing but rain-soaked shrubbery and trees

bending before the wind, and although all three searched and called till they were drenched and hoarse themselves, they found no trace of the man who had come and gone like a wraith indeed.

"We're fools!" Mott panted as at last they retreated to the house. "We'll call up old Hiram, his servant, as we should have done in the first place, and tell him to be on the lookout for his employer, for of course that's where Jack's headed for—home! He may be there already!"

Hurrying to the telephone regardless of the stream which meandered after him across the floor, he called the number of Hilltop, and when finally old Hiram replied he cried:

"Hi, this is Mr. Mott. . . . Listen, you old nut! The Major's just been here and he's on his way home now. He's sick, and you'd better have heated blankets and coffee ready. Call me if you need . . . What? He is? You tell him I just wanted to be sure he was all right and I'll run over in the morning. All the same, I'm going to be sure!"

He hung up the receiver and turned to the two who waited tensely.

"Jack's home already," he said briefly. "He must have streaked it along the short-cut through the woods. Old Hiram's in a rage—you know why, Dan, and he tried to cut me off at first; then he said Jack didn't want anybody to come near him, that he was all right. What do you think we'd better do?"

"Can't very well intrude, though I wish he'd answered you himself, Mott!" Staverton's tone was frankly troubled. "A man's house is his castle, you know, and if the old man can take care of him . . ."

"He has in the past, but I've never seen Jack as bad as this!" Mott shook his head. "Come on and we'll get into dry clothes, you fellows. Of course, Craig, you're not in on this and if you feel like going to bed, all right, but I think Dan and I will wait up for the storm to pass and the first hint of dawn to come, and then go over there, anyway. I'm not easy in my mind about him!"

"Nor am I, and I'm an old comrade of Jack, remember," Staverton remarked. "If I'm not in the way I'd like to sit up with you and hear the rest about the Tiger Lily. Is it true, what Jack cried out to us? Is the Tiger Lily really dead?"

Mott glanced at Rider, who replied:

"Tell you all about it, Captain, as soon as we get these wet things off. You'll learn it soon enough, anyway!"

When, a little later, Rider descended in a warm, dry pedestrian suit it was to find Mott in heavy corduroys bending over a coffee percolator which he had brought from the dining-room and surrounded with platters of cold meat and bread and cheese.

"You going to tell him everything?" the latter demanded. "All about the gossip and—and what I thought?"

"Of course not!" Rider laughed and clapped him on his plump shoulder. "I'll tell him only a little more than the papers have already, just to prepare him for what your excitable Chief of Police may pull before Staverton goes tomorrow."

"By Godfrey, you don't think he'll try to arrest . . ." Mott's words died on his lips, for at that juncture they were joined by Staverton, who was likewise in rough tramping attire.

"Thought I'd get into these in case you chaps wanted my company at dawn," he remarked. "Of course, I won't go into Jack's house if he doesn't want to see me, but I can wait outside."

"He'll be glad to see you when he's calmed down, and so will we be to have you with us, Craig!" Mott rejoined heartily as he handed him a steaming cup of coffee and gestured toward the food. "It's past midnight now, and we'll need something to keep us going. Let's eat and then talk."

His guests accepted the suggestion and when the pipes and cigar were lighted once more Staverton gazed at Mott expectantly, but the latter waved to Rider.

"Dan can tell you better than I can what happened to the Tiger Lily."

"Captain, have you read in the papers about a certain murder that was committed here a few days ago?" Rider asked.

"A murder?" Staverton frowned thoughtfully. "I glanced at the papers only casually on the train to-day; something about a woman found strangled in a hammock, wasn't it?"

"Yes." Rider chose his words with evident care. "An heiress who came here to visit a school friend whom she had not communicated with in ten years. She had known Major Hill in France. Her attorney came at noon to-day— or rather yesterday—and told us that this young woman was abroad with her aunt when the war broke out, and disappeared completely for the four years of its duration in spite of all efforts made in a quiet way to locate her, and influence brought to bear in high places. This information you will understand is confidential. She was well supplied with money when she vanished, but destitute, in a shocking state due to seeming privation, and overtaxed mentally and physically by some terrific experience through which she had passed, when she reappeared after the Armistice. She refused to give any account of herself then or ever after."

"She knew Major Hill?" The captain was watching Rider closely, but the latter's eyes were apparently fixed on the smoke from his cigar.

"That is the only part of this story that interests you?" Rider smiled a trifle grimly. "Her name was Gloria Warrender and she was an extraordinarily attractive young woman with masses of flame-colored hair . . ."

"My God!" Staverton interrupted, his whole body tensing. "You're not trying to tell me that the murdered woman was the Tiger Lily!"

"I told you that I had seen her once in France and I met her here a fortnight ago," Rider responded quietly.

"But who—why . . ." For once the captain was at a loss. "I can't comprehend it! It's astounding, incredible! If you're sure this Miss Warrender was the Tiger Lily, what motive in the world could any sane person have to kill her?"

"That is what the Chief of Police here figures, although he doesn't know where Miss Warrender spent those four years of her disappearance, and I doubt if he ever heard of the Tiger Lily." Rider was once more warily conscious of each word he uttered. "He does know, however, that Miss Warrender wore a curious and costly ring which has now disappeared, and that she removed it hastily whenever in the presence of Major Hill; he knows that Miss Warrender was the first to remind him that they had met on the other side, that both palpably evaded discussing where or under what circumstances that meeting took place, that they greeted each other in public formally and with constraint, but that they had a secret and violent quarrel on the edge of the golf course last Friday, and he has three eye-witnesses to the scene. Every one hereabouts knows that Major Hill left his home suddenly without warning at two o'clock on Saturday afternoon, and that Miss Warrender was found murdered in the hammock at the Mercers' at three o'clock. . . ."

"Stop!" Staverton commanded. "What monstrous thing are you insinuating!"

"I am telling you of the facts as they stand, not expressing a personal opinion," Rider asserted in level tones. "The major had not reappeared, as far as we know, until he stood in the doorway here an hour ago. You saw and heard him; you said yourself that he was half-crazed. That is why I told you the chief shares your opinion that no sane person killed her."

"I didn't say that!" the captain countered swiftly. "I asked what motive any one of normal mind could have had! So you're trying to tell me that this Chief of Police is going to hang the crime on poor Jack, eh? There isn't a chance in the world! Jack wouldn't hurt a dog, and he's as sane as the average; it's his nerves, not his brain, that's affected, isn't that so, Mott?"

"That's what I've been telling Dan ever since the whole thing started!" Mott declared with indignant emphasis. "Not that he's expressed a single opinion of his own on the case from the beginning; he's sitting tight! If it's true that Jack was still in love with the Tiger Lily and she never had cared nor pretended to, that would account for the scene on the golf course that looked from a distance like a quarrel, and account, too, for his going away the next day. He knew she was supposed to leave on Monday, and he probably came home late last night like that thinking that she was gone, and then learned from somebody of her murder. Loving her, however hopelessly, wouldn't such news naturally drive a highly nervous man into the state he was in when he stopped here? What if he's got an alibi he can prove for the time between two o'clock when he left his house and a little after three when the murder was discovered? There are several people who can't prove theirs! Nobody'll ever make me think old Jack ever killed that woman, and if they try to pin it on him, watch my smoke!"

"Mine too!" Staverton nodded. "I've got enough to stand the gaff for the best lawyers and alienists in the State if this lout of an official starts anything, and—brothers-in-arms, you know! Couldn't let an old comrade down, especially Jack!"

"But—but even an arrest would kill him, on such a charge!" Mott exclaimed. "If he loved her it's enough to do for him as it is to know she was so horribly murdered! Look here, Craig, you've known men who were splendid heroes on the field of battle and rotters everywhere else, haven't you? I'm not uttering a word of defamation against the character of Miss Warrender or the Tiger Lily, whether they were one and the same or not, but I do say, from bitter experience, that it's the nature of all women to flirt, innocently or no. Couldn't the girl who did such fine, brave work in wartime revert now to a little harmless flirtation that the man didn't take that way, and mightn't he . . ."

"No!" Staverton snapped. "Not if you're referring to the Commissioner's question earlier in the evening. She was human, she might have learned to care for some one, but the girl, whom the lowest scum in a drafted army had only respect and reverent worship for, would kill such a love or fly from it if it meant the wreckage of another woman's home, as the Commissioner suggested. There was nothing in the soul of the Tiger Lily that wasn't brave and clean and honorable."

The rain had ceased, and only the distant rumble of thunder and occasional patter on the porch roof of drops from the overladen trees came as a reminder of the passed storm. Silence had again fallen but Mott broke it by bringing his hand down sharply on the table.

"Then who killed her?" he cried. "It wasn't Jack Hill and it wasn't the person I had in mind. Is this going to be one of the unsolved crime mysteries that are shelved by the police, and dropped by the newspapers, and finally forgotten? It seems inconceivable that a woman could be killed in broad daylight in her hostess' garden within a stone's throw of the house and with servants and children scattered all about, and the murderer escape! Dan, how long are you going to let this go on?"

He had turned suddenly to Rider, and Staverton gave them a long, cool, calculating glance.

"So this was not merely a confidential conversation between a host and his guests?" His tone was cutting in its implication. "I did not know that Ex-commissioner Rider of the Secret Service . . ."

"Had become Special Deputy Commissioner of the New York Police Department?" Mott finished for him. "He is that, and my very good friend, Craig. He happened to be visiting me here as I told you, and when this tragedy occurred he was put on the case by request of the local authorities. You'll remember that it was he who recognized the Tiger Lily in Miss Warrender, and he never told even me."

Rider smiled again.

"I told you that I had seen her somewhere but couldn't place her," he remarked. "It was only this afternoon that the truth came to me. I may as well tell you now that I have never for a moment suspected Major Hill as the murderer, but it is not my province to dictate to the chief here until I have proof that the crime was committed by some one else."

"It is not your purpose, you mean, don't you?" Staverton laughed pleasantly and the lines in his face relaxed. "Sorry I jumped to conclusions, but you two rather had me going for a moment! You'd rather have the chief here barking up the wrong tree than getting in your way, eh? Still, it seems a pity that poor Jack must be the scapegoat in his condition."

"You don't know Chief Clark!" Mott shook his head. "He'll follow the first indication of a clew that comes to him to the bitter end, ignoring everything else, and the only thing that's kept him—except Dan's advice—from sending out a general alarm for Jack is that the opal ring is missing and he thinks the murder may have been committed to rob her of it. Nobody seems to remember whether they saw it on Miss Warrender's hand that day or not and it wasn't found among the rest of her jewels, but Dan and I dined there the evening before and we both noticed that she was wearing it."

"The ring Jack gave her was an opal," Staverton observed. "It had a curious fleur-de-lis effect in the heart of the stone, and Jack paid some fabulous price for it because it reminded him of her—the Tiger Lily."

"It's the same," Mott remarked and then glanced toward the windows. "Look at the gray light coming in! We've talked the night through, you fellows; don't you think it's

about time to start for Jack's place? I can't help it, but I'm worried, I tell you!"

"Let's go." Staverton rose and reached for his cap. "I'll hang about and wait outside till you give me the signal—*if* you do! Jack's probably pretty well cut up and he may not be in a mood for renewing old friendships."

The trees still dripped and the earth was sodden beneath their feet when they started out in the dim haze of light that preceded the coming of day. Mott led the others through his orchard and skirted the fields by the same route Rider had taken on the previous day, then followed a narrow, winding footpath that ran through the heavily wooded ridge.

"This is the short-cut," he announced over his shoulder. "We'll get a continuous shower from overhead and it's still pretty dark in here, but it's drier under foot and we'll save more than a mile."

It was almost as black as the open fields had been an hour before and they trudged on in silence save when Mott stumbled over a tree-root or stone and grunted in exasperation. When they neared the clearing, however, the vista before them was perceptibly lighter and a few pale streaks of rose glowed in the eastern sky.

"Rather early to break in on an exhausted, grief-stricken man if he's just getting to rest." Captain Staverton broke the stillness at last. "Is that his place there, just ahead? Hadn't we better wait till we see his old servant stirring about?"

A sudden, sharp report startlingly near them blasted the question from his lips and involuntarily he leaped to one side, then glanced at the two who had stopped and were gazing at each other in amazement.

"Did some one take a potshot at us?" Mott gasped. "Do you suppose Jack is really off his head and wandering around in these woods with his gun?"

"We'll soon see!" Rider declared, his lips set. "I thought the report came from off there to the south, didn't you?"

He turned to Staverton for confirmation and at the latter's nod he started grimly forward through the trackless undergrowth, leading the way himself this time while his two companions followed.

They had not far to go, for rounding a clump of silver birches beside a tiny, hidden pool Rider stopped suddenly. There at his feet lay Major Hill, his gun under his right hand and a thin trickle of blood coming from his temple. Rider knelt to feel for a heartbeat, but Captain Staverton stood at attention and dragged off his cap.

"Poor Jack!" he said with a break in his firm tones. "Perhaps it was the best thing for him, after all!"

14

Conspirators Three

"Think so, do you?" A nasal drawl sounded just behind Staverton and he wheeled as Rider rose slowly to his feet. Mott, for the moment overcome, was leaning against a tree with bowed head and he did not glance up as the chief of police parted the bushes and came through to them. "I heard that shot, too, but I missed the direction till I saw you three heading this way. Who are you?"

He addressed Staverton, who gave the desired information and added: "I was leaving for Chicago this morning, but of course I shall hold myself at your disposal as a witness if you require me."

"That's the coroner's business," the chief remarked. "You appeared to know the major, from what you said just now."

"I used to know him very well. We were in the service together."

"All right, Captain. I'll see you later." The chief turned pointedly to Rider. "Looks as though he made a pretty clean job of it! He was dead when you reached him?"

Rider nodded.

"I felt his heart but it wasn't necessary. Look at that hole drilled through his temple! He must have died instantly! Anything I can do, Chief?"

"Yes. I wish you'd go up to the house and tell that old man if he's there that the major has been hurt and ask him to come here. Then telephone the coroner, will you? Don't want to leave the body till he gets here."

Rider turned, dropped his hand lightly on Mott's shoulder as he passed him, and making his way to the wing of the old farmhouse where he and Mott had stopped the previous Saturday, he knocked on the door.

It opened almost instantly and old Hiram nearly fell into his arms. He had evidently been crouched on the other side of it, waiting, for his face was blanched with terror and his voice quavered as he shrilled:

"What is it? Oh, you're Mr. Mott's friend, sir! What's happened? I—I heard a shot!"

"Here, pull yourself together, man!" Rider commanded. "Was the major here late last night when Mr. Mott telephoned to you?"

"Yes, sir, he'd just come in. In a terrible state he was, worse than I told you last week! But I talked too much then! All of you trying to make out that the major killed that lady, him as wouldn't harm a fly! That was a gunshot I heard! What was it?"

"The major has hurt himself." Rider spoke as gently as he could, for Hiram had cowered back as though he had been dealt a blow. "Somebody's with him and they want you. He's down in the woods, by that bunch of birch trees beside the little pond. Know where it is?"

But Hiram had not waited to hear the question. Gathering himself together he had set out at a tottering run for the woods, and Rider entered the house.

He found the living-room clean but bare and cheerless in the cold light of dawn. It was evident that the major had not lingered there after his return the night before, for his pipes were all cleaned and in an orderly row in their rack and the humidor was full. The clean scent of tobacco was in the air, however, and something intangible of the lonely man still lingered. Rider was glad to telephone his message to the coroner and leave the house.

As he neared the little, stagnant pool in the woods once more he heard Hiram's voice, hushed and trembling, and then the slow, twanging accents of the chief.

"Yes, sir, I was up," Hiram was saying. "I sat up Saturday night and Sunday too, waiting for him."

"Did you know he was coming home last night?" the chief asked. "Get any word at all from him in advance?"

"No, sir. He came in the midst of that storm and flung open the door. Drenched to the skin, he was, and he looked like he'd been through I don't know what! He wouldn't let me do anything for him but told me to let him alone. I was used to that, but as he started for his room I went to the kitchen to fix up something hot for him and a bite to eat, when the telephone rang."

Rider waited to hear no more but strode forward to the clump of birches where he found Hiram huddled on the sodden ground beside the major's body, his face gray and pinched, and suddenly aged. The chief was standing with his back against a tree, but of Mott and the captain there was no sign.

"I've sent that message, Chief," he announced. "Mind if I stick around?"

"No. I want you to hear this man's story. Now, then, Hiram, who telephoned while you were in the kitchen? Did you answer, or the major?"

"Me, sir. It was Mr. Mott. He said the Major had just been there and he thought he was ill; he wanted to know if he had got home yet and I said 'yes' that the major was all right. He said he'd come over this morning and I told him that the major didn't want to see anybody."

"Why?"

"Well, it's like I told you last week, sir, when you came. I've been with him long enough to know what he wants without his telling me, and I can see when he feels like being by himself." Hiram looked down at the still form and a harsh sob broke from his lips.

"Did you take Mr. Mott's message to the major?" There was a softer note in the chief's nasal tones.

"I went to his room, but he wasn't there, nor anywhere in the house! He must have gone out the back way or I would have seen him pass through the living-room where the telephone is. All night I waited, and then just a few minutes ago I heard a sound like the shot of a gun! I don't know what made me, but I knew! I knew!" Slow tears were rolling down his cheeks now and he wiped them off roughly with his coatsleeve. "I went to look for his gun, and it was still there in the rack where he always kept it, but his old service revolver was gone from the drawer in his bureau! I don't know how I got downstairs and to the living-room door but I did, just as Mr.—this gentleman here, Mr. Mott's friend—knocked on it! He told me the major was hurt down here and I came a-running! Somehow, though, I felt it was the end for him."

"Hiram!" the chief spoke more sternly once more, "did one word pass between you when he came home last night that you haven't told me? Did you or he mention the murder or speak of Miss Warrender at all? Did he say anything that you didn't understand, anything that sounded as if he was rambling and sort of out of his head a little? Did you hear one word out of him, for instance, about a flower, a tiger lily?"

Rider, standing a trifle apart, smiled to himself. The chief had heard Mott tell him the subject of his telegram at the Mercers', saying that now they might get some real dope on the major, and his had been the moving shadow that leaped from the porch before them in pursuit of the major the night before! Could he have heard any of their conversation in the living-room during that howling storm? Rider doubted it. All that could have reached his ears was that agonized cry of the major's: "The Tiger Lily is dead!"

"A *tiger lily*, sir?" old Hiram stammered. "Them yellow wild things? Of course not! It was just as I told you; he said to let him alone, and I did! He never mentioned the murder and neither did I, though I meant to as soon as he was rested, to let him know what terrible things was being hinted at about him! I guess them that started it will be sorry now!"

His voice quivered with loyal indignation and as he bowed his head once more, the coroner tramped his way through the undergrowth and halted.

"'Morning, Chief!" he said. "This appears to be rather a busy season for us, doesn't it? I see that Mr. Rider is with us again! Is this the major's servant?"

"Yes, Doctor." The chief's small eyes twinkled at Rider. "I guess the job is yours alone this time, though. The body ain't been touched except that Mr. Rider felt of the major's heart, but you can see for yourself that it wasn't any use. Four of us heard the shot fired; Mr. Mott, his friend Captain Staverton, Mr. Rider and me, and we were on the spot a minute after. I got other things on my hands besides a plain suicide."

"And what were you doing around here at daybreak, Mr. Rider?" Dr. Todd turned to him and quickly amended: "You and Mr. Mott and his friend, I mean."

"We were going over to the major's to see if he was all right, for he'd seemed ill when he called at Mott's place late last night and Mott was worried about him, alone here with just Hiram." Rider paused, adding smoothly: "We'd thought of sending for you in your private professional capacity, Doctor, if we found the major really as ill as he seemed. We three heard the shot and came rushing here, and the chief appeared an instant later."

The coroner turned inquiring eyes upon his colleague and the latter drawled:

"I had a kind of a hint that the major was back, Doctor, and I was looking around a little bit before I went to the house to talk to him about the case you got through with yesterday. I didn't see Mott or any of 'em till just after the shot was fired. Then I caught a glimpse of 'em coming this way and I followed quick; four witnesses, as you might say. Do you want Rider and me to wait till you've examined the body and help you get it to the house?"

"Thanks, Chief, it won't be necessary!" the little doctor replied with dignity. "I shall want to talk to Mr. Rider and the others later, though."

Rider nodded, stopped to say a kindly word to the grief-stricken Hiram, and then, with a final glance at the still face with the streak of blood on its forehead, he turned to follow the chief, who had waited for him at the spot where they had so hurriedly quitted the path.

"What time did the major drop in at The Rafters last night, Com—Rider?" the latter began guilelessly as they turned their steps toward Mott's place.

"'Drop' in!" Rider repeated as innocently. "Burst in would be more like it! We three old-timers were sitting there talking while the thunder and lightning were raising Cain outside, to say nothing of the wind and rain, when all of a sudden the major, poor fellow, rushed in at the door, cried out something and turned and ran out again before we could stop him! We tore out after him and searched for over half an hour in the downpour, but we couldn't find any trace of him, and at last we went home drenched to the skin. Then Mott had the bright idea that he must have gone to his own place and he 'phoned, but Hiram replied, just as he told you. Mott told him we'd be over early in the morning, anyway, and then we got into dry clothes and had a bite of supper. I remember Mott saying it was past midnight then, so it must have been about eleven when the major appeared, and say!"—he lowered his voice confidentially—"what did you mean about a 'tiger lily'? I'd be willing to swear the major cried out something about a tiger lily when he dashed into the room!"

"We-ell, I ran across him in the woods on his way home and he was muttering to himself; I heard the words 'tiger lily' plain," the chief improvised clumsily, with a flat note of disappointment in his tone. "He was crazy then all right, and crazy when he shot himself just now, but I'm wondering when it took him! Was it after last Saturday, or before?"

"Where's the ring?" Rider countered slyly.

"That's what sticks in my crop!" admitted the chief. "You warned me about letting anybody leave town without giving an account of themselves, but there are two going to-morrow, from the Mercers' household at that, and one of 'em says it's on your own suggestion."

"'Two?'" repeated Rider, genuinely mystified.

"Yes, that big ox of a woman, Ingred, and her son Hans. Ingred says she asked you if you knew of any place where the boy could go in the Adirondacks for that cough of his, and you told her you'd give her a letter to a doctor, at a village that sounds like 'Saranac' as far as she can get it."

"I did! I told her only yesterday, but I forgot all about that letter; glad you reminded me," Rider remarked. "It was to be for Hans to take himself, but I didn't know he was going so soon, or that she meant to go with him. The boy ought to get away as quick as he can for his own sake, but if you want to hold them here, of course, Chief, use your own judgment."

"If you're willing to let 'em go I guess I am," the chief replied. "Ingred's only going to take him there and then come back; she's promised Mrs. Mercer to be home again by Friday. Who's this Captain Staverton?"

He returned to the original subject abruptly and as promptly Rider responded:

"A friend of Mott's from wartime. I never saw him before last evening, but I knew he was coming to stay overnight with Mott this week some time. He knew the major, too, but he'd forgotten his home was up around here till Mott reminded him. He seems to be a fine fellow. Lord, how it took us back to reminisce last night!" he added with well-feigned enthusiasm. "We were all in it, you see, Chief; Captain Staverton and that poor devil we've just left, Major Hill, and you knew what Mott did over there. I was in the Secret Service myself, running back and forth for submarines to chase me!"

"You were?" The chief spoke with an access of respect.

"Yes, and that's all we talked till the major appeared, just old experiences that we'd half forgotten now."

"Hadn't the captain even heard of the murder?" demanded the chief incredulously.

"Oh, yes, but he wasn't much interested," Rider shrugged. "I asked him and he said he'd only read of it casually on the train. Of course, Mott and I weren't giving anything away, and when we found out that Staverton had never even heard of Gloria Warrender it wasn't necessary to tell him the major had known her over in France."

The woodland path ended in the fence which bounded the tilled fields, and as they emerged the warm sunshine flooded down on them in the clear air of early morning. They started for the orchard and the chief announced with decision:

"We-ell, I'm going to find out where the major's been since Saturday. A man as crazy as he was oughtn't to be hard to trace! Then I'm going over his house with a fine-tooth comb, and as soon as that old feller is able to talk I'm going to find out if he knows anything 'bout that ring! If it turns up among the major's things I'd be willing to call it a day and the case closed, since he's dead, but if it doesn't, I'm going to hunt till I find it! That's what this whole business hinges on, to my mind, Rider—that ring!"

Mott and Staverton met them on the porch and the former tried with agonized facial contortions to signal a desperate query to Rider behind the chief's back, but for once the latter appeared dense, and at last, remembering that he was host, he suggested that they all might as well talk it over at the breakfast table.

They were scarcely seated when Rider caught Staverton's eye and asked:

"Captain, did you hear what poor Major Hill said when he burst in on us last night? I did, and the chief heard him repeat it later in the woods. It was something about a flower, a tiger lily!"

"A—*what?*" Staverton played up, while Mott gazed open-mouthed at them both. "I thought I caught the word 'tiger' and that the major was seeing things! He never drank to excess while he was in the army, but . . ."

He paused expectantly and Mott sputtered with indignation at this aspersion even while he realized its expediency.

"Jack didn't drink!" he declared. "You know that, Chief Clark, don't you? Of course, Craig, you haven't seen him for the last few years as we have, but we've realized how he was going to pieces! Not crazy, you understand, but the usual despondency and nervous attacks that led to so many suicides among our boys who'd been gassed. It's a frightful thing—hard to face the fact that he's gone!"

Throughout the meal and later, till he took himself off in a state of bewilderment shot with the vague suspicion that he was being fooled in some way, the chief was regaled with an elaboration of the same story of the previous evening's events that Rider had already told him, the latter throwing in a hint now and then to keep his fellow conspirators on the right track, but when he at length departed Mott's round countenance was frankly shining with perspiration and Staverton was grimly meditative.

Rider seated himself at the writing desk.

"You don't mind, old scout? I've got to write a letter to Doc Messiter up at Saranac. You both remember him, don't you? He was the surgeon with the Eighth, but he's got a san. now, and I'm sending him a worthy young patient from the neighborhood."

"A patient? . . ." Mott paused.

"Yes," Rider chuckled. "His mother's going to take him there to-morrow. It's Hans, the under-gardener at the Mercers'."

"Why in the world are you interested?" demanded Mott. "What's Ingred going with him for? He's old enough to travel by himself!"

Rider chuckled again.

"That's why I'm interested!" he said.

15

Deadlock

Coroner Todd came and took their depositions in time for Captain Staverton to make his train, and when Mott returned from seeing him off at the station he found that his other guest had gone out, leaving no word for him.

Rider was on his way to Hydrangea Walk with the promised letter of introduction in his pocket and a vast question on his mind. Much was working out as he had anticipated, and his own course was plain before him, but a sudden possibility had come to him during the brief talk with Mott, and wild and improbable as it was, he was forced to consider it.

Ingred herself opened the door to him, and he handed her the letter.

"Here you are!" he smiled. "I didn't know you intended to go with your son, though, Ingred."

"I t'ank you very mooch, Mister Rider." She dropped the letter into her apron pocket and her soft blue eyes opened wide. "Hans ain't been avay anyveres since I brung him here, a baby, and he ain't never been on de cars by himself; 'sides, I got to see dat he's fixed nice. I bane going, but I coom right back on account Nancy's so sick and it ain't goot dat Mrs. Mercer bane alone to run t'ings now she got sooch troubles. Hans, he gets himself well, now!"

She spoke with such happy confidence and gazed at him so gratefully that Rider mentally shrugged. Did this woman know more than her candid glance revealed? They were usually a thrifty lot, these Swedes, and she had said she had the money for Hans to go to Arizona and recuperate; was it to the interest of some one else that she take this little trip—so much to their interest that she was being paid to go? As to her probable return, Rider hazarded no conjecture.

"Of course, Hans will get well, but just when will you be back, Ingred?" he asked. "I'm sure Mrs. Mercer does need you every minute now."

"I bane home Friday," she answered. "Mister Mercer get me de times ven de trains run. Ve go to-morrow morning early and by evening ve are dere; de next afternoon I get on de cars again and I bane here Friday morning. Ve have mooch gratefulness to you, sir, Hans and me. You vish to see Mr. Mercer?"

Rider assented and Ingred showed him into the library where almost at once Stan came to him, and he saw that the strain was even more marked upon him than before.

"Glad you came, Rider, I was going to send for you!" he exclaimed as they shook hands. "Chief Clark was here again yesterday afternoon, but he doesn't seem to have an idea in his head beyond finding that opal ring, and, although I hate to say it, I'm beginning to wonder about Major Hill's continued absence."

"You needn't," Rider said dryly. "He's come home."

"No! Have you seen him? I want to ask him where he first met Miss Warrender, and perhaps we'll get some light on that four-year disappearance of hers." Stan's tone was eager.

"Yes, I've seen him, but he won't be able to answer questions now." Rider spoke very slowly. "He shot himself at dawn to-day."

"Good heavens!" Stan half-started from his chair. "Shot himself! You think that means . . ."

"It means he'd come to the end of his rope, that's all." Rider's gaze was apparently fixed in introspection on the motes dancing in the ray of sunlight which came in at one of the tall French windows. "Motives for killing oneself or another could be equally placed under the three general headings, lust, cupidity and fear. The chief still clings to the cupidity idea because of the missing ring, I think, in this murder case, but suppose we dismiss that. Could any one be afraid that Miss Warrender's continued existence would be harmful to them, their interests, their happiness, their safety? It hardly seems possible, does it? There remains lust with all its ramifications—love, passion, infatuation, jealousy, revenge! Any two of the three headings could be combined to produce endless variations; for instance, lust and cupidity. Take their ramifications, jealousy and greed, and you'll get the dog-in-the-manger attitude, that what one cannot enjoy or possess no other shall."

"I—I'm afraid I don't follow you!" Stan's face had whitened. "You'll forgive me, but the news of the major's suicide has been such an added shock I cannot seem to collect my thoughts and concentrate them on anything else for the moment. Why do you suppose he did it?"

"I was coming to that," Rider replied. "Take those three leading motivations again. Granted that the major was sane—for insanity cannot be classed as a motive—would he kill himself for love, jealousy? They tell me he was almost a recluse, and if there had been some past romance in his life he would have acted in the first passion of his disappointment, not after years of deliberation. What had he to gain by death? I can't quite see. What did he fear? Who knows?"

Stan rose and began pacing the floor.

"I don't know what to think!" he declared after a pause. "His existence was lonely, miserable, but he made it so himself; he certainly hadn't anything to gain by living on, poor fellow, for he simply wouldn't buck up. A man's got to pull himself together and go on somehow, no matter what a wreck he is, and to take destiny into his own hands is an act of madness! Perhaps that's the answer, after all! Perhaps he went mad! He seemed sometimes to be on the verge of it."

"Perhaps that is as good a theory as any other." Rider dismissed the subject. "But you said you were on the point of sending for me?"

"Yes. I 'phoned the district attorney after the chief left, but he could give me only vague reassurances and I've got to have some action! To have a guest, a defenceless woman, killed so horribly and to stand by and do nothing! I tell you, Rider, I'll go mad myself! We've led such monotonous, narrow existences here that we're stagnant, we don't know how to take the initiative! You're a man of the world, you've seen all sorts of life and you've probably been up on your toes and equal to emergencies of every kind; I want you to advise me what to do. I know it seems pretty hopeless, after all the efforts Gildersleeve made, but my wife feels that only during the period of Miss Warrender's disappearance will the motive for this terrible thing be found."

"Please persuade Mrs. Mercer to set her mind at rest on that score," Rider said quietly. "This is absolutely confidential, but there are two or three people, including myself, who know where and how Miss Warrender spent those four years."

"What!" Stan cried, staring at him. "You knew yesterday, when Gildersleeve was here?"

"No, I recognized her but couldn't place her until yesterday afternoon when memory returned, and later I obtained incontrovertible proof that I was not mistaken. No one knows this, not excepting the chief, and I must ask you not to tell even Mrs. Mercer."

"I give you my word, but can't you tell me any more?" his host spoke in an oddly choked tone. Then he added quickly: "I don't doubt you, Rider, but surely you can understand my interest! My wife—their girlhood friend-ship—why was the matter kept so secret?"

"It was the wish of this woman who is dead, Mercer, and it must be respected." Rider shook his head. "I can only tell you what you must have felt instinctively, what every one who was not skeptical of mystery would grant; that she was the rarest and highest type of womanhood."

"I—know." He turned away suddenly and walked to one of the windows, and the thought came back to Rider of Olive Mercer's response in the same words on the previous day when Gildersleeve had said, in speaking of the murdered woman: "Miss Gloria was . . . most lovable, as you know." All at once Stan wheeled about and faced his visitor. "I suppose the major knew the truth of this mystery about Miss Warrender, for she said they had met on the other side, and he was only there during the latter part of that period, and in active service most of the time, I understand. He could have had no fancied cause in that sick brain of his?"

"None whatever!"

"Thank God for that!" Stan ejaculated. "I could not bear it if it turned out that any one I knew, any friend, would be guilty of such a monstrous thing! But what is there left? What can you suggest for me to do? We're at a standstill!"

"I can only suggest the hardest thing in the world, Mercer; wait!" Rider responded as he rose. "The truth is bound to come to light in a case like this; the merest clew, the slightest word, will reveal the solution. I know how you must feel and I can sympathize with you and Mrs.

Mercer, but it's like a powder train, all set and ready to go off at the touch of a match! By the way, I only dropped in to give your maid a letter of introduction to the head of an Adirondack san. for her son; hope you don't think I'm intruding?"

"No, it was kind of you, and she's taking him up there tomorrow. I suppose we might have been more thoughtful, but we've just been drifting along. . . ." He spoke absently as he walked to the door with his guest, and Rider asked perfunctorily:

"How is Nancy?"

"There's no change." The father's face darkened. "I tell you, Rider, if this experience is going to leave our little girl with her mind impaired I would rather see her dead!"

After a few words of vague reassurance Rider took his leave and walked off down the drive, with a purposeful stride. The process of elimination was almost finished and the time for action was at hand; one more interview and then . . .

But a wholly unexpected encounter drove all thoughts of his previous intention completely from his mind. He had rounded a turn in the road where the close-set gardens of the residential section gave place to broad stretches of farmland bordered by maple trees, when a little runabout, a shade more mud-spattered and generally disreputable than Mott's, rattled up behind him and stopped. A homely woman, in a mannish tweed suit, with straight, bobbed brown hair and freckles standing out on her short, square-tipped nose, waved peremptorily as he turned, and a dominant feminine voice commanded:

"Get in!"

"Thanks, Miss Foster." Rider smilingly declined as he approached the car, hat in hand. "I promised to be at home before this to meet Mott. . . ."

"I'll take you there," she interrupted firmly. "I want to talk to you."

Trapped, Rider climbed in beside Jim Foster and they started off in silence. Then abruptly she turned to him.

"Is it true that Major Hill shot himself this morning?" she asked.

"Only too true, I'm sorry to say," he replied. "I suppose you've heard that Mott and a guest of his and I were on the scene at practically the same time as the chief?"

"What do you think of it?" She ignored his question. "Why did he do it?"

"Isn't that rather a matter for the coroner to decide?" Rider met her gaze levelly. "I scarcely knew him, and they tell me he has been ill a long time. Why do you ask me?" "Because you're one of the few men in the neighborhood that has a grain of sense." Her tone was almost grudging. "You're able to look at everything, too, from a better perspective because you're an outsider. The chief of police couldn't catch a boy robbing an apple orchard, the coroner's so full of his own importance that he can't see anything else, and the district attorney is notorious for letting things ride. I've heard all the suspicions that have been whispered against Jack Hill about this murder, and now his suicide will confirm them in a lot of one-cylinder minds, but I want to know what you think!"

"You mean you want to tell me your own opinion, don't you?" He spoke in a tone of easy camaraderie innocent of all rudeness. "My opinion doesn't count; as you say, I'm an outsider, and as a matter of fact I haven't formed any."

"Matter of evasion, you mean!" Jim retorted. "Of course you have! I want to tell you Jack Hill never killed that woman! I don't know anything about her and don't want to. I'm speaking of him. I asked him pointblank once where he'd met her, saying I'd heard they were friends over

on the other side, and he said he hardly considered himself
a friend, since he couldn't even remember her name when
they met here, but he didn't answer my question. He's
been like that ever since he came back, queer and reticent,
but he was far from crazy as some people are trying to
make out! If the coroner and the rest of the fools in office
put him in his grave with such a suspicion clinging to his
memory just to save themselves from an admission of their
own failure, I hope he haunts them! I know he didn't kill
Gloria Warrender!"

"You seem positive, Miss Foster," Rider observed mildly.
"Do you know who did?"

For a moment she was silenced by the abrupt challenge,
but only for a moment.

"I wish I did!" she asserted bitterly. "I never saw a
red-headed woman yet who didn't cause trouble, deliberately or unconsciously, but this is the worst thing that
has happened here in my memory! We've got to know the
truth, or we'll be looking at each other askance for the
rest of our lives. It sounds preposterous, I know, but it's
true. I—I shan't know an hour's peace till the murderer of
Gloria Warrender is found!"

There was a wistful, almost plaintively feminine note
in her usually forceful tones and Rider glanced sidewise at
her. It seemed to him that her face was unwontedly pale
beneath the freckles and her gray eyes had a shrinking
look of pain. As if reading his thought she went on:

"Jack and I grew up together, but it is only because I
want his memory cleared that I feel so strongly about this,
although the injustice of such a suspicion makes my blood
boil! Mr. Rider, I—I've just got to know how that woman
died!"

There was a hint of desperation now in her halting voice
as though only supreme anxiety dragged the words from
her lips, and Rider, his glance apparently fallen upon the

speedometer and glued there, furtively studied her face. Why was she confiding in him, she to whom confidences meant weakness? Was it because he was a stranger who was so soon to go out of the lives of all of them? She wanted the mystery solved, not only for the sake of the community, nor even that the memory of the dead man should be cleared, but for the wholly feminine reason that "she'd just got to know!"

"I think every one in Chichester feels that way, Miss Foster," he said. "Frankly, I can't understand why you take this murder so particularly to heart. I was under the impression that you weren't interested in Miss Warrender. Except as a matter of common interest, why does it make any difference how she came to her death?"

"It makes a great deal of difference to a woman who has any community spirit!" she retorted, stepping on the gas. "We want to know who killed her before the direct accusation is made against Jack Hill's memory, or blasts the character of an innocent living person! We want to find out if we're harboring a murderer among our associates or if he came from elsewhere!"

They turned into the side road leading to The Rafters, and Rider remarked:

"You haven't told me your own theory yet; you've assured me that Major Hill did not commit the crime, but you haven't expressed an opinion as to who did. Are you going to be as evasive as—I have seemed?"

He smiled but there was a challenge in the coolly impersonal, keen glance as his eyes met her startled ones. Then she lowered them and laughed a trifle grimly.

"It's a deadlock between us, then, Mr. Rider! You keep your theory and I'll keep mine! Perhaps when it's all over we'll compare notes!"

"I haven't thanked you yet for taking care of little Nancy Mercer for us last Saturday." He deliberately changed the subject. "Was she much trouble to you—delirious, I mean—on the way home? You had the car to manage, too."

"No," Jim Foster drew up before the driveway of The Rafters. "She was no trouble."

Rider descended, thanked her for the lift and walked slowly up to the house. Miss Foster had a theory, all right, and she wanted with all her heart to be proved wrong!

16

A Visitation

Mott was still visibly shaken by the shock of his old friend's suicide, but he grinned faintly as Rider entered.

"Saw your fair escort," he remarked. "Didn't know Miss Foster had made such an impression last Saturday."

"Not as much as she made to-day," Rider declared. "She waylaid me on my way back here to learn the details about this morning, and incidentally I learned a thing or two myself!"

His host led the way to the dining-room and as they were seated about the lunch table he asked:

"Henry, has Miss Foster ever struck you as a sentimental young woman?"

Mott stared.

"Sentimental?" he echoed, and gestured toward the dish before them. "There's about as much sentiment about Jim Foster as there was in the life of this lake trout!"

Rider smiled. "You've known her a long time?"

"Practically all her life; ever since she was a snub-nosed, brawny kid who fought all the boys in school, and took to running the town as soon as she was out of it! She's almost thirty now, but no man has ever been rash enough, that I know of, to flirt with death by suggesting matrimony to her!"

"She tells me that she grew up with the major."

"He's ten years older, nearly Stan Mercer's age, but, of course, she's known all the crowd since she could remember. You don't mean she was—was sentimental about poor Jack's death?"

"She was grieved, certainly, but not excessively shocked," Rider replied. "I guess it would take a great deal to shock that young woman, but at that I shouldn't wonder if she'd been smitten with somebody at one time in her life. Most women have at least one romance even if it's hidden and hopeless, and when they're Miss Foster's type they're apt to put on a more hard-boiled front than ever in order to conceal a tender spot."

Mott glanced at him warily.

"What are you getting at?" he demanded. "You're not interested in any hidden tenderness on Jim Foster's part unless it happens to have a bearing on this case; I know you!"

"Well," Rider's tone was admission, "I was only wondering, that's all. I was wondering how far she would permit a secret affection to bias her judgment in her own theory of the murder."

"Did she volunteer it to you?" Mott asked quickly.

"No, she refused it, but that was quite as illuminating. She was vehement as to who must be innocent, and yet I think she suspects some one and dreads to have that suspicion confirmed."

"Ha! I get you!" exclaimed Mott. "Let's see. She was always athletic and the boys couldn't stand her because she could beat most of them at their own games, but when she graduated she went around a lot with the older men— Jack and Stan and the rest—and took most of the amateur championships open to her. Stan dropped out, of course; when Olive came home from school he hadn't an hour for sports or anything else until after they were married and she gradually settled down, forcing him to go his way

alone. Jim Foster and poor old Jack got on all right in a
comradely sort of fashion while he was his old self, but
since he came back as you saw him I don't think she gave
him as much sympathy as he deserved from an old friend.
She's hard-boiled, all right, as you said! She never seemed
to realize his condition and actually teased him about it,
almost contemptuous because he couldn't apparently try
to come back. I've often seen him wince under some blunt,
unfeeling speech of hers. She's clear-headed, though, and
if she suspects any one definitely in this case, she must
have good reason for it."

"Perhaps, from her point of view," Rider returned.

"It isn't yours, then?" Mott mashed a bit of cheese meditatively down on his cracker. "And you say she doesn't
want to believe it herself? You mean she's in love with
the man she believes killed Gloria Warrender? By Godfrey,
there's only one answer to that! I'd never suspected she
could care for anybody, least of all the man you've got in
your mind, but if she did . . ."

"Hold on, Henry, you're running wild!" Rider interrupted. "I haven't any particular man in my mind; I merely said she shrank from the thought of the guilt of the
person she couldn't help suspecting. I didn't mean that
she was in love with this person—for that matter, how do
I know she was ever in love with any one? I'd like to know
her theory, that's all."

"How're you going to find it out?" asked Mott as they
rose from the table. "You said she refused to tell you."

"It isn't really important, as long as I know she *has* a
theory and hates to entertain it," Rider shrugged. "What
are you going to do this afternoon?"

"Why?" Mott's round face brightened. "Got any plan
you're going to let me in on? I supposed you'd be chasing
off by yourself, and when Holcomb called me up and asked
me to come to the club this afternoon, for a meeting to

arrange some fitting memorial to poor Jack, I said I'd be there, but I can easily . . ."

"I thought I'd go with you, if you like," suggested Rider. "Stan Mercer asked me this morning for my advice about starting some real action in regard to finding the murderer, and I could only tell him to wait. That's what I've got to do myself for a day or two, and I'd better put in the time making character as what I was before—just your guest. I've been too prominent in the investigation as it is. Don't let's even talk about it unless Holcomb and the rest bring it up; we'll have to wait now till something starts."

They spent a stupid and dolorous afternoon at the country club, returning to dine and retire early, for the previous night had been a sleepless one and the tragedy at its dawn had affected Henry Mott's kindly spirit.

During the morning the chief of police neither 'phoned nor appeared in person, and by early afternoon Mott's renewed interest in the case had mounted to actual suspense which he could control no longer.

"Dan, you said not to talk about the murder, but that's about all we heard at the club yesterday—that and poor Jack! You said something would start in a day or two, but what? What in the world are you expecting next, waiting for?"

"Just for time to pass," Rider replied. "Meanwhile I'm going for a walk. Want to come?"

The sun was hot and Mott was comfortable there by the grape arbor, but he eyed his friend for a moment and then acquiesced. There had been a hint of purpose in Rider's tone, and when they passed out of the gate together and he struck off with no indecision and at a brisk pace, his companion's suspicions were confirmed, although he asked no questions but trudged along contentedly in the heat and dust.

At the place where the road forked Rider took the narrow, winding way which led toward Hilltop, and Mott's

spirits flagged. As though sensing this, the former remarked:

"Thought I'd drop in and see how old Hiram is getting
on, but if it'll make you feel too badly, Henry, you just
wait about and have a smoke."

"I'm going with you!" Mott asserted. "You're not as
much interested in Hi's welfare as all that, though what
you expect to find out up here where—where everything's
over and finished . . ."

"I want to know something that Hiram can tell me if
he will. You're right on that," Rider admitted, adding suddenly: "Isn't this the Mercers' car coming?"

It was, but only Olive Mercer was in the tonneau,
and although she bowed pleasantly she did not direct the
chauffeur to halt.

"She looks pretty bad, doesn't she?" Mott had turned
to gaze after the cloud of dust settling again in the road.
"She's paler and more drawn and sad than when the murder was first discovered. I wonder if Nancy's worse?"

"Mrs. Mercer would hardly be driving about the country like that if the child were in danger, would she?" Rider
asked guilelessly. "She may have been to call on some
friends up this way; who lives beyond Hilltop?"

"Jim Foster for one. That is, she still keeps up the old
place and goes there now and then, but it's far out and she
spends most of her time in that brick house she built right
down in the center of town," Mott replied.

"Yet that's probably where Mrs. Mercer's been if they're
such friends," Rider observed, and then added with a sidelong glance at his friend's red, perspiring countenance:
"Going too fast for you, Henry?"

Mott indignantly dissented from the suggestion and
they proceeded in comparative silence to the major's dismal home.

It appeared more dreary and forlorn than ever, for such shutters as remained intact were fastened tight and no smoke rose from any chimney, but as they knocked at the door, shambling footsteps sounded from within and old Hiram stood before them.

He had aged immeasurably since the previous day, and now he gazed at them almost without recognition for a moment. Then a slow light dawned in his faded eyes and he nodded respectfully.

"They—they ain't going to bring him home till to-morrow, Mr. Mott," he quavered. "I got things cleaned up as well as I could for the funeral Friday. Was there anything you wanted?"

"Yes. A good drink of cold water if you'll give it to us, Hiram, and a chance to get in out of this heat," Rider interposed before his companion could speak. "We won't keep you from your work long."

Hiram regarded him with almost piteous apprehension, but opened the door wider for them to enter and then went obediently to fetch the water, while they seated themselves in the dim, cool living-room.

"I don't believe the poor old fellow will last much longer, now that Jack's gone." Mott mopped his forehead and felt of his wilted collar. "I don't know what you're going to spring on him, but you'd better draw it mild, for he doesn't look as if he could stand a lot more."

"It's keeping it back that worries him now, aside from his grief," Rider averred. "He'll be relieved to talk, once he knows he's got to."

Mott started.

"Look here, Dan, you don't mean . . . !"

He was silenced by the reentrance of Hiram with a silver pitcher of ice-cold water and tall glasses. He hovered about uncertainly as they drank, his eyes fixed upon Rider

still apprehensively, and as the latter put down his glass he
said in a friendly tone:

"Sit down yourself, Hiram. You're all worn out with
the shock of the major's death and all this extra work. We
want to know what you said to the lady who was here just
now."

Mott started again but more violently, and the old man
sank limply into a chair against the wall.

"'The lady?'" he repeated faintly.

"Yes, Mrs. Mercer. We just met her," Rider went on
smoothly. "She came to ask you about last Saturday, didn't
she? Did you tell her the truth about when the major came
home?"

Hiram's mouth opened and closed again spasmodically
and finally he stammered:

"Why, she must have known, sir! You do! Night before
last!"

"*I* know, and so do you, Hiram, and I want you to tell
the truth to Mr. Mott here before the chief of police finds
out and comes bothering you," Rider interrupted. "What
time did the major come home Saturday night?"

The old man groaned and dropped his head in his
hands, and Mott gasped, but he said nothing. Then Hiram
exclaimed in smothered tones:

"So it's come! I don't know how you knew, sir, but I
didn't tell Mrs. Mercer! I didn't tell anybody! It was the
major's orders!"

"I know," Rider said gently. "He was here all the time,
but he got away from you during the storm Monday night
and the next you knew of him was the sound of that shot
at dawn. He did intend to go away Saturday when he left?"

"Yes, sir." Hiram lifted his head and straightened.
"It was all just as I told you about his leaving. He was
all dressed with his grip packed when I brought him his

breakfast. It was long past noon then, around one o'clock or maybe after, and he shook hands and left at two, after fixing up the money matters with me. Then you came, and—and then the chief of police, and I didn't know what to make of it all! I had a kind of a feeling, though, that maybe he'd come home again, after all, and so I waited up, but I must have dozed in my chair, for all of a sudden I looked up and there he was standing in front of me!"

He was staring straight before him as though once more he saw the major, and for a moment Rider did not speak. Then he prompted quietly:

"He'd heard the news then, hadn't he? The news of the murder that the chief had already told you about?"

"Yes, sir. He—he looked like death itself standing there, and he whispered in a hoarse kind of way: 'Has anybody been here, Hi?' I told him 'yes,' you and Mr. Mott, and then the police. He said: 'My God!' Just like that. 'My God!' Then he went reeling and staggering up to his room, not as if he'd been drinking, but more like a man took suddenly blind. He wouldn't answer me when I knocked and knocked at his door, and I was near crazy myself, but I went away and sat waiting for the morning. It must have been midnight or after when he came home."

"Did you notice anything strange about him then?" Rider asked. "Anything different from when he'd gone out? His hands, for instance?"

"Not till morning." Hiram blinked in a surprised way. "I sat up and waited, and then all at once I heard him crying! Not loud but harsh sobs fair terrible to listen to when I didn't dare go near him! It seemed like hours that he kept it up, but he stopped at last, slow, as though he was tired out. I didn't hear anything more and I waited till noon the next day—Sunday—before I went to his door again. He called to me in a weak kind of way to open it, but it was locked, and then I remembered that the connecting door between his room and the next was unbolted so I went in that way. He was lying on his bed so weak he couldn't move, and I saw then that one of his hands—the right one—was bruised and swollen as though he'd knocked it against something."

"Did he say anything about it?"

"No, sir, and neither did I; he was so sick I never gave it a thought. He couldn't eat, but I got him to take some coffee, then I killed a chicken and made some broth." Hiram spoke slowly but without reluctance, as though trying to recall each detail and glad, as Rider had predicted, to get it off his mind. "Along about the middle of the afternoon he asked me to fix another room and help him to get into it, that he didn't want any one to know he was home and come bothering him and I wasn't to tell a soul! I got the bed ready in the old east room and moved a few of his things in there, but I had almost to carry him and I thought we'd both fall down more than once. By nightfall the sickness had come on him and he was out of his head."

"Do you mean that the major was raving, delirious?" Rider leaned forward. "What did he say?"

"Nothing. I told the truth about that to the chief of police to-day!" The old man spoke with every evidence of sincerity. "That must have come on him the next night, though how he had the strength to go back to his room and dress, and the cunning to get out so's I wouldn't know is beyond me, to say nothing of his taking the revolver!"

He paused, shuddering, and Rider protested:

"But you said that on Sunday night he was out of his head!"

"I mean he didn't know me or anything, but he was quiet and even took more broth when I held it to his lips. The next day he rambled a little, seemed to think he was back in some hospital again and talked a foreign tongue I couldn't understand, but he didn't say anything about any flower, like the chief of police asked me yesterday morning. Mostly he slept, especially toward night, and I thought he'd be all right till morning, and quieter if I didn't stay in the room. There's an old sofa at the turn of the hall and I went and laid down on that, for I hadn't closed my eyes, as you might say, since Friday night, and I'd have to rest if I was going on taking care of him." Hiram's voice broke. "I never meant to go to sleep! I never meant to!"

"What woke you up?" Rider asked, sharply now, for the old man seemed on the verge of collapse.

"The storm. I thought of the major first thing, of course, but he was gone, and his clothes and his revolver!" Hiram drew a quivering breath. "I didn't know where to look for him so I—I just waited, and then Mr. Mott telephoned! I was minded to tell him the truth and ask him to find the major, but I remembered orders and about the murder and all, and didn't dare! Not that I ever thought for a minute that the major could have had anything to do with it, but he didn't want anybody to know, and I said the best thing I could think of. I waited for him to come home—and waited—and then I heard the shot, and you came!"

He buried his head once more in his hands, and with a glance at Mott Rider rose.

"It's all right, Hiram," he said kindly. "Nobody else knows he was home since Saturday and never will, if you're sure you didn't tell Mrs. Mercer."

"Not me! I don't think Mrs. Mercer figured that at all, sir. She just asked how he'd been the last two weeks and when he went away and came home, and I told her what I told you and the chief, nothing else."

"Well, you stick to that story and try to get some rest now." Rider paused in the doorway, and Mott added:

"If you get sick yourself, Hiram, or you want anything, just call me up."

Hiram thanked him tremulously and they took their departure in a silence that lasted until they were beyond the broken walls and headed for The Rafters. Then Mott exclaimed:

"I don't see how you knew! What made you guess he went home again Saturday?"

"Common sense," Rider responded tersely. "The major's lived here all his life, every one must know him for miles around, he was on foot, and there were no trains leaving before the murder was discovered and the alarm out. He couldn't get away if he wanted to, he hadn't disappeared in thin air, so where else could he have gone?"

"But Mrs. Mercer? How did you know she'd been there? Why did she go, anyway?"

"I didn't know; that was just a chance shot." Rider broke off and added with a touch of impatience, "Lord, Henry, why wouldn't she? She knew the major and Gloria Warrender had met on the other side and it was her only way of finding out anything about her friend and the mystery in her life Gildersleeve had told about. Perhaps she has her own suspicions against the major, who knows? Isn't it natural she'd want to find out who had cause to murder the woman she'd known since girlhood?"

That night Henry Mott slept heavily, but he was awakened at last while it was still an hour before the dawn by the insistent ringing of the telephone bell, and drowsily he replied to it. Three minutes later he was pounding on Rider's door with the frenzy of a madman.

"Dan! Get up quick! I told you I'd never believe Jack did it, and now I know!"

"What the—" Rider's voice came from the other side of the door.

"Because Jack's dead but this infernal work is still going on! Open this door, can't you? The chief wants us at Hydrangea Walk right way! Stan's gone and Olive Mercer's been chloroformed!"

17

A Hasty Departure

Even in Mott's frenzied impatience to obey the summons of Chief Clark to the Mercers' house it seemed to him that Rider was ready in less than a minute, for he himself took only time to climb into trousers, put on a pair of shoes and throw a cloak about him, yet his guest, fully dressed, was seated in the little car with the engine running when he descended.

"Jumping Christopher, Dan, what do you suppose it means!" he cried jerkily as they shot forward. "Robbery? Where's Stan gone? Who found it out?"

"I'm a detective, Henry, not a seer," Rider responded coolly. "What did the chief say?"

"Just that, what I told you!" Mott's voice squeaked with excitement. "He said for us both to come to the Mercers' quick; that the house had been entered, Mrs. Mercer chloroformed and Mr. Mercer wasn't there, his bed hadn't been slept in! The servants were in hysterics and the chief couldn't get anything out of anybody!"

"Wasn't Mrs. Mercer conscious yet? Didn't the chief tell you?" Rider's tone was solicitous. "She hasn't a weak heart that you know, has she, Henry?"

"I wouldn't think so," Mott said in surprised accents.

His fat cheeks bulged as he drove the car forward, bounding over the rough road and skidding into the highway with a swoop that all but landed them in the ditch;

then he grazed a gatepost at Hydrangea Walk and stopped before the entrance so abruptly that Rider was almost precipitated through the windshield.

Lights were burning on the first and second floors, but the house seemed quiet enough when a dark figure moved forward on the veranda.

"That you and your friend, Mr. Mott?" It was the cheerful young policeman of the "Y." "The front door's open—you're to go straight up to Mrs. Mercer's room where the chief's waiting for you. Go quiet as you can, so's not to wake the little girl that's sick on the third floor; she's slept through it all, the doc says."

"And Mrs. Mercer?" demanded Rider.

"Oh, I guess she's all right," his informant replied. "It's a darned funny business, as you'll find out."

They pushed open the door and tiptoed up the stairs to knock softly at one above, from beneath which a subdued radiance stole out into the dim hall.

Chief Clark himself opened the door and motioned them in with an ungainly wave of his arm.

"Glad you got here so quick. Mrs. Mercer's been asking for you." His nasal drawl was lowered, and though he seemingly addressed them both his eyes were fastened on Rider's face. "Come on, she wants to speak to you."

Olive Mercer was lying on a chaise longue, decorously wrapped in a shapeless gray dressing gown which emphasized the dusky pallor of her face, but her hand was quite steady as she extended it to her guests and her voice, though low and very grave was clear and composed.

"So very good of you to come, both of you," she said. "I felt sure you wouldn't mind, since Stan is away; he depends on you, you know."

"My dear Mrs. Mercer, this is frightful!" Mott exclaimed half under his breath as he took the chair she indicated. "You know you have only to call on me—and

Rider—at any time, but tell us what has happened. The chief here . . ."

"I couldn't get a word out of anybody when I 'phoned you," Chief Clark interrupted. "See that window? It's been raised higher than Mrs. Mercer left it when she went to bed and there's a ladder against the sill that reaches to the ground. Whatever the thief was after, Mrs. Mercer must have frightened him away, but not before he put her out. Smell the chloroform?"

There was a faint, sweet, sickish odor on the air, but Olive Mercer shrugged.

"It wasn't very bad. He couldn't have given me much, for I think I awakened almost at once, when Miss Alstead began working over me."

"Miss Alstead?" Rider repeated the name interrogatively.

"Nancy's trained nurse, you know," explained Olive. "There's little to tell, really. I left Stan reading in the library and went to bed early, for I've scarcely slept since Saturday, naturally, and Nancy seemed to be doing so well, from Dr. Ross' report, that I felt I could rest. I must have been asleep for hours when I awakened to find a man standing over there, near the closet door."

"Did you—did you call out?" Mott asked breathlessly.

"No." Olive smiled faintly. "I'm not excitable, not the sort of woman who screams, and I lay quite still, thinking at first that it was Stan. Then I realized it must be very late and this man was fully dressed, and all in dark clothing. That night light there on the mantel was turned so low that I could barely distinguish his figure, but he moved and I saw he was shorter and heavier set than Stan, with something tied over the lower part of his face. I started up and I think I called out then, but not too loudly, for I remembered Nancy. The man came toward me in one bound as lightly as a cat, it seemed to me, and pressed something over my face! I smelled that heavy, sweetish odor and—the

next thing I knew Miss Alstead was bending over me bath-
ing my forehead and moving my arms, and the man was
gone."

"Has the house been searched?" Rider asked the chief,
while Mott exclaimed in horror over the attack.

"Everywhere, from cellar to attic, in our stockinged
feet, except the little girl's room, and the nurse made
sure of that," Chief Clark declared. "She's a mighty smart
girl, that Miss Alstead! She says she started downstairs
for something, leaving the child asleep, when outside this
door she got a whiff of chloroform and came in. There was
no one here but Mrs. Mercer, lying on the bed with a towel
over her nose and mouth and she was already coming out
of it, stirring a little. Miss Alstead's had experience with
chloroform and she says Mrs. Mercer only had a little, just
enough to put her out for about five minutes. The thief
didn't stop to give her any more, only enough to let him
get away. Soon's Mrs. Mercer could speak she told Miss
Alstead to telephone for me and then wake up the servants
quietly, but that fool young housemaid got hysterics and
the baby woke up and she was herding them all downstairs
to the servants' dining-room when I got here with a couple
of my men. There isn't a thing to show that the thief got
any further than this room, and nothing seems disturbed
here. It was lucky Mrs. Mercer woke up, though. I brought
Dr. Ross with me, him being the regular family physician,
and he says Mrs. Mercer won't suffer any bad effects from
it beyond the shock; he's up with the little girl now, but
she's just the same as before and didn't hear a thing."

"Where is Mr. Mercer?" Rider turned to Olive again.

"Poor Stan's had worse insomnia than I, since that terrible thing happened last Saturday, and I think he's out just
walking around, trying to get sleepy," Olive replied without the slightest trace of disquietude in her calm tones.
"He said when I left him in the library that he knew he

shouldn't be able to sleep for hours, that the house seemed to stifle him. You know how he loves the open air, Mr. Mott; I shouldn't be surprised if he walked till morning—but the dawn's coming now, isn't it?"

A faint gray light was indeed stealing in at the open window and birds began to twitter drowsily in the trees outside. The night lamp on the mantel flared redly and there seemed to be something theatric and unreal in the atmosphere of the square, substantially furnished room.

"I'm really worried about Stan," Olive Mercer went on to Henry Mott. "I wish you'd persuade him to let Dr. Ross give him something. I—you must know how my poor friend's horrible death made me feel but I've got to keep up for the sake of the children; Stan's gone utterly to pieces, and the poor major's suicide was the last straw. Do try not to—to startle him too much about this. If I could think it was the work of just an ordinary burglar, it wouldn't puzzle me so. Of course it might have been; so much has been in the papers about us lately. Perhaps some criminal from another city was under the impression that we were as rich as poor Gloria, and expected making away with a great many jewels. Yet somehow I don't feel that it was any one like that; I know it sounds absurd, but perhaps it was some one who came for—for that opal ring!"

Her voice had sunk to a whisper and her eyes were heavy lidded and dull. Rider rose, beckoning the others peremptorily toward the door, and bent over her hand.

"You're nervous and overwrought naturally enough, Mrs. Mercer, but don't let such foolish, morbid fancies disturb you. Dr. Ross gave you something to quiet you, didn't he? Well, you're quite safe now, and you must try to rest; neither Henry nor I will leave the house till your husband returns."

She smiled again faintly and her head with its thick, dark hair dropped back on her pillows as he tiptoed to the

door. Closing it softly behind him he started for the stairs
and the other two followed, but midway down they heard
footsteps in the hall below and peered with one accord
over the baluster rail.

Stan Mercer was coming from the side door with slow,
shuffling steps as though he too had been drugged, and
when, compelled by their gaze, he lifted his eyes they were
sunken with fatigue. He halted, rocking slightly on his heels,
and waited for them to descend, but as they approached
him he seemed suddenly to become conscious of what their
presence might portend and took a hasty step forward.

"My God! What is it!" he gasped. "What are you doing
here at this hour?"

"P'raps we wouldn't have had to come if you'd been
home, Mr. Mercer!" the chief replied in his provocative
drawl. "The house has been broken into and your wife
chloroformed!"

Stan started back.

"The house—broken into!" There was sheer amazement,
nothing else, in his tone, and it deepened to incredulity as
he added: "Olive—chloroformed!"

Then swiftly he dived past them and up the stairs. They
heard his wife's door wrenched violently open but closed
softly and then there was silence.

"Shouldn't have told him like that!" The chief reproved
himself with a shake of his head, but Rider dismissed the
matter with a gesture.

"Where does the chauffeur sleep?" he asked.

"He goes home nights, lives with his wife and kid in a
little cottage down the back road," the chief replied. "The
car ain't been out to-night; one of my men looked to see."

"Well, come on; we'll talk to Mercer later." Rider turned
to the side door. "I want to have a look at that ladder."

He led them out and around the house till they stood
beneath Olive Mercer's window. The light was growing

stronger every minute with a deepening rosy glow which brought every detail out sharply, and they saw that the top of the ladder had iron hooks which firmly clutched the sill, while the bottom was embedded in the soft earth so deep that its lowest rung was only a few inches from the ground.

"Mrs. Mercer was right about the intruder being heavy set," Rider commented. "See how his weight sunk the ends here into the loam? What kind of a ladder is this, anyway? It isn't new and it couldn't have been carried far. Does it belong on the place?"

"Of course," Mott answered before the chief could speak. "It's a pruning ladder, with those hooks at the top to fasten to a branch or the top of an arbor. I've often seen Stan himself on it . . ."

He caught himself up sharply but neither of his companions appeared to be attentive. The chief was rubbing his chin reflectively, his small eyes following Rider, who paced back and forth studying the scene as though from some mental viewpoint of his own, and then turned to them with an air of decision.

"When does the first train leave Chichester going east or south?" he asked abruptly.

The chief stared.

"One for Albany in half an hour, 'bout. The six-twenty," he replied. "'S all right, though. Nobody can get away without proving their business."

"Somebody must!" Rider chuckled. "That's me. I can't stop to explain, Chief, and I don't want anybody to know I've gone till night, anyway. You know my methods; I'm to have a free hand!"

The latter was added in warning as the chief opened his mouth to expostulate, and he closed it again, his eyes bulging.

"Is that what you meant . . ." Mott began but stopped at a quick glance from his friend.

"When you telephoned, Chief, and told Mott what had taken place I expected to find things very much as they are and I knew what my next move must be—I was so sure, in fact, that I've a small bag ready packed in Mott's car," Rider went on quickly. "I'm not trying to be mysterious or dramatic but I've got to work in my own way. I know what's been done here to-night and who did it, and it's time for me to take action."

"Have it your own way!" The chief shook his head in stupefaction. "I don't know how you figured this, nor what you've seen here that I haven't, but I'm up a tree myself so I've got to give you your head. When'll you be back?"

"What did Dr. Ross tell you about Nancy's condition on Tuesday when you asked him concerning a possible change?" Rider winked broadly at the chief, while an injured expression came over Mott's round countenance.

"'Bout Sunday or Monday, maybe." The chief's eyes began to twinkle shrewdly. "She'll come out of this here sort of stupor and commence to get restless and then he'll let me know."

"All right. I'll be back some time on Saturday." Rider turned to the house once more. "Let's see what Mercer's got to say."

They found Stan descending the stairs, that bewildered, incredulous stare still in his eyes, but a dull spot glowed in each cheek and when he spoke there was a note of rising excitement in his subdued tones.

"Come in here, gentlemen." He motioned toward the library. "Mrs. Mercer has told me what happened but I can scarcely believe it!"

"Didn't you see the open window with the ladder still against it?" the chief demanded. "Didn't you get a whiff of chloroform still on the air?"

"Yes, but it seems so impossible!" Stan turned to Rider. "What do you make of it?"

"Nothing but what is self-evident!" The latter shrugged. "Some one got into your wife's room, but she wakened and frightened him away."

"But if he came to rifle the house why didn't he do it after he had chloroformed her?" Stan passed a hand over his forehead.

"May have heard the nurse stirring around," Rider suggested carelessly. "The main thing is that he was scared off and no harm's been done, if the chief here has made no mistake in saying that nothing's been disturbed and the fellow isn't hiding somewhere under this roof."

"He ain't; I'll swear to that!" The chief advanced a step toward Stan. "Where was you, Mr. Mercer? Your wife said she left you reading in here and you told her you wouldn't be able to sleep for hours."

"Yes, I—it seemed as if I couldn't breathe in the house!" Stan looked from one to another of them as though seeking for understanding of something he couldn't very well express. "Everything that's happened since Saturday—it's all got on my nerves! I tried to read, but about midnight I couldn't stand it any longer and went out for a long tramp, hoping I'd tire myself out. You saw me when I came in a few minutes ago."

"Where'd you go?" the chief persisted. "Did you see anybody hanging around?"

"No. I walked straight out on the turnpike away past the country club almost to Wood's Mill. On the way back some milk wagons and trucks filled with garden stuff and crates of chickens passed me coming into Chichester, but that was all. I was tired at last when I got home and I didn't even look up at Mrs. Mercer's window or I would have noticed the bright light there, of course. I let myself in at the side door with my key and then I looked up and saw you on the stairs." Stan turned again to Rider. "What in heaven's name does all this mean?"

"The chief will tell you in his own good time, I'm sure." Rider nodded with a smile and turned to the door. "Come, Mott, let's be getting on home. Chief, if you need Mott or me you'll know where to find us. Good morning."

Out in the little car once more Mott felt on the floor for the bag of which Rider had spoken, and finding it turned quizzical eyes on his friend.

"Why didn't you tell me?" he demanded. "Are you actually going away?"

"If you can manage to get me to the train in this ark!" the other retorted. "I ought really to have gone yesterday. Don't mind me, Henry; I'll be back Saturday as I said, but don't watch for train-times—let the chief do that!"

He chuckled, but Mott asked reproachfully as they swung out into the road:

"What's this about Nancy? If that child didn't bury the ring, what was it? Do you want the doctor to let you hear her talk if she gets delirious again?"

"That's it exactly!" Rider replied. "I'll let you in on it if I can. That's the crux of the whole matter, Henry, and the biggest thing of all that I've been waiting for!"

18

Rider Takes the Trail

It was noon when Rider reached the Capital and, after writing the name "David Reid" on the register at the old Ten Eyck and leaving his bag, he strolled about the business section of the city in an apparently aimless manner until luncheon, but by that time he had carefully noted and classed in his mind all the jewelers it would be worth while interviewing, and after lunch he started on his quest.

That the opal ring with such strange fire in its heart and so strange a history had been left somewhere in Albany on the previous day he was morally certain. What Ingred and Hans had done with their combined wages he could not conjecture, for their mode of life was of the simplest and their wants almost fully supplied at Hydrangea Walk, but there had been imperative need for ready cash and a lot of it—the most imperative need in all the world, the saving of a life.

Had Hans stolen the jewel, or Ingred? It was not to be thought of that the youth in his weakened condition could have strangled Gloria Warrender, but, if she had put the ring on her finger before going out to the hammock where she met her death, he might have come upon the scene after the tragedy and succumbed to a sudden, desperate temptation.

Ingred possessed the strength for the crime, more than any one else in the neighborhood, but Rider could not associate her with such an act. She was a mother, and the boy in whom all her life centered was dying before her eyes when money alone could save him; under such stress she might conceivably have stolen, but she would not have killed. Miss Warrender had not worn the ring at lunch and it was more likely that Ingred had found it lying about her room and appropriated it, than that her son had taken it from a dead hand.

Rider decided to try that hypothesis first, and leaving the hotel once more, he went straight to the first of the jewelers on his list. There were only three of the evident financial standing to purchase so valuable a ring, and Ingred's humble appearance would undoubtedly have aroused suspicion as to her lawful ownership of it. Moreover, she had in all probability no knowledge as to its true worth and that in itself would make a reputable jewel merchant pause in his dealings with her; nevertheless Rider determined to overlook no possible clew.

At the first shop an elderly clerk came forward with an air of dignified inquiry, but his manner changed as Rider announced bluntly:

"I'm looking for a ring—an opal of unique formation which was offered for sale here in Albany yesterday."

The clerk's thin lips tensed at the corners and he replied icily:

"No such sale took place in this establishment, sir. Our settings are manufactured for us and the jewels mounted in New York and Paris, and we purchase nothing from private dealers."

"I said 'offered for sale.'" Rider's tone took on a hint of sternness and, producing a card, he laid it on the glass top of the showcase. "I didn't want to drag the local police into this and cause unwelcome embarrassment to the reputable jewelers of the city, but I shall be compelled to do so if information is withheld from me. I happen to know that the opal was shown here and I want to know which of two persons brought it. Was it a pale, thin, yellow-haired young man with a cough, or a stout, middle-aged blonde who spoke with a Swedish accent?"

The clerk glanced at the card, plucked at his under lip nervously and after a moment said hesitatingly:

"Will you wait a few minutes, Commissioner? Perhaps the head of the firm may know something of this."

He turned to the rear of the shop and in at a ground-glass door, from behind which there issued the low murmur of voices. Then he reappeared.

"If you will step this way, sir, Mr. Carson will see you himself."

A bald, plump little man arose from behind a huge, flat mahogany desk with an access of geniality as Rider entered, and held out his hand.

"Glad to know you, Commissioner!" he said, heartily. "Perhaps I can help you out. Of course, we want to avoid any unpleasant notoriety, but the law must be served. I understand you're looking for a woman who tried to sell an opal ring?"

Rider nodded. So it had been Ingred, as he surmised!

"The opal was rare, I doubt if there is another like it in the world. That is why it is so valuable to its real owner and practically impossible to dispose of by a thief."

"The woman you are looking for, my clerk tells me, was a Swede and middle-aged?" Mr. Carson asked. "I won't beat about the bush with you, Commissioner. A woman such as you describe did call here yesterday about noon with a cabochon opal which she wanted to dispose of. It had a remarkable flaw in the center, something like what we call a 'feather' in emeralds, and had great value or none, according to taste; a freak gem stone of the first quality,

known as a 'precious' opal. To a connoisseur it would be
worth perhaps four or five thousand dollars, even more,
but the woman asked twenty-five hundred. She was neat
but plainly, almost shabbily dressed, and her half-fright-
ened manner alone would have made me refuse to deal
with her even had I had a market for such a stone. In fact,
if it hadn't been for something eminently respectable in
her bearing, I should have felt it incumbent upon me to
notify the police."

Rider nodded again.

"I know," he commented. "Did she seem in a hurry, as
though she feared some one were after her? Was she nervous?"

Mr. Carson smiled.

"On the contrary, she was calm and leisurely, and when
I told her it was not our policy to buy from individuals,
particularly strangers, she took it in a stolid sort of way
and asked if I could recommend her to some one who
would buy. Naturally I couldn't and she went out without apparent disappointment but quite undeterred. Her
speech was that of a typical well-trained family servant
but with a decided Swedish accent."

"That is all you can tell me?"

"Yes. Sorry I can't help you further, but you'll undoubtedly get trace of her." Mr. Carson walked to the door
with him. "She seemed rather stupid and stubborn, and I
shouldn't be at all surprised if she tried all the jewelers in
town. I don't know of one who would have dealt with her,
though."

At Opdycke's, a smaller but equally exclusive establishment from its appearance, Rider found no hesitancy.
The lean, sharp-nosed, frock-coated individual who advanced to inquire his pleasure became eager at once and
his small eyes gleamed with avid interest behind their tor-
toise-rimmed glasses.

"Yes, sir, I thought there was something suspicious about that woman!" he declared. "She didn't look or act like a thief, though; I'd have called up headquarters if she had, for we've got to be mighty careful here. Too many stolen jewels smuggled down from Canada, you know. I had an idea she might be the maid of some rich woman temporarily embarrassed who wanted to dispose of the opal without appearing in the transaction herself, but, of course, we couldn't have handled it. A gem like that might lie in our vaults for a generation before any one came along who would appreciate it; there's no standard by which it could be valued. It would depend solely on the caprice of the customer, and I don't believe the woman made a sale here in Albany."

Practically the same information greeted Rider at the third jeweler's. Ingred had been there and offered the opal ring for sale, asking twenty-two hundred for it, but they had declined to purchase it at any price.

He spent the remainder of the afternoon visiting one after another the smaller establishments and found invariably that Ingred had preceded him with dogged persistency, but no success, if his informants were to be believed, and only when he had exhausted the list in the classified directory of the city and the shops were closed did he relinquish his search for the day.

If Ingred and Hans had gone on to Saranac, it was obvious that she must have obtained the money here by some disposal of the ring, and after dinner he called up the Messiter sanitarium.

"Hello, Doc!" He greeted his old friend. "This is the man who sent a young patient to you from Chichester yesterday with a letter of introduction. You understand, this is confidential."

"Sure!" came back the hearty, well-remembered voice. "He's here, mother brought him last night. Rather an advanced case, but I think we'll be able to arrest it. Anything you want to know?"

"Yes. Was anything paid?" Rider asked briefly.

"Three hundred in advance and the mother asked me about a bank here this morning. I directed her to the First National."

"Good!" Rider commented. "That's all I wanted to know. Thanks, old man."

He rang off, with one question settled in his mind. Ingred had sold the ring—but where? It would bring quicker results, perhaps, if he were to go to headquarters himself and get data on pawnbrokers or dealers who might be under suspicion, but he preferred to work alone. Would an old dodge serve?

On an impulse he looked hastily in the telephone book, called up his first informant of the morning and then, after a short colloquy, went to his room. In half an hour there emerged from it a different type of man, still heavy-set and huge of nose, the square jaw stuck out more prominently, for the gray mustache was gone, and on the chin appeared a bluish tinge as of too close a shave. His clothes were shabby and he slouched in them with an inimitably furtive air as he made his way down the back stairs of the hotel and around the corner where a taxi, with Carson inside, awaited him.

They drove first to the shop, where an astounded watchman admitted them, and emerged a few minutes later to part, Carson going away alone in the machine and Rider shambling off in the opposite direction, toward the river-front.

In a shack huddled between two warehouses and ostentatiously boarded up he caught a faint gleam of light from a shade which flapped softly in the night breeze through the aperture of a broken window pane, and passing around the building and down a little, narrow alley he tapped with peculiar rhythm on a small door whose boards seemed loosened from the casing.

After a moment cautious steps sounded from within and the door opened a mere crack.

"What do you want?" a low voice growled.

"Is de Twinkler here yet?" Rider asked in a rough, eager tone. "Twinkler Sam? I got a date wid him an' he give me de high sign here. Nosey Regan's what dey call me back in de big town."

The door opened wider, revealing a grizzled but powerful man who held a small, smoking lamp in his hand. He stared through bleared eyes at the visitor, but Rider's make-up evidently passed muster for he stepped back and motioned within.

"C'mon. I guess yer're all right, though I never heard the Twinkler speak about yer. When'd yer see him last?"

From the side room, through a window of which he had first caught the ray of light, came a hum of low voices and the subdued rattle of dice and clink of bottles. Rider reflected. Was there a significance in that question? Swiftly he decided to play safe.

"Not fer t'ree weeks. Dere bulls was keepin' deir eyes peeled fer him an' he had to beat it, but dis was de night an' de place if I pulled it off an' I did! Say, if he's in deir call him out, will yer? I'm new in dis burg an' I don't wanter get mixed up wid no guys I ain't wise to."

The first statement was the literal truth, for just prior to his departure for Chichester Rider had interviewed the Twinkler, when that engaging young scoundrel had stood before him on the carpet at headquarters, slim and dapper and outrageously good-looking, and blandly denied all knowledge of the theft of the Van Reisen necklace.

"The Twinkler ain't comin', not to-night," the grizzled man asserted briefly. "They got him last week in Binghamton. Didn't you get the wire?"

Rider ripped out an oath, adding:

"De McKenna gang! Gawd, we told him to lay off dat steer!"

"Them's the guys, all right." His host looked shrewdly at him. "Put you in a bad fix?"

"I'll say it does!" Rider assumed great anxiety. "Look here, yer're de guy dey calls Square Pete, ain't yer? Dis is yer dump?"

The man nodded, and Rider went on:

"I gave it to yer straight when I told yer I didn't know dis burg an' de Twinkler was to meet me an' take me to a fence dat'd hand us a fair deal on a bunch of sparklers, unset. Blue-white, de real t'ing. It was my lay, you get me, if I pulled it off, an' he was to get a fourth fer steerin' me to dis guy. I gotter beat it before mornin' an' I don't wanter take dese babies no furder wid me, see? If yer'll tip me off— come along wid me if yer like—I'll give yer de same break."

"Nothin' doin'," the other declined promptly. "Fifty-fifty or we don't play, and I gotter see the goods first. This town's tighter'n a dinge's heel!"

Wasting no further words Rider unfastened his coat, incidentally displaying a serviceable looking blackjack and the butt of a revolver, and took from an inner pocket a small packet wrapped in dingy tissue paper. This he unrolled and in its center lay a score or more of small but perfect diamonds gleaming with myriad flashes of radiance in the glow of the dirty lamp.

"That's enough!" Square Pete declared. "Wait'll I get my coat and have a word with the boys . . ."

"Dere's a coat hangin' behind yer on dat nail," Rider interrupted with a slow smile. "Guess yer better not show yerself to yer frien's in dere till we get back; dey might get kind of cur'ous an' folley along, an' maybe try some old stuff, me bein' an outsider. I'd hate to have to pull some rough stuff. Wanter play her as she lays?"

Square Pete shrugged and grinned, then set his lamp down on the stairs and reached for the coat.

"You're on," he observed. "C'mon."

Twenty minutes later they were tapping gently on the rear door of a fur shop which Rider had passed in the best part of the business section that day, and after an interval an elderly man appeared in pajamas and bathrobe. Briefly he listened to Square Pete's low-voiced explanation, of which Rider caught only the phrases: "wise old bird," "pal of the Twinkler," "real stuff and he knows it. . . . Sure, would I bring him here if I wasn't?"

The elderly man motioned up a thickly carpeted stair, and Rider followed Square Pete's lead to the top of the house and into a room which contained only two deal chairs and a long table covered with the implements of a manufacturing jeweler's trade.

"Now then, let's see what you've got," their host invited as he closed the door.

"Wait a minute." But Rider had produced the packet. "Do yer know my pal de Twinkler dat got croaked las' week? He told me de guy he did bus'ness wid was a top-notcher, and he put Big Hilda wise to him too. If yer're de feller . . ."

"I know your friend," the elderly man conceded. "Is Big Hilda a yellow-haired Swede, a woman around fifty?"

"Dat's her!" Rider cried eagerly as he shifted a step, just a step which brought him facing the two men with the door behind them. "She's a dumb-bell but real careful an' she'll do what she's told. Say, she ain't been here in de las' couple of days, has she? She's got a bird of a stone—opal, dey call it—ought to be good for seven or eight grand over de water."

The elderly man frowned.

"She didn't mention the Twinkler. I thought she was—er—an amateur. She told me the delivery boy at Opdycke's had recommended her here."

Rider laughed, but one hand slipped quietly to the butt of his revolver, and with the other he drew a card from his sleeve and palmed it.

"Sure, dat's de way she always pulls it off in a strange burg! Didn't I say she was careful—and dumb? Looks like a good old mudder, don't she? Dat's where she's aces wid us. Did yer get de opal?"

"Well, it was a risk, of course, for as you say it will have to be unloaded abroad, but we're always out for exceptional things and I gave her a good price. If what you've got is worth while, you'll find me on the level."

"I hope so!" Rider remarked with a change of tone, and drawing his revolver he threw the card on the table. "I'm Special Deputy Commissioner of Police Rider of New York, and I've come for that opal ring!"

19

The Chief's Theory

On Friday morning early Mott appeared on the main thoroughfare of the busy little city in his car, and as he drew up before the post-office the chief of police came out of the courthouse next door. His long, lantern-jawed face was red and set, and his small eyes snapped.

"'Morning, Chief!" Mott greeted him. "Just the man I wanted to see! But what's got your goat?"

"The district attorney!" Chief Clark drawled resentfully. "He's got his own men working on the case and they haven't got a step further than when they started, yet he's been hauling me over the coals because I can't turn the murderer over to him for indictment like a sack of meal! Where're you going, Mott?"

"Only to see if there's any mail from Rider." Mott descended from the car as he spoke. "I'll only be a minute. Want me to drop you somewhere?"

"If you're going back home by the usual way." The chief paused and Mott nodded understandingly.

"I get you. I was going to stop off there myself."

He entered the post-office, unlocked his box and took out the few envelopes it contained, but sorting them hastily he saw that none were from his friend and shaking his head he rejoined the waiting chief.

197

"No news?" The latter read his expression. "Say, Mott, you've known Rider ever since war days. Do you think he might be a bluff, for all the papers print about him? Do you s'pose he's give up this case as a bad job and beat it down to New York?"

"Never!" Mott exclaimed as he turned the little car around and started back. "You don't know him, and his reputation wasn't built in a day! He's got the name of 'Bull-dog Rider' because he won't let go of a case till he's finished with it! He won't talk—I've been with him nearly every minute, and I don't know any more about what he's found out nor where he's gone than you do, probably less, but he'll turn up to-morrow, all right, because he gave his word."

The chief glanced doubtfully at his face, but saw only confident reassurance there, and he drew a long, lugubrious breath.

"We-ell, maybe you know, but I'll bet he's on the wrong track for once. If he's looking for evidence anywheres but at Hydrangea Walk itself, he's on a fool's errand."

He spoke with such certainty that Mott in turn darted him a quick glance.

"You've found out something else since yesterday?" he asked ingratiatingly.

"Had it afore, but if he can keep things to himself, so can I!" The chief grinned slowly. "Stan Mercer's great on taking long walks by himself lately, ain't he? Never seems to meet anybody he knows, either, daytime or nighttime!"

"Mercer!" Mott ejaculated half under his breath. "You— you've got your eye on him!"

"You bet I have!" The chief spat over the side of the car to lend emphasis to his words. "I know you can hold your tongue, and you've been kind of in on this from the start. Mercer went out walking toward Lake Valley last Saturday afternoon, didn't he? Well, he didn't. He went along up toward the ridge and met another man and they had a fight; at least the other man struck him, but he just grabbed his wrists and held him till he'd calmed him down and they started back together towards Hydrangea Walk."

"You don't say!" Mott hesitated and asked: "Who saw them? Who was the other man?"

"I got a witness." The chief's long lanky frame swelled with importance. "Old Mis' Duxbury saw 'em—you know her? She lives out beyond Hilltop and raises guinea hens for the city markets."

Mott nodded impatiently.

"Who was the man who struck Stan Mercer?" he repeated.

"Major Hill!" The chief threw his bombshell. "I got another witness, Sam Higgins' boy, that saw them separate at the cross-roads, and he says it was around three o'clock then. That's within ten minutes' walk of the Mercer place, and the boy says the major started off in that direction but Mercer hung around for a minute or two and then followed him, though slow, as if he didn't want the major to know."

"That kid's a born liar!" Mott averred with conviction.

"Maybe, but that ain't all I got!" Chief Clark's need for an audience and praise was imperative after the rebuke he had received from the district attorney. "What would you say if I was to tell you that the coroner might be wrong about the major's death?"

"His death!" The car bounded forward as Mott involuntarily pressed on the gas. "You don't mean . . . But we all heard the shot, we were beside him in two minutes!"

"And found him lying dead, shot in the head with his own revolver that was under his hand," the chief supplemented. "All the same he needn't have fired it, Mott. Ain't no telling but what it was murder instead of suicide—the second murder in a week, and by the same hand!"

"Mercer!" Mott exclaimed again. "You mean him, don't you? But why?"

"Don't know yet, but it's common talk that he was head over heels in love with this Gloria Warrender—him with a fine wife like Mrs. Mercer! We wouldn't have time to handle the few tramps and drunks and petty thieves we do get in Chichester if we paid much attention to the gossip and scandal of you folks out at that country club of yourn, Mott, but this time there's something in it! It's a good thing it ain't come to Mrs. Mercer's ears, for she ain't a woman to stand any nonsense, as I size her up, in spite of her calm, easy-going way. The major knew the woman before in France, and we know him and Mercer quarreled the very day she was killed, but that ain't all, yet! Ingred says—"

"Ingred!" Mott cried, slowing up mechanically, for they had reached the hedge that bounded Hydrangea Walk on the north. "She came back, then?"

"On the train that got in half an hour before I met you," the chief nodded. "I got a man at the station all the time, you know, and he kept her talking till I kind of sauntered along. She's left her son at the place Rider sent her to, real pleased and happy about his getting well, and she didn't think anything when I asked her a couple of questions. Ingred's a fine figure of a woman for her years, but dumber than most! Wednesday night wasn't the first time that Mercer's gone out for a walk in the dark since the murder!"

"Jumping Christopher!" A light dawned on Mott as he turned the car in between the gateposts. "You're speaking of Monday night—in all that storm?"

"That's it." The chief slapped his bony knee. "Come on in with me, if you want to. I ain't going to pull anything yet, but if your friend Rider don't come back to-morrow he's likely to find that it's all over but the shouting! Ingred was awake and scared by the storm and she saw Mercer go out. It surprised her so that she couldn't believe at first it was him, though she saw him plain in a flash of lightning, and she went down to his room to see. The door was open, the bed hadn't been slept in, just like on Wednesday night, and he hadn't even took his umbrella with him! Ingred watched till the storm passed but he didn't come home. That's Doc Ross's car and here he comes now. I want to speak to him."

They had drawn up at the veranda steps behind the small sedan, and the young doctor appeared in the door. Chief Clark climbed out awkwardly and joined him and the two talked for a brief moment, then Dr. Ross came down the steps with a pleasant nod to Mott, and the chief beckoned.

"Come on," he said in a low tone when Mott had reached his side. "I ain't had time to tell you what I think 'bout Wednesday night, but you'll get it, maybe, while I'm talking. . . . Good morning, Mr. Mercer. I met Mr. Mott down to the post-office and he give me a lift out here."

Stan had come out into the hall and now he welcomed them both perfunctorily and showed them into the library.

"Your friend Rider went away quite suddenly yesterday, didn't he?" he asked Mott, but half-indifferently, as though merely making conversation.

"Oh, he'll be back in a day or two—just a sudden matter of business that came up." Mott hoped his tone was as easy as he intended it to sound. "Has Mrs. Mercer quite recovered from that affair the other night?"

"Quite. She wasn't badly frightened—you know what wonderful self-control she has shown through all this horrible nightmare of a week! The burglar would have driven most women into a nervous breakdown, but not her, and she got only a breath or two of the chloroform," he responded and turned to the chief. "Anything I can do for you? Ingred the housekeeper came back this morning."

"I know—saw her at the station." The other seated himself without being invited, and Mott perceived a certain difference in the manner of each man toward the other. There was an overbearing, almost insolent air about the chief and his tone was twanging with a note of assurance, but Stan, although seemingly indifferent in his attitude, held himself warily in check.

He turned to Mott now.

"Won't you sit down, too?" he asked pointedly. "If this is to be a conference, let us hope something will come of it!"

The shot told and the chief flushed darkly.

"You're right, it will!" He set his jaw. "It'll be a week to-morrow since Miss Warrender was killed, but I calc'late the end of it's coming pretty soon now! Mr. Mercer, where was that ladder kept—the one that was put up at your wife's window the other night?"

"Why, in the toolhouse with the rest of the garden implements." Stan eyed him levelly.

"Hans didn't leave it laying 'round anywheres when he went away that Wednesday morning?"

"Certainly not."

"That toolhouse fastens with a hasp and a padlock. One of my men found it open and the padlock hanging when we were sent for," the chief went on. "Who's got keys to it, Mr. Mercer?"

The emphasis on his name was purposely impertinent, but Stan only smiled slightly.

"Only Hans and I."

"Did he leave his key with you? He didn't expect to come back."

"Not with me. I don't know what he did with it; I haven't thought to ask." Stan shrugged.

"You've got yours, though?"

"Yes. Here it is." Stan produced a key-ring from his pocket and held it out. "I always carry it around with the rest and I had it with me when I went out Wednesday night."

His tone was ironical and Mott held his breath. Was Stan Mercer deliberately forcing an issue with the chief of police?

"Was that the only night this week you went out walking?"

"No. I went out Monday night."

"Just for a nice walk—in all that storm?" The chief's grin was a leer.

"For a walk in spite of it—yes," Stan maintained with no sign of aggressiveness.

"Where did you go, Mr. Mercer?"

"Up toward Mott's house—I passed it, in fact, and saw you slink across the road. Another flash of lightning showed you climbing the porch railing, and I waited for you to go in at the door, but you didn't."

Mott uttered a half-smothered exclamation and the chief's flush deepened.

"Never you mind about me!" he snarled. "What did you do yourself? Did you go up in the woods along the ridge and meet Major Hill at dawn and fight with him like you done last Saturday afternoon, *Mr.* Mercer, and did you take his revolver from him and let him have it?"

"No." Stan's tone was very quiet now, but perfectly steady. "No. I went on for a mile or so beyond The Rafters and then, as the storm had stopped, I realized I was drenched and turned homeward. When I got back here my watch pointed to ten minutes to four."

"H'm." The chief rubbed his chin and his small eyes twinkled cunningly. "You ain't denying you met the major Saturday afternoon and fought with him?"

"Yes," Stan replied unexpectedly. "I did meet him, but I didn't fight with him."

"I got a witness!" the chief shrilled. "I got a witness that seen him strike you!"

"Did this witness see me strike back?" asked Stan with lifted brows. "It takes two to fight, you know, Chief. The major was excited, almost beside himself; it was more a gesture, an expression of his highly nervous, over-wrought condition than a blow. He regained control of himself in a moment and that was the end of it."

"You walked on together to the cross-roads, didn't you? He left you there, as he thought, and started for your place here, but you followed him?"

"We separated at the cross-roads, but it was his intention, so he told me, to go to the station and take a train, and the shortest way lay past my house." Stan had ceased now to volunteer information, but waited for the other's questions, and Mott, listening, had a vague notion that the former was in reality directing the inquiry; that now, having deliberately started the chief, he was allowing him to proceed on his own momentum.

"Where was the major going?"

"I haven't the most remote idea. He mentioned simply that he was going away and I didn't ask where. It didn't interest me."

"I s'pose you wouldn't like to say what you two were quarreling about?"

"Right again, Chief. It was a private matter, a slight difference between us. I wouldn't talk about it on the witness stand."

"Thought so! How about following him from the cross-roads; ain't got anything to say about that, either?"

"I went in the same direction he had taken, but a few minutes later; you may call that following, if you choose." Stan shrugged again.

"I do!" The chief's temper was breaking at last. "If you wasn't, why didn't you walk along with him till you got to your own place?"

"Because, after he left me, I decided to return home and get some new golf balls I'd bought recently and try them out at the country club. Instead I changed my mind before I reached my own gates and hiked out, as I told you, in the direction of Lake Valley."

"That so?" The chief rose and glared at the man before him. "Golf balls ain't all you bought lately! I got just one more question to ask you, Mr. Mercer! What did you get in Flint's drugstore on Tuesday afternoon?"

Stan laughed outright.

"A bottle of chloroform!" said he.

20

Rider Returns

"Ain't heard a word from Rider yet?" Chief Clark asked. It was late the following afternoon and he had driven out to The Rafters to consult Mott, whom he found moodily smoking his pipe under the grape arbor.

"The day isn't over!" the latter protested. "There are two more trains incoming from the east and south before midnight. Aren't you going to have some one there to meet him?"

There was raillery in his tone and the chief cocked an eye at him.

"What do you mean, Mott?" he asked. "You don't think he's coming after all?"

"I think your men may have a good long wait!" Mott pulled forward a chair for his visitor and tilted his own back as he looked up at him.

"You've heard from him, then? Why didn't you let me know?"

"Not a word, but if I had, why should I tell you, Chief?" Mott asked coolly. "I'm not officially on this case, and you didn't tell me when you came snooping around the house last Monday night in all that storm."

The chief's eyes dropped.

"You thought you was going to get some information about the major from that visitor you was expecting and

207

I figgered I'd better get it, too," he explained. "If you'd wanted me here you'd have asked me, so I done the only thing I could. I was on the wrong track then, but I ain't now!"

"Sure of it?" Mott knocked the ashes from his pipe and laid it to cool on a stout support of the arbor. "Haven't heard of you making an arrest yet, Chief. What are you waiting for—Rider's return? Haven't you got enough already to send Stan Mercer up for indictment?"

"Maybe I have, and maybe I'm waiting my own good time!" he retorted. "You ain't talking the way you did yesterday!"

"No," Mott acquiesced reflectively. "I'm not, Chief, if you mean the way I talked on the road to Hydrangea Walk from the town. I don't mind telling you that I thought myself Stan might be guilty—up till then. I changed my opinion, though, while you were questioning him and if you ask me, I think he was stringing you!"

The chief swore softly under his breath.

"Because he had to admit everything?" he demanded hotly.

"Because he did it so readily—practically made your case out for you against himself. He was laughing in his sleeve all the time and he laughed out loud at the end. Have you found out yet what he and the major quarreled about? How do you know it was the woman? If you did overhear anything on my porch in the thunderstorm Monday night—which I doubt—you didn't hear a word about the major or Stan Mercer, either! You're not so certain yourself, Chief, after that talk yesterday. Circumstantial evidence is kind of like dynamite, and you remember what Rider told you on Sunday morning about getting your department held up to ridicule in case you make a wrong guess!"

Mott was enjoying himself hugely and the Chief writhed in his chair.

"I got the goods on him, circumstantial or not!" he exclaimed. "He took it that way knowing it was coming and trying to defy me!"

"And he's been sitting around all this week waiting for you to take him in?" Mott chuckled. "Why did he go outside Wednesday night and break into his own house and chloroform his wife after leaving a trail a mile wide by buying the stuff at the principal drugstore here the day before?"

"Just for a bluff, to pretend that somebody was after the ring—that opal ring belonging to the Warrender woman! That's what Mrs. Mercer herself thought, if you remember, and that's what he wanted her to think, and all the rest of us. Ten to one he took that ring as a blind in the first place, to make it look like murder for the sake of robbery. I got the whole case cinched now, and when your friend Rider comes back I'll show him what we up-State fellers can do when we get going!"

"Glad to hear it, Chief!" A new voice called out heartily from behind them, and they sprang up to find Dan Rider coming toward them over the lawn on the other side of the arbor, his footsteps making no sound on the soft, springing grass. "Too bad I wasn't here when you built your case up but you'll let me in on the finish, won't you?"

"Dan!" cried Mott as they clasped hands. "Why didn't you let me hear from you?"

"Been too busy." Rider looked worn and travel-stained as he turned and held out his hand to the chief.

"But there wasn't any train . . . !" the latter began.

Rider laughed.

"Oh, I got off at the junction hours ago and rode in on an obliging farmer's wagon. I had an errand to do first. But you've finished the case, you said?"

"We-ell," the chief shifted uncomfortably from one foot to the other, "it's circumstantial but I calc'late I'll get a confession."

"It's Stan Mercer, he means!" Mott broke in irrepressibly. "I was with him when he questioned Stan, and he admits he bought chloroform the day before that supposed burglarious entrance, he admits he quarreled Saturday with poor Jack and Jack struck him, he admits he was out in the storm Monday night . . . !"

"Oh, yes, I know all about that!" Rider laughed again. "I was wise to most of it before I went away, but I stopped at Hydrangea Walk just now—that was the errand I spoke about—and Mercer told me the rest."

"You knew most of it!" The chief spat in disgust. "Then why in Tophet didn't you tell me before you left?"

"Because it didn't have anything to do with the murder," Rider announced in a matter-of-fact tone.

Mott gulped and reached instinctively for his pipe, and the chief sank down limply into his chair.

"S'pose you got the murderer yourself?" he asked with a final attempt at bravado.

"Oh, no, I didn't go away for that!" replied Rider. "I knew about that quarrel Saturday and I guessed at the cause of it; I looked particularly to see if one of the major's hands was bruised after he shot himself and it was, all right. You remember I spoke of it the next day, Henry? That happened when he struck Mercer, but it was all over in a minute—his temper was worn to a frazzle and he wasn't accountable just then. Mercer did walk out past here on Monday night and go home again more than an hour before we heard the shot that killed the major. You see, Chief, you didn't question Ingred long enough at the station yesterday morning. She told you she saw Mercer go out in the storm, and though she waited till it had passed, he didn't come home; she didn't tell you that he did come a couple of hours later and she noticed the time—five minutes to four. She put on a wrapper and went down and spoke to him, asked if he wanted a hot drink or anything."

"Why didn't he tell me that himself?" the chief demanded indignantly. "Making a fool of an officer of the law! I'll show him!"

"Maybe he resented being accused-—people do, you know, especially when they think you're taking too much for granted," Rider suggested quietly.

"You'll try to tell me next that he did actually kill a cat with that chloroform he bought!" The chief's tone was bitter.

"No, the chauffeur did that," his informant explained cheerfully. "You didn't seem inclined to believe him when he told you, so he didn't go into details, but I can produce the corpse, if necessary!"

"I wish you could produce something else." The other's nasal tone was dismal in defeat and his ungainly shoulders slumped. "What on earth did you go away for?"

"I'll tell you if you'll come down to the Mercers' with me, both of you, as soon as I get cleaned up a bit," Rider returned. "Henry, can your cook dig up a cold bite for me? Haven't had a thing since early morning and I don't believe I'm going to feel much like eating at dinner-time, not after what I've got to do first. I saw your car out in the road, Chief; it would save time if you'd run down and get a blank warrant."

"For murder?" The chief's small eyes widened.

"No, just leave the charge blank, too. I promise you, though, that you'll be able to fill it in before night."

The two friends were waiting on the porch when the chief returned, Rider's heavy face grave and a pained look in his keen gray eyes, but his jaw was set firmly. Mott, still obviously unenlightened, seethed with excitement, and it was decided that they were all three to go in the runabout, leaving the chief's car there.

Twenty minutes later they drew up before the veranda steps of Hydrangea Walk and Stan himself came out of the door. "Hello, Chief!" he said genially. "Come to arrest me? I'm ready to give myself up . . ."

"This ain't a joking matter, Mr. Mercer!" the unhappy officer of the law replied with as much dignity as he could command, as he unfolded his long legs from the running-board and straightened. "The murderer ain't caught yet, remember!"

"What have you to tell me, then?" Stan had nodded to the other two but he still addressed the chief. "Come into the library, anyway. Rider said you had something you wanted me to know and that he'd bring you and Mott. I've been waiting."

The pleasantry was gone from his voice now, and the haggard lines stood out once more on his clean-cut face as he led the way. The chief gave a glance of agonized query at Rider and then abruptly abdicated.

"He did, did he? Then let him tell you himself!" he retorted. "I ain't going to say a word till my own time comes!"

"First of all, where is Mrs. Mercer?" Rider asked when all four were seated.

"Lying down; we won't disturb her," their host replied. "I tried to get her to go out for a short run in the car as you suggested, but she preferred to remain near Nancy; the child seems more restless to-day, the nurse tells us."

Mott darted a quick glance at the chief and saw his eyes turn significantly to Rider, but the latter ignored them.

"Mercer," he said, "when you told me about Ingred waiting up for you on Monday night and she confirmed it, there was one question I forgot to ask her. Will you send for her now?"

"Certainly." Stan pressed the bell. "She's delighted about that place you sent her boy to—it was mighty kind of you!"

"Wait!" Rider stopped him and there was a harsh note in his voice. "I'm glad myself for the boy's sake, but we've got other business on hand now."

A trifle tired looking but radiant with smiles, Ingred appeared on the threshold, and Stan said with a smile, also:

"Come in and shut the door, Ingred; we don't want to disturb Mrs. Mercer. Mr. Rider wants to ask you some more questions."

Ingred obeyed and looked with pleased expectancy toward Rider, who for once seemed at a loss how to begin. Then abruptly he put his hand in his pocket, and drawing out something held it extended before her on his open palm. It was the opal ring.

"Ingred!" he thundered, "when did you steal this from Miss Warrender—while she was living or *after she was dead?*"

The blood ebbed slowly from the woman's face as the light died out of her eyes, and her wide lips worked piteously as she gazed, as if fascinated, at the opal. A startled exclamation had burst simultaneously from the three men, but she uttered no sound till her gaze lifted to Rider's stern face. Then a little low moan was forced from her, like that of an animal suddenly stricken.

"It vas no goot, after all!" she whispered dully. "Now my Hans got to coom back—to die!"

"What!" the chief cried. "He killed . . ."

"Hans kill only himself if he got to stay here!" Ingred shifted her agonized glance to his face. "He could live vere Mister Rider sent him but here vit dat lung 'most gone—it is no use. It vas for dat I stole de ring. I send all my money back to my peoples dat are poor in de old country; I bane strong, I got years yet, I can vork, and den Hans, he shall do for me, but I bane blind, I got no eyes to see dat Hans bane sick! Ven de doctor here tells me dat Hans got to go far off for two, t'ree year or else he die, I got not'ing to send him vit, no money! I tank I go crazy, maybe, for dere is nobody . . .”

“There was Mrs. Mercer!” Stan cried hoarsely. “Why didn't you come to her—to me? Great God, did you kill . . .”

“I kill yoost my own honor, my honesty, Mister Mercer!” Ingred drew herself up to her great height and a sort of dignity settled upon her plain, stolid features. “I did it for my Hans, and yoost so he get vell, I bane not to care! I took dat ring from Miss Varrender's dressing-table, while she bane in de dining-room at noontime on Saturday, and I hide it in my dress. Vonce before—de very day she coom—she drop it and I find it, and she give me fifty dollar. I tank it too mooch, but she tell me it is vort' a ransom. After dat I bane remember it all de time—nights I see it in front of me, and days! Miss Varrender is reech, she have so mooch she maybe not miss dat one ring if it goes, and for my Hans, it is his life! I know it is not goot, not sqvare—but he coughs and he grows so pale! He dies right before my eyes! I take dat ring and I vould not be sorry, only now dat doctor he vill pay back de money and my Hans must coom home to die!”

“Ingred, tell me the truth, tell me!” Stan commanded. “You took that ring off Miss Warrender's dressing-table on Saturday? You swear it?”

She nodded, her eyes, dry and hard with despair, turned obediently to his.

“Vile you vas all eating loonch,” she reiterated. “I tank she goon Monday and dat vould be de end! How could I tell dat de poor lady vould be killed so terrible before even de sun go down dat day?”

“Look here!” the chief interposed roughly, “you're sure it was while she was at lunch? You're sure you didn't go out to that hammock and strangle her and take the ring from her finger?"

"Never, I svear it!" There was horror stamped upon her face now and glaring from her bovine eyes. "I vould not kill, not even for Hans' life! You shall not tank sooch t'ings of me, for you know it is not so! I take de ring, but I know not'ing of de murder till de little Nancy coom in screaming so! I get me a sorry, den, and I vould put de ring back—but dere is Hans! Now it is no goot! I vould not care dat I go to prison, only my boy, he got to leave dat place vere dey make him vell, vere he gets long life before him! He got—to—coom—back!"

Ingred had forgotten the murder, dismissed it utterly from her thoughts after denying her guilt, as though it were of no importance in the face of her own greater tragedy, and after studying her for a long minute Stan leaned forward.

"Ingred, if you're telling the truth I'll pay to keep your son there," he said. "You should have come to me in the first place; I saw Hans was ill and I intended to speak to you about him, anyway. *If* you're telling the truth! You did not kill Miss Warrender?"

"No!" Ingred's eyes were shining softly again. "I steal from her, yes, but I vould not harm von hair of her head!"

"And you don't know who did?"

"I don't know not'ing, Mister Mercer. Only ven de little Nancy coom crying, and den Mrs. Mercer she vent out to de hammock and called. Den I left Nancy and ran out to her, and Hans coom 'round de corner of de house and ve saw! Dat is all, I svear! Oh, if you take care of my boy for me dere, ven I coom out of prison I vork for you de rest of my life!"

"All right, you'll come with me now, and you can tell me later what else you remember and how you sold the ring!"

the chief said grimly. "The charge *now* is grand larceny, and you all three heard her confession. Maybe there'll be another charge before I get through! Come along, now, Ingred!"

She moved willingly toward the door, but at the threshold she turned again to give a final, grateful glance at Stan, and the chief spoke over his shoulder:

"Remember, Rider, what you said about somebody being strong, with a strength far beyond the normal? Looks to me as if we had that strength right here in our grasp!"

21

The Darkened Room

The church bells were ringing and Mott and Rider were seated in their accustomed place under the grape arbor, smoking, in attitudes that betokened calm reflection, when Chief Clark joined them next morning. He acknowledged their greetings sheepishly and then blurted out:

"Look here, Rider, that was mighty good of you to say what you did to Mercer! He told me this morning and it almost knocked me flat! It'll kinder even things up for me if the story ever comes out 'bout how near I was to arresting him for the murder, and makes him look at me's if I was something more'n the fool he took me for yesterday."

Mott looked inquiringly at his friend, but as the latter remained silent he turned to the chief.

"What was it Rider told Stan?" he asked.

"That I'd sent him to follow Ingred and find out where she sold the ring; he said I knew where she had it hidden all the time but waited to give her a chance to go and try to sell it, so's I'd have the goods on her. He said he'd taken an interest in my work on the case from the start and didn't mind being made my deputy!" The chief suddenly held out a large, bony hand. "Goddamighty, shake! I knew you was big, C'missioner, but I never guessed anybody'd be as big as that!"

"This is your case, Chief, and I'm only here as Mott's friend, remember. Of course all the credit goes to you."

"I'd never have guessed it in a million years!" The chief shook his head. "That's what makes me so blamed mad! Here I been thinking Ingred was the dumbest of the dumb, and she put it over on me! How in the world did you find it out?"

"I didn't," Rider chuckled. "I knew it must be an inside job—the disappearance of that ring, I mean—and it wasn't likely that either Mr. or Mrs. Mercer would take it. One of the children might have, if they'd strayed into her room, but I didn't think so, and that left only the servants. They wouldn't try to dispose of it here or trust it to the mails, even if they had an accomplice to confide in, so I waited for the first one to make an excuse to go away.

"Ingred asked my advice about a New York doctor for her son, but I told her the one here could give her just as good advice, and thought no more about it till she persisted a second time. Then she spoke of the Adirondacks, and although I said I'd give her a letter of introduction to Dr. Messiter at Saranac, I forgot it till you yourself, Chief, spoke of it to me and said she was going with Hans on the following day.

"That was enough for me, but it wasn't proof, so I went after that on Thursday. I was a day late, of course, but I knew she had to change at Albany for Saranac and have a stopover of several hours, and I figured she'd try to sell the ring there." He went on, telling in swift detail of his recovery of the ring, and added: "Ingred is so intrinsically honest that she went about the business of disposing of the stone quite openly; it's a miracle one of the reputable jewelers she applied to first didn't have her arrested as a suspicious character!"

"She looks too honest for that, somehow!" Mott's kindly face was sad. "I don't know how the Mercers look at it, but I don't mind telling you, Chief, that I'm going to do all I can to have her get off with a light sentence, grand larceny or no! She was dumb, after all, or she would have applied for help for her boy, but Swedes are moody and keep their troubles to themselves, brooding over them. If there was ever an excuse for crime, she had it!"

"Kind of like to see her get off myself," the chief admitted. "I talked to her for more'n three hours last night, but she didn't change her story and she swore up and down that Hans didn't know a thing about it, her having the ring or anything."

"He didn't," Rider asserted positively. "If he had he would have gone alone and disposed of it; that is, providing he would have been willing to take his cure on the proceeds of stolen property, and I don't think so. He seems to be a downright, honest lad."

"That's what she seems to feel worse about now than anything; that he's got to know." The chief slapped his knee. "I swear I don't know what to think! I can't look at those clear, stupid eyes of hers and believe that she committed the murder, and then I look down at her hands and I wonder! She's the strongest woman I ever saw, strong enough to throttle a bull, I guess—and I reminded you, Rider, of what you said about the murderer. You couldn't have torn that rope apart the way it was, and I couldn't, but I wouldn't put it past her! She's got the strength for it, and who else has?"

"That still remains to be proved," Rider shrugged. "I wondered myself about that once, for just a minute, while I was writing that letter of introduction for Hans to take to the doctor, and I gave it to her Tuesday afternoon."

"Say, it was Tuesday I told you she was going the next day with Hans, wasn't it?" the chief asked suddenly. "Why didn't you follow her Wednesday on the next train? Why did you wait till Thursday?"

"Because, as I told you then—just before I left, I mean—I had waited till the right time came for action. I wanted to give her a good start." Rider carefully avoided Mott's eyes as he spoke.

"But you said that attempted burglary at the Mercers' decided you!" the puzzled chief protested. "What in the world did that have to do with Hans and Ingred and the stolen ring?"

"Well, to tell you the truth, I expected that some attempt would be made soon to search that house and till it happened I didn't know that it would be well for me to leave town even to get the goods on Ingred," Rider replied slowly, drawing on his cigar. "The very first night she and Hans were out of the way, though, it was pulled off—and failed, owing to Mrs. Mercer's presence of mind. I felt free, then, to take up the trail."

"I don't get it yet, do you, Mott?" the chief turned to the third member of the party, who looked up in surprise.

"Me?" Mott exclaimed. "I never get it, not when Rider's on a case, and I've given up trying! As far as I can see, you're neither of you a step nearer finding out who killed Gloria Warrender than you were a week ago yesterday, when her body lay in the hammock with the rope twisted around her neck! I'm not, either! It would stay a mystery for all of me!"

"No." Rider spoke very gravely. "I think the end is coming very soon. In a case like this, where the murderer simply walks on the scene, picks up a weapon that happens to be there ready to his hand, uses it and walks off again leaving it there, it's bound to seem simple on the face of it, and yet it's the most difficult kind to solve of all. Even when you've got it all worked out in your mind who is guilty and every action of theirs bears it out too, you've got to have the motive and some tangible evidence if you can hope to force a confession, let alone accuse and convict a person who steadfastly proclaims his innocence."

"Yet you say the end is coming!" Mott wriggled in his chair. "Do you mean you've got it all figured out and—and you've been studying the guilty man, and know his motive, and yet haven't any evidence? Where do you expect to get it?"

"I can't tell you now, and you'd both think I was crazy if I spoke without an atom of proof. Even if I confronted the person who may be guilty, in my estimation, it would be a contest of wills now and I think I'd be beaten! Chief, you've just come from the Mercers', you say? How's the little girl?"

"Nancy?" The chief's eyes narrowed shrewdly. "What makes you think you'll learn anything from her? I met the doctor there again this morning and he said she was getting more restless and he was looking for delirium to come any time now; he was going to stay there and wait, for if things broke right she'd drop off to sleep again and then wake up weak as a kitten, but with her head all clear, and the shock of what she saw in that hammock safely passed. He's going to 'phone up here for me as soon as she shows the least sign of raving, but we've got to sneak in and stand where she can't see us."

"That's all right. I only want to hear her, that's all, and I want Mott to hear her too," Rider observed decidedly. "Dr. Ross can't refuse on the score that it will injure his patient, for she'll never know we were there, and that's the only reason he can put up against the law!"

"Well, but there's Mrs. Mercer," the chief objected. "She's wild to get in to the little girl, naturally, and it's been hard for Doc Ross and the nurse to refuse her; now she can't be convinced Nancy isn't getting worse and she demands to see her. If she knows we're allowed to, and she isn't, there'll be the devil to pay."

"Why isn't she?" Mott asked bluntly. "She's the child's mother, and if it won't hurt her to have us look at her and listen to what she may say, I don't see how it'll hurt her to have her mother peep in at her!"

His tone was filled with honest indignation, and Rider turned to him impatiently.

"Don't you know that the family are always excluded when a crisis is impending in a patient's condition?" he asked. "No doctor would allow a mother to be present, of all people; he'd be afraid she would break down and make a scene. I sympathize with Mrs. Mercer, of course, but we can't let her interfere now. Chief, the doctor's still there, you say; suppose you drive back now and contrive to see him for a minute? Say we'll all be waiting at the rear of the garden, and we'll follow you. Then you can let us know when the moment comes and we'll go up the back way, without the Mercers knowing we've been there at all."

"I guess that would be best." The chief rose. "Mercer himself would be pretty mad, especially after the bone-head play I pulled on him, and he's got a lot of influence in this town; I wouldn't like to have him get out after me! I calc'late you know what you want, Rider, but I'm jiggered if I can figure what you expect to get from the child! She didn't see any more'n her mother did, when she found the corpse in the hammock!"

He went off shaking his head, and Mott said, as they watched his ungainly form climbing into the police car:

"So it's come down to whatever it was that Nancy buried, eh?"

"Not altogether," Rider demurred. "We can't depend on that, of course, though as I told you just before I went away, it's the crux of the whole matter, the biggest thing I've been waiting for! We know your friend, the major, was in love with Gloria Warrender and so was Stan Mercer; neither of them had an alibi for the hour of her murder and both were known to be in the immediate neighborhood. It's as easy to make yourself believe that one killed her through jealousy as the other, if you're not blinded by prejudice."

"But you said you didn't think Jack did it!" Mott declared, reddening. "You told me that, and Staverton! You laughed at the chief's accusation of Stan Mercer, too! Who's there left? It may be that Ingred's stronger than any two men in the community, but if she stole the ring first instead of committing murder for it, who did? You aren't going to ring in a dark horse on us, are you?"

"I wish to God I knew!" Rider exclaimed. "Come on. It's time we followed the chief."

It was insufferably hot in the rear garden at Hydrangea Walk, for although the greenhouses screened them from possible eyes, the rays of the noonday sun, refracted from the sloping walls of glass, burned like fire, and Mott sat, perspiring but expectant, on the edge of an overturned barrow.

"Suppose Clark's forgotten all about us? What then?" He slapped at a big green fly with his handkerchief and then tucked it in under what had that morning been a stiff, immaculately clean collar. "We've been here for hours, haven't we? What time is it?"

"A quarter past one." Rider, balanced on the frame of an empty hotbed, consulted his watch and then glanced up at the windows of the house. Two at the rear on the third floor were darkened, with shades tightly drawn, and he gestured toward them. "Nancy's room. There can't have been any change; we've just got to wait."

"You've been saying that all week!" Mott grumbled. "What if there isn't any change, or—or else only a final one? What if Nancy never speaks?"

But as if in answer to his query the back door opened and Chief Clark came out, advancing toward them at a

shambling walk designed to be aimless, yet hurrying,
nevertheless. He went around the far end of the green-
house and found them awaiting him.

"It's all right, and Doc Ross says to come now!" he
whispered, although no one was within earshot. "Mercer
and his wife are at their midday dinner with the housemaid waiting on them now that I've got Ingred in jail,
and the doc has explained things to Miss Alstead. There's
nobody else in the house except cook in the kitchen, and
the nurse upstairs with Bill, and they're both busy. Let's
make a beeline for the back entry and up the stairs as fast
as we can."

"How about the chauffeur?" Mott demurred.

"He's off for the afternoon," the chief replied. "Hurry!"

They needed no second urging but walked briskly up
the path to the door which opened into the rear hall and
stairs.

"Nancy's been saying something?" Rider whispered as
they ascended cautiously.

The chief nodded.

"Nobody can make anything of it, though!" he replied.
"The nurse, Miss Alstead, says it's just baby delirium,
about a handkerchief, and violets, and somebody she calls
'Peggy'—but you'll hear her for yourself."

They had reached the second floor, and as they started
to mount to the third they glanced up to find Dr. Ross at
the head of the stairs, with his finger suggestively across
his lips and a very grave expression on his pleasant, usually cheerful face.

He led them in silence to the door of the darkened
room, where in silence he turned them over to a tall, fair-
haired, young woman, who nodded and directed them by
mute gestures to cross the threshold and step behind a
screen. They obeyed, with only the anxious squeak of one

of Mott's shoes and the chief's nasally drawn breath to disturb the utter stillness.

From where they stood they could see the head of a small, white bed which had been drawn out from the wall, with the frill of dainty pillows on each side of it and a little aimlessly waving white hand. Miss Alstead seated herself beside it once more and caught the hand, holding it gently.

"I—I buried it deep!—deep!" The faint but clear treble with its overtone of fever came at last to their straining ears. "Nobody knows! Peggy—Peggy won't tell and I won't tell! It's in my hank-shuck—my hank-shuck with the pink border, close to Peggy. It can't ever—not ever float around to let anybody know—! A-ah! Take it way! I thought the violets, the violets . . ."

The voice, which had risen in a piercing scream, droned into silence once more, and they stole from the darkened room.

22

Accruing Evidence

Mott had left his car in the back road, and the three made their way to it in silence. Then Chief Clark spoke.

"I thought so!" he remarked. "Lucky the Mercers didn't catch us, so long as we didn't get anything! It was just as the nurse said, the poor kid's wandering in her mind."

Mott said nothing nor did he dare to glance at Rider as the latter replied indifferently:

"Oh, well, it was worth a trial, and I've got a lot more to do to-day. Chief, could I see Ingred alone for a minute or two late this afternoon—around five, say?"

"Sure you can!" the chief replied promptly. "I got her in the jail, but her room's fixed up real nice. Mrs. Mercer saw to that."

"'Mrs. Mercer?'" Rider repeated.

"Yes. She came down 'bout an hour after I had Ingred safe under lock and key, and she brought pillows, and a quilt, and pictures, and a big picnic box full of food."

"Did she talk to Ingred?"

"Only for a few minutes." The chief flushed. "I thought it'd be better to stretch a point, especially after the charge I almost brought against her husband. She's terribly upset for her—because Ingred didn't ask her for help for Hans in the first place, but she told me that, of course, they'd bail the woman out when she comes up before the magistrate tomorrow and take her straight home with them. She's a fine woman herself, Mrs. Mercer! Remember how nervy she was about that chloroforming last week! Whoever that thief was, he won't come back, for I've had the place watched every night since."

"Of course, he won't come back!" Rider laughed. "You don't mean to tell me you've had men on night duty there for the past three nights? I'll be sorry for you when the truth of this gets out, and I wish I could tell you now, but take my advice and call them off!"

The chief's deepened color turned to a dull brick-red.

"Well, so long as you didn't tell me, I did the right thing, Rider!" he protested. "I'll take them off it to-night, though! You'll be down to the jail about five?"

Rider nodded and he and Mott started homeward, while the official climbed into his own little car.

"That child's talk was almost as much gibberish to me as it was to Clark, but I saw you got something out of it, Dan," Mott remarked when they were out of earshot. "She's buried something that she's afraid to have anybody know about, something that she's got a horror of. We knew that much from the few words she said when we picked her up that day and it's on her poor little mind now, but what else did her raving mean to-day?"

"A lot," Rider responded succinctly. "Take the single instance of one word; Henry, what floats?"

"'Floats?'" Mott repeated vaguely. "Cork? Wood?"

"Not in water!" his companion exclaimed in disgust. "In the air, you poor boob!"

"Dust?" Mott was too interested to resent the appellation. "Papers? How should I know? Tell me the answer."

"I will before morning," Rider promised, adding: "You've known the family intimately for years, Henry. Did the children ever have any pets?"

"They had a bird, but it died—a canary named Goldie— and there are several cats around the garage, but Mrs. Mercer never allows the children to play with them and she won't have a dog in the house; thinks it isn't sanitary for them, or something." Mott's tone expressed his surprise at the irrelevancy of the question. "I suppose you know what you're getting at, but I don't! What was that about a pink-bordered handkerchief, and violets? There aren't any violets this time of year! Apart from that thing she buried, I think the poor little girl was just plain delirious, if you ask me!"

Rider did not ask, however, and their luncheon was over when Chief Clark called them on the telephone.

"I warned you there'd be the devil to pay!" he reminded them. "Bill's nurse saw the doctor take us into Nancy's room and heard her scream that time and she told Mrs. Mercer. Now Ross and Miss Alstead have both been dismissed from the case, Mrs. Mercer's taking care of Nancy herself and she's sent 'way to Albany for a nurse and a specialist. The doc tells me, though, that right after we left the child fell into a deep sleep and the danger is past."

"Tell Dr. Ross not to worry, nor Miss Alstead either," Rider reassured him. "I'm positive I can persuade Mrs. Mercer to recall them by to-morrow."

"I must say I don't blame her!" Mott commented. "Ross is a fool! He should have known she isn't the kind of woman to make a scene, and her devotion to those children has been almost idolatry. Where are you going? Want me to come along?"

His tone was so eager that Rider hated to refuse, but he shook his head resolutely.

"Not this time, old scout. I'm going to call on some one who won't talk as freely with a third person present. I'll be home for dinner, though, and tell you what Ingred has to say."

"Take the car," his host offered. "I won't need it, and it's a long way down to town, let along where else you're going."

Rider accepted the suggestion and drove along the ridge road past Hilltop, which appeared now to be deserted in very truth. He was wondering what had become of old Hiram when, after mounting to the summit of the ridge and starting down the incline on the farther side, he came upon that individual himself in the garden of a rambling, old yellow house, ornate with the architecture of the Seventies.

"Good afternoon, Hiram." He stopped the car. "I was just wondering where you might have gone."

"I wondered myself, sir, though I've got some money laid by," the old man answered simply. "I didn't like the thought of not working any more, but I didn't expect anybody'd give me another place at my age. Miss Foster did, though; I'm caretaker here now, and when she comes out from her house down in the town she brings her hired girl with her."

Rider caught the flutter of an apron at the kitchen door as Hiram spoke, and he asked quickly:

"Is Miss Foster here now?"

"Yes, sir."

"Then open the gate, will you? I want to pay a little call on her."

The "hired girl," a sensible-looking, middle-aged woman, came to the door and showed him into a wide, sunny, old-fashioned parlor where Jim Foster presently joined him.

"You'll forgive me for the intrusion?" Rider asked as they shook hands.

"Glad to see you," she responded briefly, wrinkling her short, square-tipped nose at him. "Sit down. You've come for another theoretical discussion, haven't you?"

Rider laughed and seated himself. Then his face grew very sober.

"You've seen Mrs. Mercer recently, haven't you?" he asked.

"Not since I took Nancy home that night. Why?"

"You haven't!" he exclaimed in astonishment. "But you are her most intimate friend—at least everybody says so—I supposed of course . . ."

He broke off in evident confusion, and she eyed him curiously.

"We've been close friends, yes, ever since she came home from school, but our interests lie in exactly opposite directions and frequently we don't happen to see each other for days or weeks. If she had needed me in this trouble I knew she'd send for me, and I thought the kindest thing would be to let her alone."

"You didn't think that two weeks ago, did you?" he demanded bluntly.

Jim Foster's mouth set a trifle more firmly.

"I don't believe I quite understand you!"

"You don't want to, just as you don't want to face the suspicion concerning the murder that you can't help fostering." His tone was candidly matter-of-fact and even friendly, but her gray eyes glinted like steel. "I know this seems unwarrantable, and, of course, you can order me to go if you like, but for the sake of your friends I think you ought to know the case that's being built up against them—a case that is being built on the basis of that talk you had with Mrs. Mercer a little more than a fortnight ago."

"I shan't order you out, Mr. Rider," Jim Foster remarked with ominous quietude. "In fact, I would do my best to prevent you from going if you wanted to before you've made yourself quite clear. This is a serious matter and you've made a very serious statement. Will you explain?"

"Gladly. You went to Mrs. Mercer as a friend and told her how every one was talking about her husband and Miss Warrender, and you advised her to try to play the game with them, didn't you? Perhaps you didn't realize how long it was since she had had any practice, or bothered to make herself attractive; you couldn't foresee that she would follow your suggestions to an extent that would make herself ridiculous even in her husband's eyes, and complete the work you were too late to stop."

"I certainly didn't, and I don't realize it now!" she retorted. "In fact, I think you're talking nonsense, or worse! No cause for gossip or scandal existed or could ever exist except in the minds of the country club set. Mrs. Mercer was so secure from such petty stuff that it didn't worry her in the least, and she only exerted herself to go about more because she thought she wasn't paying enough attention to her guest! Do you mean to say that some one is trying to implicate the Mercers in the murder of Miss Warrender?"

"Where have you been this past week, Miss Foster?" countered Rider.

"Listening to accusations against the memory of one of my best and oldest friends!" she replied bitterly. "I told you that in our talk the other day."

"That was Tuesday," he reminded her. "You are speaking of Major Hill, aren't you? Public opinion has veered since—public opinion and that of the police."

"You seem remarkably well informed for a mere guest in the neighborhood, Mr. Rider!" Jim Foster smiled grimly. "You thought it strange that I took such an interest in the death of this woman; I find myself curious now as to your own interest in the investigation."

"It is odd," he admitted coolly. "I don't know why it is but people seem to single me out for their confidences, perhaps because, as you suggested before, I'm an outsider."

She colored faintly.

"Score one, but you haven't satisfied my curiosity! However, let's get to the point. The police suspect the Mercers of guilty knowledge of this murder, is that it? On what grounds?"

"Jealousy," Rider answered as directly as she had put the query. "Call it infatuation or whatever you please, Mercer was mad about Miss Warrender from the first moment he laid eyes on her; it was like a flame applied to dry tinder. Any one who does not deliberately shut his own eyes can see it in the man's face now, hear it in the tones of his voice when he speaks of her, read it in his every action. If there's such a thing as this love at first sight that you read about, it was what hit him, and you warned Mrs. Mercer too late that she was losing him, though only four or five days had passed since the other woman came. That is hardly fair to Miss Warrender, though, for Mrs. Mercer had practically lost her husband long before, through neglect and lack of interest. You were frank enough to tell her this, weren't you?"

The shot told and Jim Foster's faint color deepened.

"Some one was listening, then?" She caught herself up and added defiantly, "What if I did? Some one had to tell her just to stop the silly gossip, but for no other reason. Stan may have been bored and—and a little lonesome, and this woman was of a type foreign to his experience. I don't say that he wasn't perhaps infatuated with her for the time being, but if she had finished her visit and gone that would have been the end of it. He'd soon have settled down again, glad enough that he hadn't made a bigger fool of himself, and Mrs. Mercer's eyes were opened; she would have seen to it that such an opportunity didn't occur again. Instead of that, somebody had to come along and murder this woman, and now we're all in a horrible mess!"

"You would like to think it would have ended that way if Miss Warrender had lived to complete her visit, but you

can't, can you?" Rider bent slightly toward her. "You don't
want to face the fact that you yourself perhaps precipitated
the tragedy by what you call opening Mrs. Mercer's eyes.
In her attempts to follow your advice she only succeeded
in arousing a sort of pitying distaste in her husband and
forced him to compare her to the woman who innocently
had aroused the strongest passion of his life. You're too
square with yourself, too honest, to hide the knowledge
from your own intelligence that Miss Warrender's departure would not have been the end of it! It would, on her
part; that I can assure you, for I know more about her and
her character than any one in this community except one
living man and one dead one, but being a woman yourself
you must naturally blame her."

"I don't!" Jim Foster rose to the taunt. "The whole
unfortunate situation was Mrs. Mercer's own fault for not
realizing what miserable, weak specimens all men are, and
taking the trouble to hold hers! I don't say that Miss Warrender was to blame in any way; if you and poor Jack and
some one else know so much about her—for you mean
Jack, of course—and you're certain that when she went
away it would have been the end . . ."

"On her part, I said," Rider interrupted. "It wouldn't
have been on his, though. While she lived that flame
would have consumed him and he knows it; perhaps it will
consume him while he himself lives! The pity of it is, now
that she is dead, that if you had not spoken his wife might
never have known and suffered humiliation."

"Don't you suppose I realize that!" The low cry broke
from her and she struck her hands together. "Don't you
suppose I know the needless unhappiness I caused? Do you
think that hasn't been before me, day and night, since . . ."

Her voice ended in a gasp and she caught her throat
with both hands as though to choke back the words rushing unbidden from her lips.

"Since Gloria Warrender was murdered?" Rider finished for her, but she was on guard once more. "There hasn't been any deadlock between us, Miss Foster; I think we've both held the same theory, right along."

"Stop!" she cried. "You—you've misunderstood me! Whatever your theory is, it's running away with you! When I said just now I knew what I'd done I meant that Miss Warrender was dead and it was all over, and if I only hadn't repeated that spiteful gossip to Mrs. Mercer she need never have known her husband was—was attracted by any one else! I made her unhappy without any reason, any—any necessity, and she is my friend, she will always remember it! That has nothing to do with the murder itself, and you are absolutely wrong about my theories! I have none. I was curious when we last met and I wanted to lead you on, find out what you thought about the murder. Can't you understand? Miss Warrender must have been killed by a stranger—a stranger to us, I mean! Any other thought would be monstrous, impossible!"

"Then why did you tell me an untruth when I first came to-day?" Rider asked quietly. "The excuse you gave me for avoiding the Mercers since the tragedy might have been offered by a formal acquaintance, but not an intimate friend of years' standing! You realized how weak it was while you spoke."

"If that is so, perhaps you will tell me why I have not seen them?" Jim Foster tried to speak coldly, but there was a tremor in her voice and her flat breast rose and fell with her quickened breathing.

"Because you couldn't face them!" he challenged her. *"Because you knew the truth!"*

She stared at him for a moment and then suddenly buried her face in her hands.

"I do not know!" she sobbed, desperately. "Please go! Oh, God, I do not know!"

23

The Violet Grave

"I told Ingred you were coming to see her," the chief remarked as he greeted Rider a little later at the jail.

"She's a funny woman, don't seem to hold a bit of a grudge against either you or me for finding her out, and now that she's sure her son will be taken care of, she's as contented at the thought of a long term ahead of her as she would be on a vacation!"

"Has any one else tried to see her?" Rider asked.

"Yes, Mercer himself was here an hour ago, but I told him nothing doing. He said he only wanted her to be assured he'd put up her bail to-morrow and she'd be home with them again, but he looked pretty anxious and I calc'late there's something more than that on his mind!"

"What did he say about the doctor's allowing us to see Nancy?"

"Asked me pointblank what my object was and why I brought you and Mott," the chief shrugged.

"What did you tell him?" Rider frowned.

"We-ell, the truth, except that I took it on myself. I said I thought the child might have seen more than just the body in the hammock and she might talk about it in her delirium, and that I'd brought you two along as witnesses. I don't think that last went down with him very well, but he can't say anything because our being there

237

didn't do her any harm. He asked if Nancy had said anything and I told him she'd just talked about violets and
things floating and then called out: 'Take it away.' That's
all I could remember and it didn't seem to mean anything
more to him than it did to me. I guess he thought it was
pretty high-handed of us, but he wasn't mad, only anxious
on his wife's account."

"All right," Rider dismissed the subject. "Where's Ingred? What cell?"

"I ain't got her in a cell!" the chief admitted. "I know
the charge is grand larceny but she's such a—a *nice* woman, somehow, that I let her spend to-day in the matron's
sitting-room. We ain't as strict as you folks down to New
York."

He led the way and Rider followed into a pleasant
room, bright with chintz and highly colored pictures and
the rays of the westering sun through the barred windows,
which latter gave the only sinister note.

Ingred was sitting quietly with folded hands, but she
rose respectfully as they entered and stood waiting, un-
smiling but serene.

"All right, Ingred?" the chief asked. "Mr. Rider wants
to talk to you."

"All right, I tank you, Mister Clark," she replied in her
soft, full tones. "I tell to Mister Rider anyt'ing I can."

"I'll come back for you in half an hour," her jailer whispered in an aside to his companion and went out, locking
the door behind him.

"Ingred, I'm sorry you did this, and that I was the one
who had to go after you," Rider said. "Sit down again. I
want to tell you I'm going to help Mr. Mercer all I can to
get you off with the minimum sentence."

Ingred shook her head.

"It vas wrong," she said simply. "I steal and it is right
dat I should go to de prison. My Hans shall be vell! He

must know dat his modder bane a t'ief, but dat also I should have because I bane vicked vomans."

There was a little pause and then Rider spoke.

"Ingred, I want to ask you some questions that I don't want to trouble the Mercers with while their little girl is still so ill, but they're things the chief wants to know in connection with the murder of Miss Warrender. What time do the family breakfast in the morning?"

"At eight o'clock, sir."

"Does Mrs. Mercer come down or have hers sent up?"

"She ain't sick!" Ingred looked her surprise. "Alvays she coom to breakfast."

"Did Miss Warrender come to the table that morning—the morning of the day she was murdered? Did you wait on the table?"

"Yes, dat housemaid, she don't know not'ings. Miss Varrender vas dere, and I mind now I didn't tank she look so goot. She vas very qviet, and she vouldn't go out riding like odder mornings."

"Do you remember any of the conversation?"

Ingred thought for a moment.

"Only she said somet'ing 'bout letters to write, but after she plays vit' de children. At loonch she say dat she goes out in de hammock to read and maybe she vill sleep a little onless Mrs. Mercer coom out, too, but Mrs. Mercer, she goes to her own room instead." Her voice lowered. "It vas vile dey were eating de cheese and fruit dat I see de ring bane gone from Miss Varrender's finger, and vat I tank of all de time comes back in my head like de blood rushing. I make de excuse to go up de stairs and dere bane de ring on de dressing-table! I take it and ven I coom down dey are yoost going out of de room. Dat vas de last I see Miss Varrender till I run out to de hammock after Mrs. Mercer cried out for me!"

"What did you do yourself after lunch?"

"I set dat housemaid to clean de silver and I go to mend linens in de sewing-room." Ingred waited for the next question as though uncertain how to proceed, and Rider prompted her.

"Tell me everything that happened from the moment you finished your own lunch. You went up to mend—Mrs. Mercer was sewing too, wasn't she?"

"Yes. I go to har room to ask if I should mend a towel dat bane mooch vorn and Mrs. Mercer bane sewing a feadder fan to vear at de dinner party dat night. I go back and vork, and de house bane so qviet and still, and den all at once little Nancy scream out terrible!"

"Does the window of the sewing-room look out on the place where the hammock was hung?"

"No, de odder side of de house, sir."

"Did the screams seem to come from outside or right down in the hall?" Rider bent forward. "Think, Ingred. I want to find out if Nancy started screaming the minute she came on Miss Warrender's body or waited till she reached the house."

Ingred hesitated.

"I don't tank she scream till she get to de door, maybe yoost outside," she said at last. "I have a scared, because I tank she vas still vit' har modder. . . ."

"Oh, she was in Mrs. Mercer's room when you went there?" Rider interrupted.

"Yes. She have not'ing to do—she don't play like odder little girls—and I bane tell har coom vit' me and I tell har stories vile I sew, but she bane tired vit' de hot veat'er. Ven I hear dat screaming I run down, and she bane all small-like on de floor, as if she try to crawl inside harself, and she shake and cover har face vit' har hands, and all de time de screams dey come qvick as she get de breat'. Den Mrs. Mercer coom and pretty soon everybody else, even Bill, toombling down de stairs, but Nancy, she scream vorse ven ve touch har and she bane more vorser vit' har modder as all! At last ve get out of har somet'ing about de hammock, to go look in de hammock."

"Then Mrs. Mercer called and you went to her?" Rider urged. "Where did you leave Nancy?"

"In de hall. I tank she bane all right vit' de odders to take care of har; she bane stop screaming and vipes de eyes vit' de hands till dey look like two little mud-holes, poor little von!"

"Were her hands so dirty?" Rider smiled. "I always thought she was a neat, dainty little youngster! Didn't she have a handkerchief, either?"

"She did have von vit' a little pink border—I see it ven she bane in har modder's room before, but I guess maybe she dropped it ven she bane scared," Ingred hazarded. "She ain't got it, anyvays, ven she coom in de house dat time, and har hands dey bane all dirt. Ven I coom back to de house myself, after I see poor Miss Varrender and de awful t'ing dat bane done to har, I bane so troubled in my mind 'bout dat ring and who should have killed har and all, dat I forget Nancy, and ven I tank of har again, she bane gone!"

"Miss Foster brought her back safely, though, at about seven o'clock, didn't she?"

"She bring har back sick, so sick she don't know not'ings! Dere are scratches on har face and hands and she bane hot vit' fever! De doctor coom and get a nurse right avay because Nancy she bane clear out of har head, and fight and scream ven har modder coom near har. I tank she maybe die, but ven I coom back from—from taking Hans to get vell, she bane better."

"When Miss Foster brought her home, did Nancy say one word that you heard distinctly?" Rider asked very slowly. "It doesn't matter whether you understood it or not; did you hear her say one word?"

Ingred shook her head.

"No. It vas like she bane dreaming somet'ing dat vas not goot, and she try to talk, but de vords, dey von't coom, only little, little sobs."

Chief Clark rattled the bolts of the door and Rider rose.

"Just one more question, Ingred. Who is 'Peggy'?"

"'Peggy'?" Ingred repeated. "Dere bane nobody . . ."

"Some one or something that Nancy knew," Rider explained. "Didn't she ever have a pet or a little playmate named 'Peggy'?"

Ingred shook her head, but all at once a faint smile came to her lips.

"Nancy had a doll vonce, dat she called dat."

"A doll!"

"Yes. Bill dropped it last year and it vas all broke—a beautiful, big doll, vit yellow hair. Nancy vould not let it be t'rown avay, she said it bane dead, and she bury it in de garden."

"Where?"

"In de spot vot she loves, vere dere are vild violets in spring. It bane by de hadge near vere de hammock vas hung."

Ingred's voice had lowered, and Rider turned as the chief entered.

"Good-by, Ingred. You'll be home at Hydrangea Walk again by this time to-morrow, Chief Clark tells me. Maybe I'll see you there."

"Did you get anything out of her?" the chief asked anxiously as he accompanied the visitor to the main entrance and stood for a moment, beside him, looking out on the street. "Do you think she knows anything more about the murder than she's told?"

"I didn't ask her," Rider smiled. "By the way, court opens at ten, doesn't it?"

"Yes. She ought to be free, if Mercer is there with the bail bond, before twelve, anyway," the chief replied.

"All right. I'll call you up late to-night—nearer morning—and if you'll be ready to do what I ask, I may be able to turn some one over to you that you've been looking for since a week ago yesterday."

"The murderer!" gasped the chief. "Goddamighty, Rider, can't you tell me, even now? What if you're on the wrong track yourself, whatever it is, and I make a worse fool of myself than ever?"

"You won't," Rider responded gravely. "Unless I'm very badly mistaken you'll hear a confession first!"

Dusk was falling as he took leave of the bewildered official, and the lights were just flaring up in the little shops that lined each side of the thoroughfare. At one of these Rider stopped and purchased a small, sharp-edged trowel which he put in his pocket together with a flashlight. Then he drove straight to Hydrangea Walk.

As he entered the gates Stan Mercer's tall, lithe figure emerged slowly from a mass of shrubbery and came toward him. The buoyancy of his carriage was gone and he stooped slightly, walking with the dragging, weary steps of a man from whom all youth had gone.

"Hello, Rider." He spoke with an evident constraint. "Anything I can do for you?"

Rider stopped the car midway the drive.

"I came principally to make my apologies for what occurred this morning," he announced, adding mendaciously: "It was quite your chief's fault here; I understood you knew we were going to peep in at your daughter when the change in her condition came, but that the doctor didn't wish Mrs. Mercer to know, for he had forbidden her to go near the child; her presence, so the chief said, seems to make Nancy more restless. I hadn't any more intention of intruding than Mott had, and I'm sincerely sorry."

"That's all right; it's too bad Mrs. Mercer was told, that was all. Come in and have a highball?"

"No, thanks, but I'll get out here and walk with you for a little if you don't mind; like to stretch my legs." Rider descended from the car as he spoke and joined Stan on the path. "All little Nancy said that we could understand was something about wanting some violets. Do you grow any? I thought you had only hydrangeas."

"There's a little patch of wild violets over there." Stan gestured toward the northern hedge, near which stood that semi-circle of bushes with the trees rearing dark branches within it against the darkening sky. "I wanted to root them up, but Nancy pleaded so hard for them that I left them there; they only bloom for a few days in the spring, anyhow."

At his gesture Rider had stepped off the path and drawn his host insensibly across the lawn toward the hedge, and the latter came with obvious reluctance.

"Was it there that Nancy once buried a doll that was broken?" Rider asked with a trace of amusement in his tones. "Mrs. Mercer mentioned something of the sort one day."

"Yes. She's a strange, rarely sensitive child with the queerest whims and fancies, and sometimes it strikes me that she's far older than her years." Stan was talking absently with palpable effort, his eyes straying as if fascinated toward the spot where the hammock had hung. "That doll was very real to her, and when it was broken she naturally felt that it was dead. Here's the place she buried it, all this space around here is a mass of purple bloom in May. But for heaven's sakes, let's go to the house and get a drink! This place gets on my nerves!"

Rider had noted the tiny patch of dark, shiny leaves, and before turning to follow his host, he marked with his eye the distance to the bordering hedge and the nearest tree which would serve as a landmark. He could well understand how the proximity of the scene of the crime had wrought upon Stan's nerves and for the next quarter of an hour he tried to erase the thought of it from his host's mind.

"The truth will come out, and sooner than you think, Mercer," he said as he took his leave. "The chief of police is a shrewd man in spite of the mistake he made in regard to you, which was too absurd, of course, to take seriously—and if you and Mrs. Mercer will have just a little more patience I think he'll solve the mystery."

Stan shook his head gloomily.

"I think," he said, "that the mystery will never be solved!"

24

Sleeping Strength

At ten o'clock the next morning Chief Clark's long, lanky figure rose up from its cramped position behind a clump of trees near the gates of Hydrangea Walk as Mott and Rider approached in the mud-spattered car, and leaped upon the running-board almost before it had come to a halt.

"What is it?" he demanded. "What in Tophet did you mean by that message you telephoned at two o'clock this morning, Rider? I'd have come right up then to find out if you hadn't threatened to leave town if I did!"

"I meant just what I said," Rider replied seriously. "Got that warrant I told you to bring?"

"A blanket one, charging murder in the first degree." He nodded. "You told me to meet you here and not to stop anybody I saw going in or out, but there's nobody left in the house except Mrs. Mercer and the servants and children, for Mercer himself has gone; down to court, I calc'late, to bail Ingred out when she's held for trial, but I fixed it with the magistrate to delay her case an hour, like you told me. Where're we going to find the murderer? Not here at Hydrangea Walk?"

"I have every reason to believe that the murderer will come before we go, but I want to ask Mrs. Mercer a few questions first." Rider turned to Mott. "Go on, Henry. We'll drive straight up to the door."

The little car leaped forward and the chief protested:

"Look here, ain't you going to tell me even now? I've given you your head for a week and you let me make a fool of myself! What'll folks think to have their own police chief stand aside and let a stranger that's just supposed to be visiting here run his job for him? I don't want the credit that's your due, but I asked for you to help me, not take this case out of my hands!"

"You're right. That's why I wanted you to meet us first, for I'm not sailing under false colors any longer. I'm Commissioner Rider now, loaned to you for special duty on this case." There was no mistaking the earnest ring in his tones. "Mott's kind enough to say he can square himself with his neighbors for keeping the nature of my profession from them, and you can put off any blame on me that you like."

The chief looked slightly dazed.

"All right, if you say so!" he assented. "Who'm I going to arrest, then?"

"Miss Warrender's murderer," Rider said tersely. "I tell you flatly that we haven't enough circumstantial evidence to hold any one and we've got to force a confession. Give me my head once more, and when I tell you, take in your prisoner. Is that good enough?"

"It'll have to be!" the chief responded as they drew up before the veranda steps and he dropped off. "I'll bet you don't ask Mrs. Mercer any questions this morning; not after we sneaked in to see Nancy yesterday. She won't even come down!"

It seemed that his prediction was to be verified, for the housemaid who admitted them returned from conferring with her mistress to inform them that Mrs. Mercer could not leave her daughter's bedside and begged to be excused.

"Go back and take this to Mrs. Mercer." Rider drew a card from his pocket, scribbled two words on it and handed it to the astonished maid. "Say to her, please, that if she does not receive us the Chief of Police and I will come upstairs."

The maid stared a minute, her eyes starting from her head, and then turned and flew out into the hall while the three men left in the drawing-room seated themselves.

"That was your departmental card?" the chief asked in a whisper.

Rider nodded.

"Yes, and I wrote upon it 'official business,'" he replied grimly. "No matter how offended Mrs. Mercer is, curiosity if nothing else will bring her here."

As if in echo of his confident words there came a footfall on the stairs, the curtains at the doorway parted, and Mrs. Mercer stood before them. The pallor was accentuated in her sallow face by a sharp touch of bright color, and her dark eyes gleamed as she said, frigidly:

"I should not have understood your extraordinary message had it not been for the card which accompanied it, Commissioner Rider. May I ask who has retained you on this case? I do not think your authority extends beyond the limits of your own city."

She spoke as though he were an utter stranger, and Rider bowed.

"It does when I am detailed elsewhere on special duty— loaned out by my own chief to another, as in this instance. Mr. Mott introduced me here in a purely social capacity, but when a grave crime took place and I encountered Chief Clark he recognized me and wired my own headquarters for my official aid."

"We knew, of course, that you were something more than the merely intrusive guest of our neighbor, when you followed Ingred and found the ring she had stolen." Olive Mercer's lip curled. "I shall be glad to assist you in any way, but I hope you will be brief, for I must return to my sick child."

"Then I must ask you to listen patiently for just a few minutes." Rider motioned toward a chair as though he were the host and Olive sank into it, her eyes fixed upon his face. "Mrs. Mercer, we know every movement of every one under this roof on the day Gloria Warrender was murdered, we know why she was killed and the identity of the person who took her life. She was your friend; wouldn't you care to hear the truth?"

"Naturally." There was, however, a scornfully incredulous note still in her tones. "I could perhaps receive it with greater faith if the guilty person were already under arrest, but please go on. You insinuate that some one under this roof killed Miss Warrender?"

"You must judge for yourself." Again Rider bowed. "You had been in your friend's company much more during the second week of her visit than the first, Mrs. Mercer; your friends and neighbors all remarked it and Miss Foster, whom I called upon yesterday afternoon, explained why."

"Jim?" Olive started slightly and the color reddened on her cheekbones. "I don't quite understand! Of course, I exerted myself to entertain my guest!"

"Of course," Rider agreed. Mott was staring roundly and the chief sat with his bony hands clenching and unclenching on his knees. "She was to have left you on the following Monday, I believe. Why did you avoid her on the day of her death—or was it she who avoided you?"

"Commissioner, you are impertinent!" Her dark eyes flashed. "Find the murderer! That is your business, isn't it? Why do you catechize me?"

"That, too, is part of my—official—business," he replied slowly but courteously. "You left Miss Warrender to her own devices all that Saturday morning; after lunch she asked you to join her out on the lawn, in the hammock, but you preferred to go to your room. You were mending a fan then, weren't you—a black feather fan?"

"Yes, I think so. It was some such trivial thing." Olive nodded and the bright spot of color began to fade from her cheeks.

"Your little girl came to you while you were mending this fan, and then Ingred appeared to ask you about some linens she was at work upon," Rider continued, his eyes gazing straight into hers. "Ingred went back to the sewing-room, and your little girl went out to play. She wandered about the garden for an hour or more—that part of the garden which lies on the side of the house farthest from the spot where the hammock was swung—and she talked to the undergardener, Hans, who was pruning the pergola. Then she recalled that Miss Warrender had said she was going to read in the hammock and Nancy went to look for her. You know what she found."

"Certainly!" Olive exclaimed hurriedly. "She ran screaming up to the house. But haven't we gone all over that a score of times? What has Nancy to do with it?"

"Everything," Rider returned. "You know that she saw your friend's body lying there, but perhaps you do not know what else Nancy found?"

"What—else—!" Olive's face was quite colorless and strained now, and she moistened her lips.

"Something she recognized; something that told her who had been there before her—*who had murdered Gloria Warrender!* Her childish but psychic instinct re-vealed to her the truth, but even in her overwhelming fear and horror, her loyalty was steadfast and she had pres-ence of mind enough to pick up the thing she had found and recognized, wrap it in her little, pink-bordered hand-kerchief and hide it in the safest place she could think of. Then, her self-control gone, she ran shrieking to the house, the only haven she knew, but she would never have told—never, if delirium hadn't unsealed her lips."

"I thought it would be some such conspiracy as this!" Olive rose. "That was why you induced the doctor to allow you to enter Nancy's room yesterday! Do you think that you can fasten a crime on any one, on the mere testimony of a sick and delirious baby?"

"No. She told, however, in the presence of witnesses, what she had found and where she had buried it, and in the presence of witnesses I unearthed it, still wrapped in its tiny pink-bordered shroud. She had told Mr. Mott and me about it before, when we found her miles away in a thicket on the evening following the murder, half-dead from exhaustion and the horror that had almost crazed her brain, but not until yesterday did we get from her the details that enabled us to complete our case. The object which she had found was only a fragment, but we have the article of which it forms a part. Mrs. Mercer, when you sat mending your fan that Saturday afternoon, after Ingred had left you, and then Nancy, what were your thoughts? Can you recall them?"

She shook her head, but seated herself once more.

"How could I, Commissioner Rider?" she asked. "I presume I was thinking of the dinner we were to attend that night at the Waterfall Inn, perhaps my mind was engaged with my household duties—how can I remember after this lapse of time?"

"Perhaps they were fixed on something far more vital," he suggested. "Something that would not let you rest. How long did you sit there in your room, Mrs. Mercer? How long did you brood over the wrong that had been done you till you got up and went out to the hammock to have it out with the woman who had stolen your husband from you?"

"How dare you!" The low cry burst from her lips and then they set stonily.

"You went to tell her that he belonged to you and that you would never let him go! That you would hold him,

fight for him, keep him at all odds from her—and you
found her asleep, her head hanging over the edge of the
hammock, her face hidden, her round neck under your
hands! The impulse to kill came to you, to kill this creature who had entered your home as a guest and stolen
from you your mate, who meant to take him away with
her, away from you forever! You went to the opening in
that circle of shrubbery, but no one was in sight, no one
had seen you enter it. You turned and looked again at that
woman helpless before you, and then, in a blind fury, you
seized the rope tied to the tree, jerked it apart and flung
it about her neck, winding it tight, round and round so
that her screams would be choked back in her throat, and
holding it tighter and tighter while she struggled, until
at last her struggles ceased! You didn't realize until later
that your swollen, abraded hands would betray you and
you cleverly, nervily overturned a burning alcohol lamp on
them; you didn't know that you had brought with you, and
dropped at the scene of your crime, an object that would
inevitably point to your guilt, the object which Nancy
found and buried to shield you—*this!*"

As he spoke Rider drew from his pocket a tiny, earth-
stained handkerchief with a narrow pink border, and un-
wrapping it, disclosed a single black feather.

The chief swore a startled oath, Henry Mott choked, and
Olive Mercer sprang once more to her feet, her face livid.

"Yes, I killed her!" she cried. "I throttled her as I would
a snake! It wasn't because she had taken from me the father
of my children, because she would break up my home, but
because she had stolen my mate! He was mine, mine, and
I had a right to kill!"

"Goddamighty!" The chief rose also and advanced a step
toward her. "I've got to put you under arrest, ma'am . . . !"

Olive laughed with a rising note of hysteria in her
harsh, husky tones.

"Do you think that it matters now?" she exclaimed. "That girl shared my bed at school for three years! She was always cleverer than I, brilliant, daring! Everything she wanted, everything worth while came to her without effort, while the rest of us worked and struggled, and she fascinated all of us, we were her slaves! Years passed and then I heard of her again and invited her to my home. She came—you saw her, you saw how every one fell under her spell, and how blind I was, how blind!

"A friend came to me and opened my eyes, and I began to watch! I tried to enter into the life she led—she and my husband—to keep up with them in the things I had forgotten for my duties as a wife and mother, but it was too late! I saw my husband's infatuation, but I hoped it was only idle amusement on her part and that she would go away and leave me in peace with my own. Oh, how I had grown to hate her! How old she made me feel! I knew I was losing my dignity, making myself ridiculous in the eyes of my friends, but I didn't care, I was trying to win back Stan! It was only when I saw with his eyes that I realized how futile it all was—when he pitied me, showed me how distasteful I was to him, and I saw the comparison he must be making between her and me! I didn't blame him—I've never blamed him, it was she!

"He urged me to ask her to stay on and I did, but with the bitterness of death in my heart! She refused—and then he announced that he was going to New York in a few days, and I saw it all! In despair I said I would go with him, but he refused to take me, put me off with lying excuses when I urged, and finally told me pointblank that he was going alone. That night . . ." Olive crouched over the table toward them, her face distorted till her heavy black brows seemed to writhe, and her voice sunk to a hoarse whisper. "That night I saw them in each other's arms! I heard her tell him she loved him, I heard him say that it was the beginning of a new life for them both—and I knew then what I must do! Wherever she went she would call to him and he would follow! Out of all the men in the world she had chosen him—mine! It wasn't amusement, she wanted him and she meant to have him just as she had always taken anything in life that she wanted!

"When I stepped back from the pergola where I had followed them, and out into the moonlight so that they should think I had just come from the house, Gloria Warrender was a dead woman! I didn't know how or when the opportunity would come, but I knew she must not leave my home alive to draw my husband after her! All that night I thought, all the next morning, and I could feel something rising in me that I'd never known before—a strength, a power to crush, to destroy! I felt dizzy and yet clear-headed too, only everything was in a red mist before me. They tried all day to avoid each other in order to deceive me, and I laughed at them—laughed in my heart!

"That afternoon it was hot—the heat seemed beating into my brain, beating in what they had said to each other the night before, and something kept telling me 'now! now!' I couldn't stand it any longer! I put down that black feather fan I was mending and went to her! I found her, as you said, asleep, and I killed her!"

The harsh, guttural voice ceased and she brought her fist down with a dull, heavy thump on the soft cover of the table. The chief was still standing, his lantern-jaw dropped, staring at her with blank eyes, and Mott was breathing stertorously while the perspiration stood out on his forehead. Rider regarded her with a keen, matter-of-fact scrutiny, and when he spoke the words were clipped cleanly.

"You broke the swing-rope from the tree? . . ."

"I snapped it as though it were a piece of thread!" Olive cried, with a fierce note of exultation. "I wound it round and round her white neck and held the ends taut, while she whipped about in that hammock like a fish in a net! I think she tried to cry out, but the sound gurgled away in her throat, and in a little while it was all over! Long, long after she was limp and still I held her so, then gradually I loosed my hold on the rope ends till they dropped from my hands. She didn't move, and then, all at once, I began to tremble and the strange strength which had come to me, which had seemed to awaken inside of me, left me and everything whirled and grew black!

"I was afraid I should faint and they would find me there, and I fought off the weakness somehow and got back to my room. I don't know—I only remember finding myself there once more and wondering if it wasn't all a nightmare! I bathed my face in cold water and sat down to take up my fan again so that I should seem never to have dropped it— and then, for the first time, I noticed my hands! It wasn't a nightmare, after all, for they were seared as though I had clung to a rod of fire! It was true, then, she was really dead and out of my way, she couldn't take my husband from me!

"I could have shrieked for joy in the thought that he was mine again, but I knew the summons would come at any time, and I planned what I must do, how I would put that hour from my mind and tell my story! I was sure of myself, sure that no one would ever know; Stan would come back to me and we would go on as though that woman had never come into our lives. What a fool I was! Living, she threatened my happiness, but dead, she had taken it with her to the grave! Her memory would always stand between us, Stan would never forget her—she had taken him from me after all!

"When I realized that, why, nothing seemed to matter. I kept on—instinctively, I suppose—studying myself, guarding my every word and action, but it hardly seemed worth while. Now and then I've had a creeping fear that Stan suspected me! He couldn't have, of course, it was only that I was losing my grip, but even if he knew, what difference could it make? I don't suppose we could have gone on—this way. I don't know what the end would have been, but I'm glad I did it! Glad! Glad! She took what was mine, but I killed her for it!"

"Stop!" The curtains at the doorway were dashed aside and Stan Mercer flung himself into the room. "I've heard you! I heard what you said and I thought I was going mad, just as I thought I was going mad all these days past, for I *did* suspect you, though I prayed for forgiveness for the thought! I can't judge you, you're Nancy's mother, and Bill's, and I suppose you've been what they call a model wife, but there's one thing you've got to hear! You've got to know what you've done!"

He was breathing as though he had run a long, exhausting race, and his face worked with emotion. Slowly Olive straightened and faced him, and slowly the words fell from her lips.

"Can you deny that you loved her?"

"No!" He fairly hurled it in her face. "I loved her and I always shall! Such love as that you don't understand, a woman like you never could! There's no more right nor wrong to it than there is to a man's actions when he's carried along in a whirlpool, a tornado! What had you given me for years? A single hour of companionship, a moment of tenderness that was really spontaneous, really *you?* I'm not blaming you for that, God knows, but you've got to know what a thing this is that you have done!"

"Stan!" Mott gasped, but the man before them did not hear.

"Gloria Warrender loved me—you heard her say it, but it is a pity you didn't wait to hear more! She was a good woman—good, and brave, and sweet, and true—true even to you, who killed her! We'd never spoken of love until that night, I don't think she even knew what had come to her! I caught her in my arms because I couldn't help myself, because this thing which had come to us was too big for me, but it wasn't too big for her! I pleaded with her, told her that I would never let her go, but she said that I must! She would go away and that would be the end forever, that moment must never come again! It was because of you, because she would not bring unhappiness to you! Because she *wouldn't* take the love that was rightfully yours! It was the beginning and the end there, that night in the garden—and you killed her!"

He stood panting and staring into her face, and her eyes met his for a moment that seemed interminable to the three watchers. What she saw there must have convinced her of the truth, for all at once she swayed and turned gropingly, blindly toward the chief of police.

"Take me away!" Her hoarse, toneless cry rasped on the silence. "Take me away!"

25

In Perspective

Chichester was pleasantly astir with the market-day bustle of another summer when Rider climbed into Mott's car at the station. It was a new car, with low, rakish lines and sporty lamps, but Henry Mott's rotund form was as shabbily comfortable as ever, and his kindly face as beamingly good-natured.

From the steps of the courthouse a tall lanky figure waved ungainly arms and halloed in defiance of his own rules concerning orderly conduct, and Rider nodded and waved in return.

"The chief seems flourishing," he commented.

"Like the young bay tree," Mott supplemented. "That affair last year made him solid for life. By Godfrey, it seems more than a year! There've been a lot of changes here."

"Town appears the same," observed Rider.

"Not in the town; I mean, the folks," Mott explained. "You'll notice one or two landmarks gone, though, out my way. Poor old Jack's place has been made over into a boys' school and—well, wait."

"Is old Hiram still working for Miss Foster?"

"Working for her? He's running her! You'd think he owned the place, and when she's out there she doesn't dare call her soul her own," he chuckled, and then his face grew grave. "She's one of the folks I meant had changed; she's still rampaging around for votes, and doing a mighty lot of good, too, cleaning things up, but she's softer and more gentle—turning out to be a real nice woman! I guess she won't ever take it into her head again to go around telling people how to run their own lives!"

They had left the business streets behind them and turned into the road Rider remembered so well, leading past the larger estates on the way to the country club, and he found himself looking for, yet dreading to see, a square, solid gray house with wide, red-roofed verandas and massed blue hydrangeas everywhere. He watched and waited, and then suddenly gasped:

"Why—where's it gone? Surely that's the place! What on earth has become of Hydrangea Walk?"

Row upon row of flat glass greenhouses spread before him, shimmering in the sun like a broad lake, and Mott replied:

"Razed to the ground. Stan wouldn't leave a stick nor stone of it when he took the children and went out to California to live. The place looked like a battlefield when he got through with it and he sold it to a nurseryman."

"Do you ever hear? . . ." Rider began but paused.

"Oh, yes. The Board keeps in touch with things, you know," Mott responded, reading the other's meaning. His tone was dry as he added: "She's a model prisoner, I understand; she ought to get quite a little off that twenty-year manslaughter sentence for good behavior."

"And Ingred?"

"Her pardon's pending and Hans is getting well fast." Mott s voice was cheerful once more. "How's your golf? The course is a lot improved and I went around in seventy-eight the other day—not bad for me, eh? We'll run over after lunch and see if we can make up a foursome."

But after lunch they somehow found themselves under the grape arbor as of old, with pipe and cigar alight and chairs comfortably tipped back. For a while they smoked in silence and then Mott exclaimed.

"Oh, what's the use? We might as well get it talked over and forget it! You promised that when the trial was over you'd tell me how you doped out the case, but before she pleaded guilty to manslaughter you had to beat it back to New York on that big bank robbery. I know what your memory is, and I haven't forgotten a single detail. What was it that first made you think Olive Mercer killed Miss Warrender?"

"Let me see. It was more a feeling than a thought, as I remember it." Rider watched the smoke-wreaths from his cigar retrospectively. "I'd studied her a little more carefully than I do most people I meet in a social way because there was a certain incongruity about her that interested me. Every line in that full, heavy face of hers denoted passion, a terrific passion that would sweep everything before it and leave wreckage behind if it were ever roused. Those thick, black brows, too, that almost met over her forehead—I never saw a woman with them yet that wouldn't make a man's life a h—l through jealousy if she ever grew suspicious, whether she had cause or not."

"But until Gloria Warrender came she was wrapped up in her home and the children and never seemed to give Stan a thought!" Mott protested.

"That's how she had you all fooled—she was placid and contented because she was so sure of him; he belonged to her and that was all there was to it. It was *his* home, those were *his* children, do you see? It wasn't love with her, not the love that sacrifices and renounces—it was the mate-instinct, and when that scented danger she took the trail!"

"Like an animal!" Mott shuddered.

His companion smiled.

"What are we, all of us, underneath?" he asked, and then went on. "When we got there after she telephoned that there was trouble, the minute I saw her face I realized that she was roused at last, and I began to study her every word and look and gesture, and she overreached herself! Her announcement of the tragedy was a little too dramatic, and when you had rushed off to see the body I asked her to tell me the whole thing over again in detail. Henry, no woman, laboring under such shock and strong emotion could have been able to tell a connected, concise story like that unless it had been carefully rehearsed! You've only to contrast it with her own account, verified by the servants, of little Nancy's incoherent outburst to understand. Her eyelids were very red, I remember; too red, but there wasn't a sign of tears, and carefully as she had planned what she would say and do about her own discovery of the body, she had forgotten one significant detail. She said she looked at it, called for help, and then telephoned to us. She just *looked* at it. Wouldn't it have been natural for her to try to find out whether life was extinct or not, *unless she already knew?*"

"Jumping Christopher! And I never got it!" Mott exclaimed.

"Of course, I knew what motive she might have had, from the common gossip about her husband's infatuation, but I tried to discount that. When he came, do you recall how she broke the news to him? She hurled it at him in a sort of triumph that you took for hysterical horror, but she gloried in it! Do you recall, too, how careful she was to impress on us then and later how little she had known of her friend's life during those ten past years? That was for an opening to throw suspicion elsewhere if the scent got too close. You all thought her a marvelous mother, yet she hadn't any thought for Nancy's condition of fright that afternoon, to comfort her; her only desire was to get off to her own room by herself to think and plan further subterfuge. I went away with you to send my telegrams morally certain that she herself had murdered her friend."

"Why in the world didn't you tell me . . ." Mott began, and stopped suddenly.

"Exactly," Rider replied to his unspoken thought. "You never would have believed me for a moment. When we returned and sat in that conference between her, the coroner, and the chief of police, she assured them that she didn't know anything about Miss Warrender, but insinuated that Major Hill might. Were you watching her face when the coroner 'phoned and found out he'd left town suddenly that afternoon? She saw another possible avenue of escape if she were ever suspected. Do you remember her blank astonishment at the discovery that the opal ring was missing? That was entirely beyond her calculations, a complication utterly unforeseen. When I shook hands with her then, and again on Monday after the inquest, I noticed how hot hers was, and I handed her that telegram from my New York operative so that she would have to extend her palm for it; I saw that it was bruised and seared, and when you exclaimed, she told us she had overturned an alcohol stove. I verified this by Ingred, but I knew it was only a cunning and rather courageous ruse to conceal the effect of the rope!

"Then, when Gildersleeve came she turned him over to me for interrogation . . ."

"I remember that, all right!" Mott interrupted. "I couldn't understand why, though."

"Because she knew I'd question him later, if not then, and she wanted to hear the replies," Rider responded. "When he said she must know how lovable Gloria Warrender was, she said: 'I know!' in a tone that spoke volumes. It was that lovableness that had caused all the tragedy!

"After the inquest I examined the hammock and found a bit of black fluff clinging to it; I didn't know about the black feather fan then, but I put it in my pocket, anyway. The next day—Tuesday—I told you at lunch about Miss Foster's suspicions. You thought I meant that she suspected Stan, but I told you I hadn't any particular man in mind. I hadn't. It was a woman—Olive Mercer. As for Miss Foster, she alone beside myself suspected the truth from the first. Do you wonder that she dreaded to have it proved?"

"You said too, something about a romance in her life. I've often thought of it, watching her and the change in her. Do you really think she cared for Stan?" Mott asked, but Rider shook his head.

"No. It's presumptuous of me—of both of us—to pry into a woman's heart, but I think if Miss Foster ever cared for any man, that man is dead. . . ."

"You told me, too, that day, that you'd have to stop your investigation for a while and wait, and when I asked you 'what for' the next day, you said simply for the time to pass," Mott reminded him after a pause.

"Yes. I was waiting for Ingred and Hans to go."

"But you didn't follow them for over twenty-four hours!" Mott objected.

Rider laughed and eyed his friend quizzically.

"Yes. I wasn't waiting to follow them, though. I wanted to get them out of the house. It meant two less to encounter, and Ingred had an embarrassing habit of being watchful at night."

"By—Godfrey!" Mott dropped his pipe but caught it as it touched the ground. "So it was you! No wonder that burglary was never solved! You took a long chance when you resorted to chloroform, though, Dan!"

"Had to, or be discovered," Rider shrugged. "I'd searched her room pretty thoroughly before she woke up, looking for the dress she had on the day of the murder to see if any bit of trimming or something had dropped from it, that Nancy might have picked up and buried, recognizing it. I knew the child must have hit on the truth. Only that would account for her horrified aversion to her mother which persisted even in delirium, though she was loyal to her instinctively. I found the broken black feather fan, but still didn't connect it with that bit of fluff I'd picked off the hammock, so I left it there on the shelf in Mrs. Mercer's closet. It was sheer luck that Mercer himself had gone out tramping around in the night with his sorrow and his frightful suspicions! I was more successful the second time I broke into Hydrangea Walk."

"'The second time!'" Mott ejaculated.

"The night before we confronted Mrs. Mercer. We'd learned then from Nancy's own lips that whatever she found was light enough to 'float around,' and she had wrapped it in her handkerchief with the pink border and buried it near 'Peggy,' where there were violets. Ingred told me when I visited her in jail that 'Peggy' was a doll for which Nancy had made a grave in the violet bed, and later Mercer pointed it out to me. That night late I went back with a trowel I'd bought, dug up the bed, found the doll and the black feather wrapped in the dirty little handkerchief. I remembered the fan then, and the whole thing was clear." Rider paused to relight his cigar and then resumed: "I went into the house the same way as before, got that fan for evidence and this time nobody spotted me, nor ever knew of my presence. You remember the fan when the chief produced it at the trial? It was of uncurled ostrich, and the broken tip that Nancy had found beside the body fitted exactly to the one short feather."

"That was the single link needed!" Mott nodded slowly. "Why do you suppose she went out to see old Hiram and ask about the major the day after he killed himself?"

"She was uneasy, getting fearful of herself—call it guilty conscience if you like," Rider explained dryly. "She had begun to look for suspicion on every hand and wanted to see if she couldn't somehow fasten the guilt on his memory if the need came. We had a pretty slim case against her, even if we put her own child on the stand, but she confessed, as I figured she would, and saved us the trouble."

A little silence fell then between the two friends and they smoked on, relaxed in the warm sunshine. From a neighboring field came the whir and droning hum of a mowing machine, and the fragrant scent of new-cut hay lay heavy on the air.

All at once Mott spoke again.

"The only thing I can't understand is how Olive Mercer had the strength to do what she did."

"You heard her explain that herself as well as she was able. She said that all that day she felt a strength rising within her, a power to crush, to destroy. There's an old French saying—'le chat qui dort,' beware of the sleeping cat. You've heard of women, and men, too, for that matter, raised to Herculean strength to rescue some loved one from danger? Why not to destroy a rival whom Olive Mercer thought had deliberately stolen her mate?" He paused and after a moment added: "I shouldn't wonder if there were a 'sleeping cat,' a hidden strength, in all of us, Henry. Heaven help us if we waken it!"

About the Author

Isabel Ostrander was born to a wealthy New York family in 1883. She eloped with songwriter Arthur J. Lamb in 1907 (breaking the news to her startled mother with a quick telephone call), but the marriage did not last long. Her stories started to appear in magazines and newspapers in 1911 and 1912, with the crime story 'The Heritage of Cain' being among the first. The serial publication of 'At One-Thirty' in 1915 (published in book form that same year) introduced detective Damon Gaunt, one of the first 'blind detectives.' She was a prolific author, and wrote under several male pseudonyms as well. One 1922 newspaper advertisement noted 15 'detective and mystery' books and over 60 short stories to her credit. Several of her mysteries included serial detectives Timothy McCarty and Dennis Riordan. Her untimely death in 1924 was reported as from heart disease, after several weeks' illness, at her home in Long Beach, New York. She left behind a number of manuscripts, which were published posthumously over the next several years.

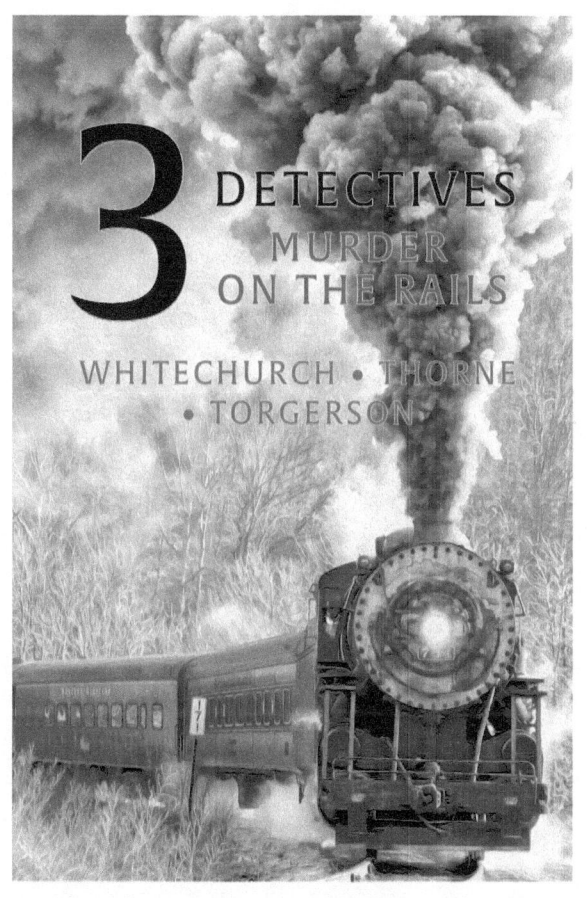

3 DETECTIVES
MURDER
ON THE RAILS

WHITECHURCH • THORNE
• TORGERSON

Also Available

Coachwhip Publications

CoachwhipBooks.com

MURDER'S COMING

GRAVE WITHOUT GRASS

BY
DONALD CLOUGH CAMERON

Also Available

Coachwhip Publications

CoachwhipBooks.com

THE CASE OF THE ADVERTISED MURDER

MINNA BARDON

Also Available

Coachwhip Publications

CoachwhipBooks.com

No Face to
Murder

EDITH HOWIE

Also Available

Coachwhip Publications

CoachwhipBooks.com

THE
BEACON HILL
MURDERS

∞

THE
BACK BAY
MURDERS

THE ROGER SCARLETT MYSTERIES
VOL. 1

Also Available

Coachwhip Publications

CoachwhipBooks.com